The

Patron Saint

of

Second Chances

The Patron Saint of Second Chances

a novel

CHRISTINE SIMON

ATRIA BOOKS

NEW YORK   LONDON   TORONTO   SYDNEY   NEW DELHI

ATRIA
BOOKS

An Imprint of Simon & Schuster, Inc.
1230 Avenue of the Americas
New York, NY 10020

First Atria Books hardcover edition April 2022

ATRIA BOOKS and colophon are trademarks of Simon & Schuster, Inc.

For information about special discounts for bulk purchases, please contact Simon & Schuster Special Sales at 1-866-506-1949 or business@simonandschuster.com.

The Simon & Schuster Speakers Bureau can bring authors to your live event. For more information or to book an event, contact the Simon & Schuster Speakers Bureau at 1-866-248-3049 or visit our website at www.simonspeakers.com.

Interior design by Kathryn A. Kenney-Peterson
Images used under license from Shutterstock.com.

Manufactured in the United States of America

1   3   5   7   9   10   8   6   4   2

Library of Congress Cataloging-in-Publication Data

Names: Simon, Christine, 1978– author.
Title: The patron saint of second chances / Christine Simon.
Description: First Atria Books hardcover edition. | New York : Atria Books, 2022.
Identifiers: LCCN 2021024185 | ISBN 9781982188771 (hardcover) |
ISBN 9781982188788 (paperback) | ISBN 9781982188795 (ebook)
Subjects: GSAFD: Humorous fiction. | LCGFT: Humorous fiction.
Classification: LCC PS3619.I56189 P37 2022 | DDC 813/.6—dc23
LC record available at https://lccn.loc.gov/2021024185

ISBN 978-1-9821-8877-1
ISBN 978-1-9821-8879-5 (ebook)

To the founding members of the Read, Write, or Draw Club:
Jack, Emily, Juliet, and Zoey
I love you

The
Patron Saint
of
Second Chances

1

Who Will Pray for the Pipes?

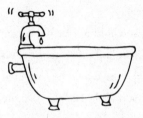

Signor Giovannino Speranza, self-appointed mayor of the diminishing village of Prometto, population 212, knew from his sixty-two years of experience in this world that, in dealing with plumbers, one must never show even a hint of weakness. A plumber was the circling vulture of home repair, smug in his knowledge that pipes were the very circulatory system of polite society, and that his poor dope of a client, whoever they might be, was undoubtedly in over their head, and therefore as putty in his unscrupulous hands. These scoundrels were also organized. They had gotten together, perhaps on a plumbers' getaway weekend, and decided that their services ought to cost a minimum of a hundred and fifteen euros an hour. If one still thought in lire, as Signor Speranza did, that came to two hundred and twenty-two thousand, six hundred and seventy, a number that, if one could even fathom it, was patently criminal.

This knowledge of the depravity of plumbers, and all their known associates, was why, on this particular July morning, Signor Speranza was taking great care to maintain the upper hand. He was standing in the bathtub eating his breakfast, which, of course, was a power move, while a junior plumbing inspector from the Regional Water Commission prepared to cut a meticulous hole in the plaster under the bathroom sink.

"Are you sure you would not be more comfortable at the table, signore?" the young man had asked timidly, upon regarding the circumstances under which he would be expected to work.

"I always eat breakfast in the tub," Signor Speranza lied, not breaking eye contact and producing a salt shaker from behind the bottle of Ultra Dolce di Garnier. *Go ahead*, he thought, twitching his black moustache from side to side. *Tell me that I don't.*

The young man coughed and dropped his gaze, and Signor Speranza gave a small snort of triumph.

The Speranzas' hotel, a ten-room establishment with a coin-operated Jacuzzi and a rooftop terrace, where they lived and which they had inherited from Signor Speranza's wife's parents, was not the first place in the village the inspector had visited; indeed, it was the last. He had already made the rounds, he and his little clipboard, to a random sampling of homes and businesses throughout the rocks and cliffs of Prometto. His visit had been a long time coming. In fact, Signor Speranza had been putting it off for two years now, through a coordinated system of avoidance. Whenever the Water Commission's number had shown up on the caller ID at Speranza and Son's, the vacuum cleaner maintenance and repair business Signor Speranza had inherited from his father, and whose premises doubled as his mayoral office, he would shout for his assistant, Smilzo. Smilzo would then race to plug in the

Hoover WindTunnel 2 floor model and hold the nozzle up to the receiver.

"SORRY, I CAN'T HEAR YOU!" Signor Speranza would shout. "BAD CONNECTION!"

This method of postponement had worked like a charm until some diligent civil servant had finally followed up in writing. The date had been set. The inspector was to come and examine the pipes. Any pipes discovered to be in disrepair were to be fixed at the expense of the municipality. For small municipalities that could not afford the cost of repairs and who did not qualify for a payment plan, the water would be cut off, and the commission would assist with the resettlement of displaced individuals.

Signor Speranza had lingered over this last line, and in particular those two words, *displaced individuals*, with a queasy feeling in his stomach. Then he had laid it aside and in its place opened the large volume he kept on his desk for just such emergencies, titled *The Complete Compendium of Catholic Saints and Blessed or Beatified Persons*. He had opened to the *P*s, running his finger down the appropriate column, and found what he was looking for—St. Vincent Ferrer, patron saint of plumbing. He'd closed the book with a satisfied snap and begun immediately. *Ciao, Vincenzo*, he had prayed, clasping his hands—with the exception of the rosary, he liked to keep things casual. *It's Signor Speranza. I'm sorry to bother you, but could you take a look at Prometto's pipes? I know it's a pain in the ass, but there is no money here.*

Now, from his perch in the tub, Signor Speranza glared at the junior inspector. *Just look at him*, he thought, shoveling the last of his scrambled eggs into his mouth. The young man was crouched alongside the sink, carefully affixing a square of blue painter's tape to the area he meant to cut open. When he had finished, he leaned back to examine his handiwork, and, finding it infinitesimally crooked, patiently peeled it off and began again.

"Why don't you just smash it?" Signor Speranza asked, when he couldn't stand it any longer.

The junior inspector was aghast. "Oh, no, signore. You must never smash plaster. That makes it very difficult to repair."

Signor Speranza rolled his eyes to the ceiling. The entire village was facing the wrecking ball, dependent on the report of this giant toddler with his clip-on tie and his sensible four-cylinder car, but yes, by all means, let us be careful with the plaster.

Signor Speranza balanced his clean plate on the edge of the tub and fidgeted. He had not been in this particular bathroom for some time, as there had been no guests on this floor of the hotel for at least two years. He had chosen this spot for the junior inspector to work because it was out of the way, but, as he looked around, he frowned. A memory stirred. A leak? Had there been a leak? And if there had been, how had they fixed it? He studied the checked linoleum, which was unique to the third floor, and got a sudden flash of it, swollen around the base of the sink: an enormous, water-filled bubble. His hands went clammy.

"You know," he said, clearing his throat, "I wonder if you might prefer to see the pipes in the kitchen? It's cooler there."

The junior inspector looked up, surprised. "I have already taped, signore."

"Yes," sighed Signor Speranza. "I've seen you do that." They both gazed bleakly at the blue-taped square.

"Well . . ." said the junior inspector into the awkward silence. He bent over his bag, and at that precise moment Signor Speranza glimpsed, gleaming around his adversary's neck, a silver medallion imprinted with none other than the pallid image of St. Vincent Ferrer himself!

"Signore," whispered Signor Speranza, his voice trembling with emotion. "You're a friend of St. Vincent?"

The junior inspector glanced down at his medal and smiled.

Feeling that it was now safe to let his guard down, Signor Speranza dropped to a sitting position, propping his elbows on the rim of the tub. "I'm very impressed," he enthused. "You do not often find this kind of devoutness now, in young people."

The junior inspector nodded and pulled on a pair of goggles. "It's very important, signore. My father says people do not take care of things the way they used to. Someone has to pray for the pipes." Then he switched on the saw and began to cut into the plaster.

The junior inspector's words, along with the buzzing of the saw, seemed to bounce and ricochet off the porcelain sides of the bathtub and ring in Signor Speranza's ears. *Someone has to pray for the pipes?* He was reminded of a similar argument he had made to the village priest, Don Rocco, regarding vacuum cleaners. "How has the Vatican not considered the need for their protection, Father?" he had asked fretfully after yet another customer had failed to show up for their yearly service appointment, and a search of the otherwise "complete" *Compendium* had yielded nothing.

Signor Speranza gasped and put his hand to his mouth. He understood everything now. This upstart clerk was not praying that the nation's pipes might outlast their prescribed usefulness, as he himself had been doing. No! This dastardly pup had been praying instead for their deliverance!

At this instant of terrible reckoning, two things happened. The junior inspector, switching off the saw and pushing back his goggles, gently eased the freshly cut block of plaster from its place in the wall, sending a chalky shower of white dust onto the linoleum, and Signor Speranza, his black moustache trembling, recalled the means by which he had repaired the sink. It came to him as a kind of vision—Smilzo, in shirtsleeves, perched on the edge of the tub, chewing pack after pack of pink bubblegum.

It was the junior inspector's turn to gasp, as he shone his flashlight into the hole.

"Signore!" he cried. "What is this?"

Resuming his earlier sangfroid, which at this point was the only thing he had left, Signor Speranza glanced into the hole, crossed his arms, and sniffed.

"I think it's Hubba Bubba."

2

Do You Want Me to
Show You a Real Problem?

$\mathcal{S}$ignor Speranza was subdued after that. He stood there, in the bathtub, as the junior inspector filled out a form in triplicate and handed it to him.

"Here is the estimate, signore. The town will need to remit payment within sixty days or the commission will cut off the water."

Signor Speranza stared at the form. The junior inspector had written the total in blue ballpoint, and circled it. Seventy thousand euros. The numbers swam on the page. Seventy thousand. It might as well have been a million.

"Signore?" the junior inspector called to him from somewhere very far away. "Would you like to see if you qualify for a payment plan?"

Signor Speranza must have nodded, because the junior inspector turned to a fresh sheet on his clipboard and rattled off a string of questions. Was Prometto home to any major form of industry? Did it have a shopping mall? Any unique or culturally significant tourist attractions? Was there perhaps potential for mining in the area, such as natural gas, or coal deposits?

No . . . no . . . no . . . Signor Speranza shook his head. Prometto didn't have any of those things. It was just a nowhere place. A *going*-nowhere place. Had the junior inspector ever seen it on a map? It was like a tiny speck at the bottom, just at the point where Italy's narrow boot might meet the pavement if it were grinding out a cigarette.

The junior inspector didn't answer, but just checked his boxes, and when he was finished, he sighed and returned his pen to his pocket. "I am very sorry, signore, but it appears your village does not have the resources necessary to qualify for a payment plan at this time."

Signor Speranza looked at him, dazed.

"No money," the young man said loudly, as if Signor Speranza were deaf. "There is no money here, signore. There is not even the chance of money."

❈ ❈ ❈

The Lord works in mysterious ways. Signor Speranza would not be able to see it until much later, when everything was over, but the pointless, maddening time he spent at work that afternoon was destined to change the course of his entire life.

Three hours after the departure of the junior inspector, he sat at the back of the once-flourishing Speranza and Son's on the Via Sant'Agata, just him and his terrible secret: that they were all doomed. He had avoided his wife, Betta, on his way out of the door, and she had called after him not to forget the balloons for his uncle's birthday party, and just hearing the words had brought tears to his eyes. A party? What was there to celebrate? He had the town's ledger open on one side of his desk, and the *Compendium* on the other. He was no longer on speaking terms with St. Vincent Ferrer. He had, in fact, taken a permanent marker and, in full sight of God, run a line through his name. He should have known better than to trust the patron saint of plumbers.

The ledger had yielded no hope. As he had known already, there was no money in the coffers. He glanced around his shop, at the quiet ranks of vacuum cleaners and the dim coils of replacement tubing, and sighed. There was no money here, either.

He had discussed the matter only a week ago with Don Rocco.

"Understand me, Father. It's not the population," he had told him over glasses of lemonade at the café. "It's a matter of percentages. If one hundred percent—two hundred twelve people—were all to bring their vacuum cleaners to my shop, then . . ." Here, Signor Speranza had kissed his fingertips. *"Mwah!"*

Don Rocco, who was a young priest, and a thoughtful one, had stirred the ice in his glass. "Two hundred and twelve, signore?" he asked, his forehead rumpling. "But wouldn't that mean that every husband and every wife would have their own vacuum? And each of their children, also?"

Signor Speranza pulled a face. "If you want to split hairs, Father. You know what I mean. You have the same issue. It's the young people; they are the problem. We cannot even get them to stay in the town where they were born. They would rather have internet service."

Don Rocco frowned. "Just because they have left Prometto,

that does not mean they have left the church, signore. It's possible they are going to Mass in those new places where they are."

Signor Speranza shook his head. "That's a very nice dream, Father, but we have to face the facts. Young people do not take care of vacuums, and they do not go to church. That is just the way it is. How many young people do you have going to Mass now?" Then he held up his hand. "And spare me Christmas and Easter, Father. Even the devil goes to church at Christmas and Easter."

But Don Rocco would not be drawn into talking numbers. "It's something we're doing, signore," he said instead, glancing forlornly at the little church. "We are doing something wrong."

Signor Speranza had taken a contemplative draft of lemonade. "People also like Ash Wednesday," he mused. "They enjoy the drama of that, I think. Have you considered giving out ashes on other days, Father? Might drum up business."

Yes, clearly, the young people were to blame. Hundreds of years, and Prometto had never been in a mess like this before. Signor Speranza closed the ledger now and glared across the shop at his own personal young person, Smilzo, who was perched atop a vacuum canister in the showroom and scribbling in a notebook, the tip of his pointy nose pink with concentration.

Signor Speranza and his assistant were not currently on the best of terms. A little over a month ago, in response to the customary yearly dip in business following spring-cleaning season, the two of them had undertaken an informal campaign of interoffice pranks, as a way of livening things up. Signor Speranza had difficulty now in remembering who had started it, and indeed it might have been accidental—one of them had mixed up the salt and the sugar, or something like that. But, last week, Smilzo had gone too far.

It was just as Signor Speranza was calling a meeting of the

local business owners to order. He had a special gavel and block, of carved walnut, and stored in a walnut box lined with dark blue velvet, which he kept in the top drawer of his desk and brought out for just such special occasions. All the council members had sat ranged in a semicircle in front of Signor Speranza's desk. Smilzo, who was not on the council but had been prevailed upon to take notes, had been sitting off to one side. Everyone was chatting when Signor Speranza rapped the gavel.

"Order. Order, please," he had called.

The room had fallen silent.

Signor Speranza had smiled pleasantly. "Now," he'd said, and leaned forward at his desk.

At that precise moment, when all eyes and ears were riveted in Signor Speranza's direction, there had come—and most definitely emanating from Signor Speranza's chair—the loudest, most terrific fart anyone had ever heard.

PBBBBBBBBBBBBBTTT!

"You should have seen your face, boss," Smilzo had said, when the meeting was finally over. Then he had keeled over and clutched his stomach, engaging in the kind of helpless laughter that is so filled with mirth, it produces no sound. A black box, with a blinking red light, was revealed, taped to the underside of Signor Speranza's chair, and a matching remote with a single button produced from Smilzo's pocket.

"See, boss? Simple." And Smilzo had demonstrated, pressing the button and releasing another thunderous explosion.

Signor Speranza had done the only thing he could do under the circumstances, which was to plant his heavily booted foot on the seat of Smilzo's pants. He had realized later that he should have immediately confiscated the box and remote control. Now, while he wasn't exactly living in fear, it might be said he was living in a state of *heightened awareness*.

Closing the *Compendium* with a sigh, Signor Speranza went for a fitful walk around the shop. When he came to Smilzo, he stopped and kicked him gently in the shin. "What's happening now?" he demanded, nodding at the notebook.

Smilzo was writing a screenplay. Signor Speranza didn't approve of screenplays, obviously, but it was sort of interesting that a person could just write something down as if it had actually happened.

Smilzo looked up, his pointy face aglow.

"You'll never believe it, boss. A tornado comes and picks up the house. And then it puts it down in a magical world."

Signor Speranza considered this, his mouth disappearing up into his moustache. "Like ruby slippers?" he asked finally.

Smilzo was very still for a moment, and then a muscle under his eye twitched, and he dived back into his notebook, scrubbing his eraser across the page.

Signor Speranza rolled his eyes and then circled around behind his assistant, so he could read over his shoulder.

"'Enter leading lady, Arabella, twenty-three. Tall, skinny, black hair. Bubbly personality.'" He snorted. "That sounds just like—"

The little bell over the shop door jingled. Smilzo, looking up, yelped, turned three shades of pink, and then sat on his notebook, just as Antonella Capra burst onto the scene. She was the only person Signor Speranza knew of who was skinnier than his assistant—like a walking stick of spaghetti. Today, she was wearing approximately fifty bangle bracelets on each narrow wrist, and a pair of enormous pink plastic hoop earrings, one of which had gotten stuck in her voluminous black hair and was sticking out at an odd angle. Her thin face was bent over her phone, and she was typing very fast.

"*Ciao*, signore," she said, aiming two air kisses in roughly the direction of Signor Speranza's cheeks without looking up and without ceasing typing. "Do you know where Smilzo is? He's supposed to take a picture of me with a vacuum. For a joke."

Signor Speranza's moustache bristled.

Smilzo jumped up. "Is not really a joke, boss," he said hurriedly. "Is more like an ironic statement."

Antonella looked up. "Oh, there you are."

Signor Speranza sighed. He had known Antonella since she was a baby. She was twenty-three years old now, and for the first twenty-two and a half years of their acquaintance he had, whenever he'd seen her, enjoyed an unobstructed view of her face. This had all changed now, since she had acquired this new gadget of hers.

"What are you doing on that thing?" he asked crossly. He had used his own cell phone exactly twice: the first time when Betta had called him to be sure it was set up properly, and the second when he had hurled it across the room to kill a spider. "Are you talking to someone?"

Antonella nodded, causing one pink plastic earring to jounce up and down, and the other, which was stuck in her hair, to tremble maddeningly on the very cusp of freedom.

"Who is it?" Signor Speranza persisted.

Antonella let one hand go for a second and waved it around in the air. "I am talking to everyone, signore."

"What does that mean?" Signor Speranza frowned. "You are talking to everyone? Are you talking to me?"

Antonella sighed and with some effort peeled her eyes off her phone's screen long enough to turn it around so Signor Speranza could see it.

"Social media, signore," she said, scrolling. "I have seventeen followers now, but really, anyone, anywhere, can read it."

Signor Speranza tried to concentrate as words and images flashed by. "Mm," he said, nodding as if he understood. "It's the worldwide web?"

Antonella giggled. "*Sì, signore.*"

"Who is this one?" Signor Speranza poked his finger at the screen, trying to stop on a particular picture he kept seeing scroll past again and again.

Antonella angled the phone back toward herself and tapped it. "This one?" she asked, incredulous, turning it back around.

Signor Speranza blinked at the tank-topped young man who was smiling at him from inside a neon-pink heart, and whose bicep was roughly the size of Smilzo's waist. The face was familiar.

"I know him," he said, pointing at the screen. "Who is it?"

Antonella's mouth dropped open.

"Dante Rinaldi," she said, in a tone she might have used if Signor Speranza had asked her to explain what pasta was. "*Dante Rinaldi.*"

Signor Speranza frowned, searching the young man's face. Rinaldi . . . Rinaldi . . . He couldn't place the family. Had Giulia Scarpa married a Rinaldi? He glanced at Smilzo, who appeared to be studying the ceiling tiles.

He turned back to Antonella. "He's your boyfriend?" he asked.

"*Boyfriend?*" Antonella threw her head back and squawked. "Signore! It's Dante Rinaldi!"

"He's a movie star, boss," mumbled Smilzo.

Oh. Signor Speranza lost interest. A movie star.

"Just look at him, signore." Antonella had apparently switched over to a page devoted exclusively to pictures of Dante Rinaldi sporting a lurid assortment of multicolored tank tops, and was now scrolling tenderly through them, the phone tilted outward so that Signor Speranza and Smilzo might enjoy them, too. She sighed. "Isn't he beautiful?"

Smilzo made a sound like a strangled cat, and covered it with a fit of coughing.

"Look at this one," she said, tapping the screen, but then did a double take and stuck her lip out. "The internet is glitching again." She pointed her phone accusingly at Signor Speranza. "You really need to do something about this, signore. It's a serious problem."

"Yeah, boss." Smilzo nodded, having recovered his composure. "Is a very serious problem. I was watching a movie on my phone last night, and right at the end—*fft!*" He drew one finger across his scrawny neck. "All gone."

Signor Speranza's eyes widened. A serious problem? *This* was their idea of a serious problem? *Do you see, Lord?* he asked, gazing heavenward. *Do you see what I am dealing with here?* He opened his mouth, and in another second he might have spilled his secret, and told these two idiots what a serious problem really looked like, but he was interrupted by the jingle of the bell.

❋ ❋ ❋

"I hope you don't mind, signore, if these two young people listen to our conversation." Signor Speranza was ensconced at his desk at the back of the shop. Signor Rossi, a loyal constituent, sat in the upholstered chair opposite him, while Smilzo and Antonella sat alongside the desk in a pair of folding chairs, Smilzo sneaking looks at Antonella out the corner of his eye, and Antonella scrolling through her phone and twirling her hair. "I'm trying to show them the difference between serious and nonserious problems."

"Oh, this is a very serious problem, signore." Signor Rossi leaned forward in his chair and twisted his hat in his hands. "It's a problem I am having with my dog."

Antonella snorted.

Signor Speranza threw her a warning look and then gestured. "Please, signore, continue."

"Well, it's—it's that she's being attacked."

Signor Speranza raised one eyebrow. "Attacked, signore?"

Signor Rossi nodded. "She's being attacked by my neighbor's new litter of puppies."

Signor Speranza preemptively glared at Antonella and produced a small spiral notebook and a stub of pencil.

"What kind of puppies?" he asked.

"Miniature schnauzers," said Signor Rossi. "You know, the German ones, with the ears."

Signor Speranza nodded over his notebook. "Yes, I have seen some of those. They look like the Huns, marching, marching."

"That's exactly right," agreed Signor Rossi. "And these Huns, as you call them, will not leave Bambolina—that is my dog—alone. They jump on her and they bark, and they bite her ears and her tail." Signor Rossi's eyes filled with tears. "She's a very old dog, signore. She deserves her time in the sun."

"I completely agree, signore." Signor Speranza made a notation in his notebook. "And have you approached your neighbor with this complaint?"

Signor Rossi's deeply tanned cheeks flushed, turning his face a kind of dusky purple. "Yes, I did. I spoke to both of them, and they just laughed. They said, 'How can you tell she's bothered by them? Have you checked to see if she's still alive?'"

Signor Speranza gasped. "Signore!"

Signor Rossi nodded. "I couldn't believe it myself, signore." The bell at the front of the shop jingled, and he glanced over his shoulder. "But here—here is Bambolina now. My wife has brought her out for a walk. I will bring her in so you can meet her and see for yourself how sweet she is."

Everyone moved to the front of the shop, where Signora Rossi was negotiating the entrance. When she was finally inside, Signor Speranza saw that she was dragging a large red wagon.

"Here she is. This is Bambolina, signore," said Signor Rossi.

Signor Speranza blinked at the contents of the wagon, a little bit of the wind going out of his sails. "So this is the famous Bambolina," he said, and then, weakly, "Is this how she goes for a walk?"

Signor Rossi and his wife exchanged indulgent smiles.

"Bambolina has always been a bit of a princess, you see," said Signor Rossi. "I will take her out so you can say hello."

Before Signor Speranza could object, Signor Rossi had removed Bambolina from the wagon and placed her heavily atop the toes of Signor Speranza's shoes. There she sat, the world's largest Pomeranian, her tongue lolling out of one side of her mouth, bright pink against a fluffy profusion of orange fur. She did not move, except for panting and blinking, and as Signor Speranza watched, mesmerized, the frequency and duration of her blinks gradually increased, until, finally, she was sleeping.

Everyone was silent for a moment, until Antonella knelt beside Bambolina.

"You are right, signore," she said, giggling. "This is the most serious problem I have ever seen." Then, holding her phone up, she fluffed her hair and snapped a picture.

3

Betta Finds Out

$\mathcal{S}$ignor Speranza closed the shop at five thirty, turning the crank that lowered his awning and taking care to shake out the all-weather mat outside the door. When he had finished, he glanced around the little cobblestoned square. Everything was just as it had been when his father was still alive. There was Bisi's Emporio to his right, its tin roof baking in the late-afternoon sun, and the café beyond it; the dentist's office was to his left. Directly across the street was Maestro's butcher's shop, and, diagonally to the left, the little whitewashed building that was Sant'Agata, Prometto's church. It was all anyone could ask for. Maybe there were not so many people milling about as there had been in his father's day, but there were a few. Signor Speranza watched them, and his heart sank. Unless he came up with some kind of answer to this spectacular problem they were having, in sixty days, there would be no one. Everyone would be gone.

Seventy thousand euros. The number squeezed at Signor Speranza's chest and wrung the air out of his lungs as he walked down the Via Sant'Agata toward home. How much would that be in lire? He had to stop to do the computation. Almost one hundred and thirty-six million!

"What do you make of *that*, Papà?" he asked out loud. Luigi Speranza, despite having departed this earth nearly three decades earlier, as yet occupied a small corner at the back of his son's mind. There he sat, on an upturned bucket, threading red peppers on string—because that was how Signor Speranza pictured him. Today, however, Luigi Speranza had no answer, no words of advice for his son. He only hunched over his peppers and sorrowfully shook his head.

Signor Speranza got all the way to the hotel before he recalled that tonight was Zio Franco's birthday party, and he had been meant to pick up balloons. As he opened the front door, his four-year-old granddaughter, Carlotta, careened toward him.

"*Nonno!*" she shouted, and blew a party horn in his face.

❆ ❆ ❆

Zio Franco, who was now ninety-three years old to the day, sat at the Speranza kitchen table. He was not happy to be there; he was not happy to be anywhere. He was sitting beside Carlotta—who, in contrast, was having a marvelous time—and glowering at everyone, his arms crossed in billowing linen shirtsleeves, silvery patches of psoriasis showing on his elbows, and a pointy orange party hat on top of his balding head.

"Go on, Zio, open it." Signor Speranza leaned over the table and nudged the little foil-and-ribbon-wrapped package closer to his uncle. "You'll love it, believe me."

When everyone's eyes were on Zio, Signor Speranza dabbed his forehead with a napkin and took a long drink of water. It was exhausting, smiling like this as if everything were fine, and avoiding his wife's searching eyes. He glanced around the table. It was just them for the party: Zio, who had been picked up earlier that afternoon; Betta; little Carlotta; and Carlotta's mother, their daughter, Gemma. Gemma had come to Signor Speranza and his wife late in life, an astonishing gift after they had stopped hoping. His eyes lingered on her now, as was his habit these last five years, ever since the news had broken, just after her nineteenth birthday, that they were to have a grandchild, but no son-in-law. Was she getting smaller? Signor Speranza narrowed his eyes and frowned, watching her pick at her cake with the tines of her fork.

"Let me help you, Zio," said Carlotta, who was dazzled by the shiny paper. Hopping down from her chair, she wrested the box from Zio Franco's not-altogether-cooperative hands and tore it open. "LEGOS!" she crowed.

Zio Franco slouched in his chair and grunted. "What the hell am I supposed to do with that?"

Signor Speranza managed a manic grin and shoveled an enormous forkful of cake into his mouth. "You're a builder, Zio. I thought you would like to *build* something." He continued his grinning and shoveling, until his black moustache was dotted with white frosting and he looked insane.

"I think it's offensive," said Gemma, putting her fork down and clamping her arms over her chest. "Who gives a ninety-three-year-old man a kid's toy for a birthday present? It's rude."

Signor Speranza's mouth dropped open. This cutting little statement constituted almost a full-blown speech for his daughter, who didn't ordinarily go out of her way to speak to him at all.

Betta motioned to him to keep quiet from the other end of the table.

"I don't think that's how Papà meant it, Gemma," she said, her voice soothing. "It's just a little joke. Something for Zio to play with Carlotta. Isn't that right, Nino?"

Now Signor Speranza crossed his arms and scowled.

Carlotta clutched the box to her chest, almost bursting with excitement. "Can I open it, Zio?"

Zio Franco muttered that she could keep it for all he cared, and within seconds she had the box open and had popped one of the plastic bags, sending Lego pieces skittering everywhere, including one that landed in the remains of Signor Speranza's cake. He picked it out and brightly changed the subject.

"I've been wanting to talk to you about your house, Zio."

Zio Franco's already petulant face hardened into a stiff mask, and Betta made a tsking sound, but Signor Speranza did not back down. If he was going to have to convince this uncle of his, who was stubborn as a mule, to leave Prometto peacefully in sixty days' time, he needed to get cracking on it now.

"Zio, please understand. I know you're attached to your house. But I think it's time. It is not good for you to be there all alone."

Zio Franco shook his head. "I'm not moving."

Signor Speranza persisted. "Did you see the advertisement I left for you last week? That place looks very nice. Units starting at four thousand euros."

Zio Franco snorted. "That was a mausoleum."

Signor Speranza's eyebrows lifted. "What are you talking about? It's a condominium complex."

Betta, at her end of the table, stifled a whoop of laughter. "No,

Nino," she said, when she got ahold of herself. "Zio is right. I looked at the ad myself. The Garden of Everlasting Roses is a mausoleum."

Signor Speranza was baffled. "It said they have air-conditioning," he marveled. And then, mystified, "Who is the air-conditioning *for?*"

Zio Franco ignored all this and pounded his fist. "It would take three armies of men to remove me from my home."

Signor Speranza rolled his eyes to the ceiling. *Or one oversize toddler with a clipboard.*

"Papà," said Gemma. "I think that Zio should be able to make up his own—"

Signor Speranza turned to her, beseeching. "*Cara mia*, please."

Gemma's quiet eyes flashed. "Oh, right," she said, her lip trembling. "Who am I to have an opinion?" She stood up, her chair knocking over behind her. "Maybe for *my* birthday you can get me a Barbie doll!" She ran out of the kitchen and into her bedroom, slamming the door behind her.

Carlotta looked up from her Legos and started to cry. Betta folded her hands on the table and sighed. "Oh, Nino."

"*What?*" Signor Speranza shouted, throwing his hands in the air. "What did I say?"

* * *

"All right, that's it."

With Zio gone and Gemma and Carlotta in bed, Betta closed the bedroom door behind her and put her hands on her hips.

"You tell me what's happening right now. You were like a crazy person tonight. What is bothering you?"

Signor Speranza sank onto the bed, and Betta sat beside him. The story came out in fits and starts.

"Oh, Nino." Betta covered her mouth with her hand. They sat there for a while in silence, and then the cogs of her brisk and practical mind began to turn. "Well, there has to be an answer. You have to talk to Don Rocco," she said. "He'll take up a collection."

Signor Speranza sighed. "To collect from whom? Betta, we are in this mess because no one has any money. You know how many people have not paid their taxes?" He knew. He had their names marked in the town ledger, with their excuses alongside, on sticky notes. It was a mess. It was all a mess.

Betta chewed her lip. "What about Signor Maestro? He has to have money. Have you seen that ridiculous house?"

Signor Speranza grimaced. He had not had cause to enter Signor Maestro's domicile, thank God, but he saw him every day outside the butcher's shop, a large gold-and-diamond ring sparkling on his pinkie finger. Imagine the blood and guts that must be stuck in the prongs of that ring. He shuddered.

"Signor Maestro is a barbarian," he said. "He will not be interested in helping anyone but himself." He shook his head and got into bed. "Try not to worry. We will have a place to live. Tomorrow, I'll call Alberto."

Betta, who had her own views on said Alberto, pulled a face and got into bed also. As she pulled up the covers, her eyes wandered to the wall that separated their room from Gemma and Carlotta's.

"Do you think they'll want to move with us?" she whispered.

Signor Speranza was startled. "Of course they will move with us. Where else would they go?" But even as he spoke, he felt uneasy. The last time Betta had asked him a question like that, in that worried voice, had been five years ago. "Nino, you don't think Gemma is getting too serious with this Ricci boy, do you?" And he had been sure then, also.

"I've seen her texting him, you know," said Betta quietly, looking at her hands. "He's in Rome, I think. We cannot afford Rome, Nino."

Signor Speranza sat up. "So what?" he blustered. He could feel his blood pressure rising, and a pounding in his temples. It was the feeling he always got when he was boxing an invisible enemy. "So what? No one is keeping her here. If she wanted to go, she would go. She likes it here."

"Shhhhh," said Betta, her eyes flicking again to the wall. "Yes, Nino. She likes it here. She likes the school for Carlotta. She doesn't want to take her away from her friends. But . . ." She shrugged. "What if there is no school? What if the friends are gone? What then?"

Signor Speranza had no answer for this.

"I worry about her, Nino." Betta sighed. "It's as if she has given up. No friends. No interests. She's angry or depressed all the time. I worry. Maybe . . ." She hesitated. "Maybe it's not the worst thing that could happen, if she and Carlotta were to move away . . . start their own life . . ."

Signor Speranza grunted and turned out the light. In the dark, he saw himself and Carlotta, four years ago. He was walking the floor with her as she cried in the middle of the night, while her mother cried in the room next door. "*Gallinella zoppa, zoppa, quante penne tiene 'n coppa,*" he sang softly, the old song about the little lame hen, and how many feathers she had on her back. When he stopped singing, Gemma had called out, in her thin, stretched voice. "Sing it again, Papà," she said, and he had sung it over and over, until both his little girls were sleeping.

Now, tonight, he bunched his pillow under his head and pretended to sleep, until he heard the sound of Betta gently snoring.

Then he climbed out of bed and knelt at the side, as he had when he was a child. He grunted a little as his knees struck the hard floor and that electric jolt of old age shot through his joints. He made the sign of the cross and scrunched his eyes shut. In his mind, he paged through the *Compendium*, trying to decide to whom he should appeal for help.

In the end, given the dire circumstances, he went directly to the manager.

"Please, Lord," he said, whispering aloud. "I do not know what to do. If you have the answer, please show it to me."

He waited a few minutes, in case God wanted to make a really grand gesture and tell him what he should do on the spot, but, when nothing happened, he climbed back into bed and stayed awake, deep into the night, arguing with Betta in his mind. Because she was wrong. Gemma and Carlotta moving away was the worst thing that could possibly happen.

4

The Mysterious Whereabouts of George Clooney

At dawn, Signor Speranza was dreaming of when Gemma was young.

"Papà."

He was in the hotel's living room, but it was the living room of twenty years ago. At the windows there were the pink watered-silk curtains with puffed flounces, which Betta had found at a flea market, and he was sitting on the old, scratchy couch with the crewelwork flowers on the cushions. He peered over the top of his newspaper.

"Papà, you said that you would come to my tea party."

There was little Gemma, as real as anything. She was standing with her arms crossed, the way her own daughter did now.

Then Signor Speranza found that he was no longer his younger self, sitting there on the couch. Rather, he seemed to have floated up, and was looking down on the scene from above. He had been here before, he realized, in this actual place; he had participated in this actual conversation. He wasn't so much dreaming as remembering. He saw his younger self lower the newspaper and raise one eyebrow. He watched his old moustache, at the very peak of its luxurious lushness, twitch from side to side.

"Will there be biscuits?" he heard himself ask, in a mock-serious tone.

They moved to the table, and Gemma told him about school. "I don't like it," she said, staring fiercely at the little china teapot. "Everyone is mean there. Why can't I just stay home?"

The young Signor Speranza had not gotten the moment right. He had miscalculated. He had teased. And the older Signor Speranza, who was watching from the ceiling, did not remember in time, and missed his chance to do it over again, a different way. He watched his younger self rumple his daughter's hair.

"You can't stay home forever, *cucuzza*," he said. "Pretty soon, when you are big, your *mamma* and I will kick you out."

Little Gemma had flung her head back and gasped, just as if her father had slapped her across the face. "I am *never* going to leave!" she'd cried. "Never, never, never!" And then she had thrown the teapot, and it had smashed on the floor.

Signor Speranza woke with a start. It was morning. The events of long ago faded, and the events of yesterday trickled back to him, and he fell back on his pillow and sighed. Just outside the door, he heard the scuffling sound of his daughter's slippers.

"Gemma?" he called.

He heard her pause, and then walk on. She didn't answer.

❈ ❈ ❈

With no word yet from God, Signor Speranza took his coffee in bed and activated the municipal phone chain, alerting residents to a town meeting on a vague but critical topic, to be held two days hence, at eight o'clock Monday evening, in the church. He would have preferred it to be tomorrow, but there wasn't any sense in wrecking everyone's Sunday. Then he rang his old school friend, Alberto Martini, who now lived twenty miles north in Oliveto, about renting a three-bedroom apartment.

"He says we have to act fast, or we will miss our chance," Signor Speranza told Betta after hanging up the phone. "He says places are going like hotcakes."

Betta, whose usual equanimity was more or less restored this morning, was folding towels. She shook one out and raised her eyebrows. "In Oliveto? *Tuh.*" Swiftly, she gathered the towel into a neat square. "That man is a con artist. I don't know why you are friends with him."

"He might be a useful friend to have," Signor Speranza said, glancing at the notepad on the nightstand, which was covered in penciled computations. "We are not dealing with a lot of capital here."

Betta clapped her stack of towels between two hands and started for the linen closet. "If the apartment is in Alberto and Maria's house, I would rather live on the side of the road."

Thirty minutes later, Signor Speranza parked in front of the Martini home. They lived on the outskirts of town, in one of the newer houses with a clay tile roof. Alberto was waiting on the portico, smoking a cigar, the smoke mingling with the hazy July heat, and, when he saw Signor Speranza pull up, he began waving his arms.

"Hello, Speranza!" he hollered. "How are you doing, you magnificent son of a bitch?"

Signor Speranza climbed out of his car, uttering a quick prayer of thanksgiving that Betta hadn't insisted on coming with him. He could almost hear her—*That's it; we're done.*

"Where did you steal that thing?" Signor Speranza called, pointing at the garage. He could just make out the bumper of a red Alfa Romeo.

Alberto grinned, twirling his cigar. "What can I say? I got lucky."

❖ ❖ ❖

With Alberto, there was no going to see the apartment and then going home. He had to make a production of it.

"I told Betta I would not be too long," said Signor Speranza, glancing at his watch. They were in the Alfa Romeo now, with the top down, riding around town.

"She'll be fine," said Alberto, cranking up the radio. He was a spry sixty-three, and, driving, he gave the impression of a little kid playing a car-racing game at an arcade, bouncing on the seat, his feet scarcely reaching the pedals. "Besides, this is part of the tour. You are not only renting an apartment—you are renting all of *this*!" He made a flourish with his hand to encompass the surrounding area, with its dusty trees and its haphazard traffic signs, and the car veered sharply, nearly careening into a pair of indignant chickens on the side of the road.

Signor Speranza sighed. As he looked around, the eleven o'clock sun broiling the top of his head, and the wind whipping his moustache into a froth, he could not help but notice that things were different here from the last time he had visited. When was that? He frowned. Six months ago? A year? However long it had been, something had happened. The Oliveto he remembered was even sleepier than Prometto, if that were possible, but today the Alfa Romeo wound through streets filled with life. There was a velvet rope outside the poky little café, with a line of people behind it, waiting to get in. The car turned onto the main boulevard, and Signor Speranza did a double take. Was that a McDonald's? Betta would never believe it.

Signor Speranza turned to his friend and shouted over the radio and the roar of the engine. "What's all this? What has happened here?"

Alberto grinned. "Isn't it great?" he shouted back. "It's a great story. You know George Clooney? Movie star? American?"

Signor Speranza considered. Movie stars were not his speciality. He turned the radio down. "What movie?"

"You know." Alberto rolled his eyes. "The *Ocean* movie. They rip off a big casino."

Signor Speranza racked his brain. "Oh, right," he said finally. "*Il biondo?*"

Alberto shook his head. "No, no. That's Brad Pitt. The other one. Black hair. The one with the aunt. You know—'Mambo Italiano.'" He did a little dance in his seat.

"Okay." Signor Speranza was getting impatient. He could just see Betta, making her hand into a puppet, talking, talking. *Chiacchierone*, she would say, exasperated.

"So," said Alberto, looking directly at Signor Speranza and not at the road at all, his disconcerting blue eyes shining. "About six months ago, a big magazine runs a story. George Clooney thinks he will buy a house in Oliveto."

"No kidding?" Signor Speranza said aloud. *Why would he want to do that?* he said in his head.

Alberto was looking at the road again, but he took one hand off the wheel to snap his fingers. "Just like *that*, everything changes. People come from all over. *If this place is good enough for George Clooney*, they say, *then it's good enough for me.*"

"No kidding," Signor Speranza murmured again.

Alberto whipped the Alfa Romeo into a parking space on a cramped, ill-lit street. "We're here," he announced, snapping off his seat belt.

Signor Speranza looked around. There wouldn't be anywhere for Carlotta to ride her bike on a street like this. He didn't like the look of one of the houses, either, with an old washing machine rusting on the lawn, and a dented sign tacked to the fence — BEWARE OF DOG. He got out of the car and stepped gingerly over the broken curb.

"And?" he asked, curious. "Where is George Clooney?"

Alberto pressed his key fob, making the red car beep, and grinned so widely that Signor Speranza could see one of his silver crowns.

"I don't know," he said brightly. "If I see Brad Pitt, maybe I'll ask him."

❀ ❀ ❀

"Needs a spruce-up," said Alberto, picking his way through the layer of rubbish that carpeted the living room floor of the limited-time-only, get-it-while-it's-hot, three-bedroom apartment.

"You said it had a backyard," said Signor Speranza, staring out of the back window.

Alberto joined him. "It does," he said, pointing. "See? The property goes to the tree line."

Signor Speranza suppressed the urge to wring his friend's scrawny neck. "It's a ravine!"

"Mm," said Alberto, looking down. "You did not want a ravine?"

Signor Speranza gazed at the ceiling, noticing an alarming brown patch of water damage. Alberto's eyes followed his.

"Look, Speranza, I know it's not perfect," he said, in that smooth-talking tone Betta hated. "But you just have to think of it as a starter home."

Signor Speranza laughed bitterly. "I am sixty-two years old. I'm past the point of starter homes."

"Listen . . ." Alberto was getting bored. He kept fidgeting and glancing toward the door. "I can give it to you for seven hundred a month."

Signor Speranza's mouth dropped open. "Seven hundred a month? I thought you said you could give me a deal!"

Alberto threw his hands in the air. "Seven hundred *is* a deal! Wake up, Speranza. How much do you think things cost? Where are you going to go, Rome? For seven hundred a month, they might let you piss in a bucket."

Signor Speranza closed his eyes and rubbed the sides of his head. It had not been helpful, Alberto mentioning Rome like that. With his eyes closed, he noticed the smells—the mildew and the wood rot and the mouse droppings. Finally, he opened his eyes and held out his hand.

"*Grazie*, Alberto," he said. "*Mille grazie.* I will talk to my wife."

5

Signor Speranza
Consults His Conscience

$\mathcal{W}$hen Signor Speranza arrived back in Prometto, he sat in the car for an hour, trying and failing to picture Gemma in that apartment of Alberto's. Then he turned off the ignition and walked into town. He had not smoked a cigarette in twenty-five years, but he was smoking one now. He stood outside Maestro's butcher's shop, glaring up at the battered stuffed boar mounted over the awning and sucking his cigarette down to the filter. He had spent a fair amount of time contemplating this boar over the years. It was missing one tusk and stared beadily over the horizon, and sometimes, when Signor Maestro came outside and stood on the step in his white apron, gazing stupidly in the same direction, they looked like brothers.

"Maestro is not my friend," Signor Speranza muttered aloud.

Then he pointed his cigarette stub at the boar. "He was not your friend, either."

The boar did not answer.

Signor Speranza looked up at the sky. "This, Lord?" he asked, raising one eyebrow. "This is what you want me to do?"

There was no answer from that quarter, either.

Signor Speranza sighed. There wasn't any other way forward that he could see. No one else in Prometto had any money. He tossed his cigarette on the ground.

"Signore!" he called heartily as he entered the shop, throwing his hands in the air. "So good to see you. You look as if you could wrestle a bear. Business is good?"

Signor Maestro, who was standing behind the counter like a pillar of wood, made a guttural sound in his throat. "What do you want, Speranza?"

Signor Speranza meandered around, trying to keep it casual and perusing the merchandise. He wondered if Signor Maestro went home smelling like salami and copper.

"This is good. Very good," he said, nodding at the rack of cured salamis. "You have a wonderful selection. I tell everyone that. You must be making a lot of good money here."

When Signor Maestro remained silent, Signor Speranza decided he had better put his money where his mouth was. He bent in front of the largest glass case and pointed at a pair of pork chops. "I'll take these," he said. "Betta will be pleased."

Signor Maestro took down an order slip and licked the point of his pencil.

"Where do you want me to send it?" he asked.

Signor Speranza balked. "I don't need you to send it anywhere. I am standing right here."

Signor Maestro swung his pencil out, pointing at a laminated sign.

ALL MEATS THIS CASE

MAIL ORDER ONLY

"New policy," he grunted. "I had to make some changes. How else am I to make money in this town? The world is out there, Speranza." He slugged one of his giant paws in the same direction the boar outside was looking.

Signor Speranza blinked, first at the sign, and then at Signor Maestro.

"How long does that take?" he asked, incredulous.

Signor Maestro shrugged his fat shoulders. "Three to five business days. Depending on where you're located."

Signor Speranza felt his blood pressure shoot up ten points, and he forgot why he was there. "I'm located directly in front of you!"

He regretted this outburst immediately, of course. There was silence for a moment, and then, from the back room, the sound of chairs scraping against the floor. That would be Maestro's sons, no doubt, coming to defend their father's honor, and his right to sell meat exclusively via mail order. Could all fifteen of the sons fit back there? Signor Speranza wondered dizzily, trying to peer over Maestro's shoulder. Was it still possible to make a run for it?

Signor Maestro, meanwhile, had crossed his arms over his gore-smeared apron.

"Do we have a problem here, Speranza?" he growled.

Signor Speranza held up his hands. "I was just joking. Send them to me. I don't care how. Post office. Carrier pigeon. I would love to eat them for dinner next week."

Signor Maestro counted Signor Speranza's bills into his stuffed cash register. Signor Speranza stared balefully at the thick stacks of money, remembering why he had come here in the first place.

"Signore," he said, in as pleasant a voice as he could muster, "you are a businessman. Have you ever considered investing in Prometto? Putting money back into the community?"

Signor Maestro snorted and slammed the cash drawer shut, tearing off the receipt. "Speranza," he grunted, "don't be an idiot."

❊ ❊ ❊

The next day was Sunday. Signor Speranza slept late and woke with a headache.

"Where is your mother?" he grumbled to Gemma when he padded into the kitchen. Gemma was at the table, sitting in front of an untouched glass of orange juice, and hunched, like Antonella, over her phone. She didn't look up.

"She took Carlotta to church."

Signor Speranza grunted and dragged out a chair. "What about you?" he asked peevishly. "You don't have to go to church?"

Gemma glanced over the top of her phone and stuck out her tongue. "And what about you, Papà? You have a dispensation?"

Signor Speranza frowned, drawing his mouth up and into his moustache and emitting an indistinct burbling noise, which indicated he was not currently available for theological debate.

"Who are you talking to?" he asked instead.

There was a pause. Then, "Nobody," said Gemma, shrugging, her voice half an octave higher than usual.

Signor Speranza felt the old, familiar well of panic. Better if his daughter were like Antonella, trying to talk to "everyone." Everyone was better than what he suspected was this particular nobody.

He cleared his throat and made his own voice light and casual.

"Do you ever talk to Luca Ricci anymore?" he asked, his eyes wide and innocent. "You know, I saw his cousin—"

It was a mistake.

"*Papà!*" said Gemma, her eyes flashing, just like the little girl who had thrown the teapot. She clutched her phone to her chest and flung back her chair. "I'm going out," she muttered, and stalked out of the kitchen.

Signor Speranza listened as the front door slammed. He gazed at the ceiling and sighed. Where had he gone wrong? Where had it *all* gone wrong? He looked at the cracks in the ceiling, and his mind wandered . . .

"Am I on that sign, Nonno?" he could hear Carlotta asking, dimly, as if from somewhere very far away. "Am I one of the numbers?"

It was five months ago, and he and Carlotta were walking home, in a wet February wind, from the beach. They had just come upon Prometto's weather-beaten sign, mounted crookedly on a stake at the side of the road, and Carlotta was staring up at it, awestruck.

PROMETTO
POPULATION: 212

Signor Speranza had looked down at his granddaughter, so small and so eager, and utterly disbelieving that she could merit such an honor, and his throat had felt strangely constricted.

"Of course, *tesora*," he had choked. "Of course you're on that sign, what do you think?"

She had clapped her little hands with the joy of it.

He had not lied to her, Signor Speranza told himself sternly as they continued their walk. She was one of the numbers. She was. He had just not seen any need to tell her the whole story. Why would a little girl need to know that the sign hadn't changed when she was born? The baby had come, and, before even bothering to see her, the father had left. It had been a one-for-one switch.

* * *

At six a.m. Monday, the day that Signor Speranza was meant to stand up in front of his friends and neighbors, and weep, and tell them that they were all going to lose their houses, he woke with a strangled cry.

The sound woke Betta, and she sat bolt upright. "What is it? Nino, what happened?"

Signor Speranza, who was tangled in the sheet, struggled to sit up.

"I was robbing a casino," he gasped, his heart still pounding. He squinted, trying to remember the details. Yes, he had been rappelling down the side of a shiny building, a pack of money on his back, but when he'd looked up he had seen the junior plumbing inspector looming at the top, his clip-on tie whipping in the wind, sawing through his rope with a knife.

"Alberto was there, too," he said, frowning at the memory. "I think he was singing 'Mambo Italiano.'"

Betta groaned and dropped back on her pillows. "A nightmare," she said. "Any dream with Alberto is a nightmare. Now go back to sleep." She turned on her side and pulled the blanket up to her chin.

But Signor Speranza was fully awake now. "Did I tell you George Clooney—the actor—was supposed to buy a house in Oliveto?" he asked. "Alberto told me." He related the whole story about the magazine article.

Betta snorted. "George Clooney? In *Oliveto*?"

Signor Speranza nodded. "That's what the magazine said."

"And who told the magazine, huh?" Betta closed her eyes to go back to sleep. "Three guesses, and they are all Alberto."

❉ ❉ ❉

Three guesses, and they are all Alberto. Betta's words knocked around in Signor Speranza's head as he got up and washed his face, and as he walked to work two and a half hours early. They kept bobbing back to the surface as he sat at his desk and paged through the *Compendium* in search of a last-minute rescue team, until all the saints' names blurred, and ran together. *Three guesses, and they are all Alberto.*

Well, and so what if it were true? Signor Speranza thought, with a surge of defiance. What if Alberto *had* started that rumor himself? Maybe it was wrong, technically speaking, to lie, but in this case, wasn't it also sort of . . . brilliant? People nowadays didn't know what they wanted. Or they thought they wanted one thing, until a celebrity on TV told them they wanted something else. Everything had to be bigger, better, new-and-improved. A fading place like Oliveto, or Prometto, didn't stand a chance without a little edge. And what harm did it do? George Clooney wasn't sweating it. It was a victimless crime! If a few vapid people believing that some movie star wanted to come to Prometto could jump-start the economy and save people's houses, then what was it to anyone, really?

What is it to God? Signor Speranza thought, with a twinge of conscience. He glanced up then, through the front window, and spotted Don Rocco across the square, sweeping the little pathway in front of the church.

Signor Speranza hastened across the shop and opened the front door, the bell jingling.

"Good morning, Father!" he called, waving. "How about breakfast? My treat!"

❅ ❅ ❅

Fifteen minutes later, Signor Speranza and Don Rocco sat at their usual table at the café, the one next to the dusty olive tree that the café's proprietress, Signora Catuzza, watered with leftover cooking liquids, and which therefore always smelled vaguely of chicken soup. Signor Speranza was eyeing the unwitting young priest, who was shoveling frittata into his mouth without a care in the world, as one would an opponent. How, he wondered, could he put this so as to get the answer he was looking for?

"Let me ask you something, Father," he began lightly, and then drained his cup of espresso in a single gulp. "Pretend that I say something to you, hypothetically speaking, only you take me at my word. Would that mean that I have lied to you?"

This, Signor Speranza thought, was his best shot at avoiding mortal sin. If he were just to let slip, casually, that it would really be something if some famous person—Brad Pitt, for example—were thinking of buying a house in Prometto, then he wouldn't actually be lying, would he? Linguistically—*grammatically*—he wouldn't have done anything wrong.

Don Rocco wiped his mouth with his napkin and considered. "That does not sound like a lie to me, signore. That sounds like a misunderstanding."

"Ha!" Signor Speranza clapped his hands and pointed at the priest. "A misunderstanding. Yes! That's perfect. Thank you, Father."

Don Rocco frowned. "But if you're *hoping* I'll misunderstand, then that changes matters, signore. That's different territory altogether."

Signor Speranza's momentary exuberance fizzled out, and his moustache drooped. "Of course, Father. Of course," he mumbled. Moodily, he pushed his food around his plate. It was all over, then. There was no answer to his problem. It would take a miracle to save them now.

With his fork, he flipped over his piece of toast, and, happening to glance at it, he gasped.

"Father! What does this look like to you?" He plucked the toast off the plate and showed it to the priest.

Don Rocco squinted. "Semolina?"

"It's Baby Jesus, Father!" Signor Speranza pointed. "See the halo here, and the manger." He tilted the toast so the priest could see it better. "I think there is even a cow, or maybe a donkey."

"Let me see that, signore."

Signor Speranza handed the toast over and waited on the edge of his seat. "Could be something big, Father," he said, excited. "People would come from all over to see something like that."

Don Rocco examined the toast, turning it over and holding it up to the sun, and then, when he was finished, he shrugged. "Sorry, signore, I don't see it," he said, and took a big bite.

6

Signor Speranza Finds the Answer

Signor Speranza spent a fitful day at work, and, with several hours left until the meeting, closed early and went to the Bosco di Rudina to argue with God. This was the ancient forest that was located at the highest point of Prometto's elevation, about a twenty-minute walk from the center of town. Signor Speranza often felt it was holier than any church.

He lay on a moss-covered stone the size of a helicopter launchpad and stared up at the crisscrossing canopy of branches and leaves and sky. It was very quiet, and if Don Rocco, stalwart defender of truth and justice, had been there, he might even have admitted that the forest had the same cool, bottled air as his church, and the same stillness.

"Why do you not answer me, Lord? What do you want me to do?" Signor Speranza called. "You want me to let Prometto fail? Is that what you want?"

A greenfinch called back to him, and nothing else.

"A *sign*, Lord," Signor Speranza grumbled. "Would it hurt for you to send a sign?" He lay there a few minutes longer, stripping olive tree leaves down to their veins to pass the time, just in case there was a time delay on his prayers traveling upward and reaching the Lord's ears, although he did not think the Almighty actually constrained himself to the same laws of physics He imposed on everybody else.

When he grew tired of waiting, he walked, picking his way over roots and vines and so many layers of dead leaves that it was like trudging through the bottom of a fish tank. He paid no heed to where he was going, and at a certain point the air changed, and there was a whiff of wood smoke that brought him back to an evening last October, when he and Don Rocco had talked about people who were gone.

"Do you ever miss your parents, signore?" Don Rocco had asked as they sat outside the café with a bottle of Chianti, the shops around them lit up like lanterns, and the sky filled with stars.

Signor Speranza had shrugged. "I talk to my father all the time, Father. It's not so different."

Don Rocco was startled. "You do not actually hear him, right?"

Signor Speranza had rolled his eyes. Then he'd rooted in his pocket for a piece of card and a stub of pencil. He'd scribbled something on the card and flipped it over, slapping his hand on top. "Father!" he'd bellowed suddenly. "On Sunday—and I don't care what you say, or the Pope, either—I am not going to Mass! I am going to have my own Mass in the forest instead, and I don't think God is going to give a damn about it."

Don Rocco had sat bolt upright. "Signore! A forest is not a church! And you are not a priest! And don't say *damn*!"

Signor Speranza had turned the card over. SIGNORE! it said in blocky letters. A FOREST IS NOT A CHURCH! AND YOU ARE NOT A PRIEST! AND DON'T SAY DAMN!

Don Rocco had gasped, and Signor Speranza chuckled. "Do you see, Father? If you know a person well enough . . . if you know what he *might* say . . ."

And so Signor Speranza did not have to miss his father, not really. They talked about all the same things they had when he was alive—new vacuum models, the rising cost of gasoline, the ludicrous Nativity scene made entirely of delicatessen meats that Signor Maestro insisted on placing in his shop's window every blessed year. It was different with his mother. She had died when he was only two years old, and he could not remember her, at least not clearly. She was still there somewhere in his mind, the ghost of her, but she was always disappearing around corners. Unlike his father, she would not sit down.

He exited the Bosco di Rudina on its northern side, where there was a small clearing and a couple of ramshackle houses, and, beyond them, the sheer drop of the cliffs, and the sea. As he did so, he came upon a clump of pulmonaria, that delicate purple flower with a name like a lung infection, and must have trodden on one of the blooms, releasing its fragrance, because, in one of those miracles of half-remembered scents, his mother, Caterina, suddenly appeared before him.

"*Mamma!*" Signor Speranza gasped, and he reached out, as he had when he was small, to touch the hem of her dress.

At that precise moment there came an unearthly cacophony from the yard of one of the houses, and Caterina Speranza vanished as quickly as she had appeared. Signor Speranza fought his way through weeds and vines to find her, and found Signor Rossi instead, standing in the middle of the lawn, his hands covering his eyes.

"Signore," Signor Speranza panted, bending to catch his breath and hide his disappointment, his hands on his knees. *"Che cosa?* What is happening?"

Signor Rossi peeked out from between his fingers. "It's my Bambolina, signore," he groaned. "Just look."

Signor Speranza straightened, and shielded his eyes, peering out over the horizon. He followed the dreadful sound, which was simultaneously like the honking of cars and the squealing of pigs, and his eyes alighted on a spectacle such as he had never seen, awake or dreaming.

A scant thirty feet from where they were standing, there lay a great, fluffy orange mound, and, teeming over it, seven or eight small, furry, salt-and-pepper-colored creatures.

"My God," Signor Speranza marveled, watching the furred demons swarm and re-form, swarm and re-form. He bit his knuckle. "She is covered in schnauzers." Finally, he could stand it no longer. "I'm going in!" he announced, and charged across the lawn, even as he heard Signor Rossi cry after him.

"Be careful, signore! Careful!"

The closer Signor Speranza got, the less sure he became. He had assumed that as he approached, squawking and waving his arms like a mad windmill, the beasts would scatter, but they did not. One even jumped off the mound to stand guard, yapping at Signor Speranza and alternately darting forward and dashing back, daring him to come closer.

Signor Speranza panicked, and his eyes swept the yard. He spied a wooden bucket off to one side.

"Lord!" he prayed, shouting to the sky, and veering sharply to the left. He snatched up the bucket and rejoiced: it was filled with water. Then he charged, sloshing and uttering a strange, yodeling cry.

Whooooosh!

Eight small schnauzers shot outward, like eight rays of the sun, and Bambolina, who was too slow to get out of the way, took the brunt of the cascade.

※ ※ ※

"I want to thank you, signore," said Signor Rossi. "But you understand, I cannot simply throw a bucket of water on Bambolina every time this happens."

Signor Speranza was wet. Bambolina was wet. They were both sitting near the fire wrapped in blankets, Signor Speranza with a cup of hot coffee, and Bambolina eating a plastic cup of tapioca pudding, which was being fed to her on a spoon by Signora Rossi.

"Isn't there something you can do to help us, signore?" Signor Rossi pleaded.

Looking back on this moment later, when he had come to the end of things, Signor Speranza could see where God had intervened again. He had been on the point of opening his mouth, of telling these humble people that Bambolina would not be plagued by schnauzers much longer—only fifty-seven more days, as a matter of fact, since they would all be moving out of their houses—when Signora Rossi interrupted.

"*Shh*, Bruno," she scolded. "Can't you see Signor Speranza has had enough today?" She turned to Signor Speranza and smiled. "Please, signore. Would you like to stay for dinner?"

And something—or Someone—made Signor Speranza say yes.

❄ ❄ ❄

"I think my mother used to make this, signora," Signor Speranza said of the cooked beans and toasted bread, trying to grasp at the thread of memory. "It is delicious."

Betta had made the same thing many times, but he had never made the connection before. It must have been the added smell of Signora Rossi's woodstove that brought the memory back. For the second time that day, he fancied he saw his mother out of the corner of his eye, just for a second, before she whisked softly away from him.

"This is a very nice house," he said, looking around. "It's like the one where I grew up." There was the wooden table where they sat, with four wooden chairs. There were wooden racks on the walls, with battered tins for flour and spices. Everything was scrupulously clean. In the corner, there was a wooden broom, its bristles made from dried rushes. It was as though he had stumbled out of the Bosco di Rudina and into the past.

After dinner, they sat in the living room, on a flowered couch with broken springs and doilies draped over the armrests, Signor Speranza in the middle, and Bambolina ensconced on a tufted cushion at their feet. Together, they perused the family photo album. There were a great many photos of Bambolina, from the time she was a tiny, brownish ball of fluff, to now, and in all of them her pink tongue lolled out the side of her mouth, and it seemed almost possible, if one were to hold the photo album up to one's ear, to hear her gentle, relentless panting. There was also a little girl in most of the photographs.

"Serena!" said Signor Speranza, pointing at a photo of the Rossis' daughter. "She has grown so big." Serena was one of Antonella's friends, and, as in the case of Antonella, Signor Speranza had not seen her actual face in at least six months.

Signor Rossi sighed. "Too big," he said.

Signor Speranza shrugged. "We cannot stop them from growing up, can we?"

Signora Rossi made a small clicking sound with her tongue. "We're worried that Serena will not want to stay here," she said, a thin, worried crease appearing in the middle of her forehead. "She is always somewhere else." She gestured at the ceiling. "Talking on her phone. Dreaming about movie stars." She shook her head. "I think she'll want to leave us . . ." she said, her voice trailing off.

Like the rest of them, Signor Speranza thought, finishing Signora Rossi's sentence for her. Like the rest of the young people who have left this place and never looked back.

"She will stay," said Signor Rossi firmly. "Where else would she go?" And then he and his wife and even Bambolina, who lifted her head from her cushion, all looked at Signor Speranza, as if he, perhaps, might know the answer.

❊ ❊ ❊

It was a funny thing about signs, thought Signor Speranza, as he hastened down the mountain, away from the Rossis and the Bosco di Rudina and toward Speranza and Son's. The sun was sinking in a bank of fiery clouds to his left, and a fresh breeze was frisking over the sea a thousand feet below him, so that his lungs, which were practically bursting with exertion, also burned with an occasional zing of salt. Every so often, he removed his cell phone from his pocket and waved it around, hoping to find a signal. His heart was thudding in his ears, and he kept glancing behind him, as if concerned that the devil, or perhaps a pack of miniature schnauzers, might be pursuing him.

It was a funny thing about signs: they were subject to interpretation. For example, in the moment that Signor Rossi had turned to him so appealingly, and repeated his own words of the other night back to him, the words he had used about his own daughter, Gemma—*Where else would she go?*—a funny feeling had come over him. Signor Speranza had been sitting there, on a couch that looked very like the couch of his own childhood, with a bellyful of food such as his own mother used to feed him, and sandwiched between Signor and Signora Rossi, as if he were their own enormous child, and a very funny feeling indeed had come over him. A feeling that was very like the feeling one might imagine one would experience if God Himself were attempting to deliver a Very Important Message—an answer. He really could not account for his words and actions after that.

"Your daughter likes this actor, this Dante Rinaldi?" he had heard himself say, plucking the name out of the air in the most appalling, cavalier tone. He told them he had it on very good authority that "this Dante Rinaldi" was interested in Prometto. No joke. Not only interested—he was thinking of buying a property here. What might Serena say about that? Would she still want to leave if *that* were the case? "Tell her," he had said, with nerves of steel. And then, shamelessly, "Tell her to tell her friends."

Now, as Signor Speranza hurtled down the mountain, his nerves coming apart at the seams, it did not seem quite so clear any longer that he had been acting according to God's Holy Will. It seemed much more likely that he had just perpetrated a serious infraction of the Ninth Commandment.

For the second time ever, his cell phone rang. He fumbled with it and managed to press the button that Betta had shown him.

"WHAT?" he shouted in the direction of the mouthpiece.

"Boss?" Smilzo's voice crackled over the line. "Boss, where are you? There are some people waiting by the church. Don Rocco wants to know if you are coming—if he should let them in."

Signor Speranza froze. He thought of the report from the Water Commission, folded into thirds in the top drawer of his desk at the office. He thought also of Serena Rossi, arriving home later this evening to the fantastical fabrication that Dante Rinaldi—in one of his famous tank tops, no doubt—was on the point of showing up any day now. He thought of her shrieking and hugging her mother and jumping up and down, and then of her tapping the big news out on her phone, and sending it to Antonella—maybe sending it to "everyone," whoever "everyone" might be. An image flashed through his mind of Alberto Martini, bouncing around the front seat of his red Alfa Romeo, a cigar in his stupid mouth, and whipping the steering wheel this way and that, like a kid at a video arcade. *What if?* A little frisson of hope tickled Signor Speranza's nose, and rippled over his moustache. What if this plan could actually work?

I'm sorry, he mouthed at the sky, and shrugged. The little frisson of hope had grown and expanded, until it tingled in his fingertips. He held the phone four inches away from his face.

"CANCELED!" he shouted. "TELL THEM THE MEETING IS CANCELED!"

7

A Once-in-a-Lifetime Investment Opportunity

"It's remarkable," said Don Rocco. He was perched on top of Signor Speranza's desk, eating a large bag of potato chips and watching his freshly charged, manufacturer-refurbished Roomba s9+, which he had purchased against Signor Speranza's express wishes, traverse the low-nap carpeting of Speranza and Son's.

"It's an idiot," muttered Signor Speranza absently. As if he didn't have enough problems already, now the priest had gone and put a perfectly good vacuum cleaner out of work and replaced it with a robot. He didn't have time for this kind of nonsense.

He lingered by the front windows, peering this way and that, looking for any evidence that the colossal lie he had told the night before had borne immediate economic relief. What he had witnessed thus far was not promising. The square was empty. Beppe Zello sat on a chair outside his dental practice, ostensibly reading a newspaper, really dozing. Signora Catuzza had placed a placard in the ordering window of the café that read CLOSED FOR LUNCH. This, as Signor Speranza understood it, referred to Signora Catuzza's lunch, and not anyone else's. When the proprietress of a café had ceased caring about anyone's lunch but her own, things had come to a pretty pass, indeed. If this were an American Western, Signor Speranza thought grimly, a tumbleweed might be expected to roll past at any moment.

"Have you heard from Antonella today, Smilzo?" he asked, pacing up and down.

"No, boss." Smilzo, who was toiling over a tricky act break in his screenplay, looked up, surprised. He fished his phone out of his pocket and examined it hopefully. "Was I supposed to?"

"Well, *I* think it's very clever," Don Rocco resumed, crunching into a handful of chips. "And it's cute, too, like a little dog."

This observation was infuriating enough to command Signor Speranza's full attention. He stopped pacing. "You want me to tell you how clever your robot is? This story has a dog in it, too, so you will like it." Signor Speranza proceeded to regale them with the tale of a man who had left his Roomba and his dog alone at home together. The dog, who was not an idiot but was poorly trained, had had an accident on the kitchen floor, and the Roomba, who, despite being trained, was an idiot, had attempted to vacuum it up, dragging the pungent mess over every square inch of the owner's home, afterward docking itself proudly at its charging station. "*That* is how smart your robot is," he concluded, with a sharp clap of his hands.

Don Rocco took another contemplative crunch of chips. "That sounds like user error to me."

Signor Speranza's blood pressure scarcely had the opportunity to rise before Smilzo jumped up. "Antonella's coming, boss! I can see her." He pressed his pointy nose up to the glass.

Signor Speranza could see her also, a frizzy-haired speck in the distance, running toward the shop. He acted quickly.

"One more test, Father, and you'll be all set," he said, snatching the bag of chips from the priest's hand.

"Signore!" Don Rocco protested. "What are you doing?"

But Signor Speranza was already at the front door. It jingled merrily as he wedged himself in it, turning the crinkly bag over and shaking the crumbs onto the step.

"Go get it!" With his foot, he nudged the Roomba over the threshold, and then shooed the priest out after it. "Enjoy your robot, Father!" he called, waving. "I'm sure you will be very happy together."

Antonella, out of breath and this time with a pair of plastic turquoise-and-yellow-spattered hoop earrings stuck in her hair, careened into the shop not thirty seconds later. Signor Speranza was relieved. Lying was one thing; lying in front of one of God's own officers was entirely another.

"Oh, signore!" Antonella gasped. "Is it really true?"

Everything came out then.

"Dante Rinaldi?" Smilzo squeaked. "Here?" He glanced sidelong at Antonella and swallowed repeatedly, his Adam's apple bobbing in his narrow neck. "That is so great," he croaked, and pasted a tremulous smile on his face. "So great."

"But you're not telling me everything, signore! It's not just a house," Antonella scolded, wagging her finger. She turned her phone around so they could see it and tapped the screen. "Look at what he said this morning."

Signor Speranza and Smilzo huddled. There was a picture of a stretch of beach, just clear blue water and sand. Underneath was a block of all-caps text. Signor Speranza's lips moved as he read.

GOING OFF GRID. NEW PROJECT. CATCH
ME IF YOU CAN. #DANTERINALDI
#BACKTOBASICS #VIVAITALIA
#IMMOREFAMOUSTHANYOU #BLESSED

Signor Speranza frowned. "What's all this with the number sign?"

But Antonella was practically crowing. "Imagine you—pretending that you didn't know who he was a couple of days ago!"

Smilzo looked back and forth from Antonella and Signor Speranza. "What is she talking about, boss?" he asked, nervous.

"It's obvious," said Antonella. "Look." She flicked the screen, zooming in on the picture of the beach. "This is Prometto."

Signor Speranza wrinkled his nose. "How can you tell?"

But Antonella wasn't paying any attention. "It makes total sense," she said, twirling a chunk of hair and causing one of the turquoise earrings to fall suddenly free. "Dante doesn't get along with the corporate suits. He's too much of a bad boy."

So it was "Dante" now, was it? thought Signor Speranza, an uncomfortable feeling starting in the pit of his stomach.

Antonella waved her hand in the air. "He wants to be free to do what he wants to do. To make his mark, you know. As an artist."

"Mm?" said Signor Speranza, still not seeing where this was going.

"And so that's why he's coming here!" Antonella finished with a flourish. "I figured it out."

Signor Speranza blinked.

Smilzo whimpered.

Antonella beamed.

"He's coming to make a movie here, signore!" she cried. "Tell me that I'm right."

* * *

"You told them *what*?" gasped Betta.

It was night. The summer air was close and humid, and clouds obscured the stars. Signor Speranza and Betta were on the hotel's rooftop deck, clustered on two wicker stools around a brazier fire. A long time ago this had been a gathering place, not just for the hotel's guests, but for the villagers as well. Signor Speranza could still recall the first time he had come here, at age seven or eight, with his father and one of his aunts. If he closed his eyes, he could still see it—his Zia Valentina with her poodle-cut hairstyle, sitting with the other ladies on fleets of lawn chairs, his father and the other men smoking over the balcony, and Betta, the young daughter of the hotel's owners, skinny as a colt, the hem of her dress falling down, and her hair in two streaming pigtails. In the old days, at this hour, they would have had to stay very quiet, so as not to disturb the guests on the floor below, but now it was where they went to talk without Gemma or Carlotta hearing.

Signor Speranza threw his hands in the air. "Alberto said—" he began.

"Alberto said!" snapped Betta, throwing her hands up also. "You know that is not a very good beginning, right? Alberto said!"

"They have a McDonald's now," Signor Speranza muttered in his own defense.

Betta crossed her arms. "So okay, Signor Big Shot. You thought you would tell people that Dante Rinaldi wanted to come here, and then—what? Everyone would run out to get their vacuum cleaner fixed?"

Signor Speranza pouted, and Betta softened. "Oh, Nino," she sighed. "Let me see what you have there."

Miserably, Signor Speranza passed her the notepad on which he had scrawled the names of three dozen families and businesses around Prometto, and the back taxes that they owed. Betta squinted at it in the leaping light of the fire.

"Do you see?" he said plaintively. "I just thought that if things picked up a little . . . if people could afford to pay even *some* of what they owed, we could have enough. Seventy thousand euros is a lot, but it is not unattainable."

Betta passed the pad back, shaking her head. "It's not going to work, Nino. What happened with Alberto and Oliveto was different. It was in a big magazine, right? You cannot just tell Antonella Capra something and expect the whole world to know it."

Signor Speranza pondered relaying the miracle that was social media to his wife, but decided against it.

"It's too late for Prometto," she said, sighing. "In fifty-six days, they are going to shut the water off. There is no getting around that. You have to tell people, Nino. Right away. Tomorrow. And then . . ." Betta's eyes, in the firelight, were liquid. "We just have to let the pieces fall where they will."

Signor Speranza looked down at his hands in the light of the fire. They were the hands of an old man, which still surprised him sometimes. The years had snuck up on Giovannino Speranza, loosening his skin and tightening his joints, putting a pain in his back and a creak in his knees, but he had never felt truly different, not in his heart, where it mattered. As a little boy, when he heard of an earthquake a hundred miles to the north, he had told his father that he was not afraid. If an earthquake did come to Prometto, and even if it knocked their house into the sea, he would still not be afraid. He would simply wade into the water and drag it back out again. That—that was how he had always felt. Until now. Now, in the face of all this, he felt old in his heart.

When he spoke, his voice cracked.

"What if they don't come with us, Betta?" he whispered. His wife held his gaze. "What if Gemma gets it into her head to go to Rome? What if she goes looking for *him*?" He thought of Gemma, slamming the door on him at Zio's party the other night. He pictured her moving away, and slamming the door on him forever.

Ordinarily, at a juncture such as this, with her loud and blustering husband laid low, Betta would have stepped in. She would have taken over, briskly shooing away his worries, and explaining, matter-of-factly, and in defiance of all evidence to the contrary, why he didn't actually have any troubles to begin with. But this time she didn't answer. She just looked off, into the blotted night sky.

Signor Speranza closed his eyes. "I have one more idea," he said. "One more idea that I think might work."

Betta sighed. The fire was dying down now, almost out, and Signor Speranza could only see the shape of his wife in the darkness. "I'm listening," she said. Listening, but guarded.

Signor Speranza drew a deep breath and let it out in a rush.

"I got the idea from Smilzo. He was telling me about how a movie production gets started. That someone has to pay for it. Someone has to take a chance. An investor."

He paused, but Betta said nothing.

"What if *we* get an investor? What if someone gives us money to make this movie? That will buy us time. We can use the money to pay the Water Commission, and then, later, we say the movie is canceled."

There was silence. There was just the soft crackle of embers in the grate.

"If there is no movie, you cannot keep the money," said Betta stiffly. "You would have to pay them back. How would you be able to do that?"

Signor Speranza's pulse quickened. If Betta was asking questions, then she was not just saying no.

"Betta, believe me," he said, a pleading note in his voice. "This Dante Rinaldi person is a big deal. The young people will hear he's coming, and then they'll come here, too, the same as they went to Oliveto. The money will come with them. People will get back on their feet again. They will be able to pay their taxes. I know it in my heart. We just need to buy a little bit of time."

Signor Speranza waited, his pulse pounding in his ears. Asking Betta for permission was not the same as asking God, but, in this moment, it felt very close to it. If Betta said it was okay, then it was.

Finally, slowly, she spoke.

"All right, Nino. If you believe that this rumor will work, then I will believe it, too. But you have to pay everyone back as soon as possible."

"Of course!" Signor Speranza found his wife's hand in the dark and kissed it. "Of course, *cara mia!*"

She snatched her hand back, and wagged her finger at him. "And I am not going to jail for you! If this blows up, I'll deny I know anything about it."

"Yes, Betta! Yes!"

"One week," she said. "One week to see if you can find someone to invest, or you'll have to tell people about the water right away."

Signor Speranza nodded. "One week." He stared at the fire. A glowing ember collapsed onto itself and turned to ash. "I promise."

"But, Nino," Betta said, her voice puzzled now, "who can you ask that has that kind of money? Who?"

※ ※ ※

Signor Maestro, who was engaged in mopping chicken slime off the stainless-steel counters of the butcher's shop with a clean white cloth and bleaching spray, was unaware that he was being watched. Outside, a scant ten yards from the entrance of his shop, were ranged Signor Speranza, Don Rocco, Smilzo, Antonella, and, for some reason, Beppe Zello, the dentist.

"All fake," said Beppe Zello, shaking his head in wonder. "I heard he had all of his natural teeth extracted and replaced. He had to go all the way to Milan to do it."

Don Rocco wrinkled his nose at the dentist and then turned to Signor Speranza. Antonella had done her job, at least within the confines of Prometto, and over the past twenty-four hours everyone had learned of Dante Rinaldi and his supposed new movie.

"I still do not understand, signore," said Don Rocco, perplexed. "Why do you have to raise money for this movie? Aren't these things paid for by movie studios or something like that?"

Signor Speranza squirmed under this direct interrogation by the priest, but he was rescued by Antonella.

"Dante doesn't want to be beholden to the studios, Father," she explained, sniffing, and tossing her hair with the new air of sophistication she had cultivated in the past twenty-four hours. "He explained it all in a post last summer." And she read aloud from her phone. "'Do your own thing. Be beholden to no one. Hashtag

Dante. Hashtag rebel. Hashtag owe nothing to nobody.'" She allowed this to sink in.

Don Rocco frowned. "Nothing to nobody? I think that is a double negative, no?"

"Besides, Father," said Antonella breezily, "Signor Speranza is an old friend of the family. He knew Dante's father back in the day. They worked together. In the mines."

Signor Speranza began to cough.

Don Rocco narrowed his eyes. "The *mines*, signore? What mines?"

"He's coming, boss!" yelped Smilzo.

The little group banded together, as if they were just chatting on the street. Signor Maestro emerged from the butcher's shop, his vast expanse of white apron covered with gore. He did not appear to have any particular errand there, but simply stood on the step, in the shade of the awning, and stared off into the distance.

"What are you going to say, boss?" Smilzo whispered.

Signor Speranza peeped over the huddle at Signor Maestro and considered.

"I'm going to say it's the opportunity of a lifetime." He thought of Betta, and the one-week deadline. "And I'm going to say that he has to act fast," he added quickly.

"Are you sure you want to do this, signore?" asked Don Rocco. He shivered. "I would not want to borrow money from a man like that."

They heard the door of the butcher's shop creak and then close, and they all looked up and fanned out again to resume their watch.

"I just think you should be careful," Don Rocco warned. "Signor Maestro is not a man to trifle with."

Signor Speranza regarded the pig's carcass hanging in the window of the shop, and his spirits quailed. Don Rocco was right, of course. Maybe this was crazy. If it all blew up in his face, as Betta had said, he wondered which would be worse: being carted to jail, or having Signor Maestro after him.

Beppe Zello sighed. "I just wish I could get a really good look inside that mouth of his," he said wistfully.

Everyone turned to look at him.

"That is a weird thing to say, Zello," said Signor Speranza.

❊ ❊ ❊

Signor Maestro had the same bell over his door as Signor Speranza had over the door of Speranza and Son's. It jingled reassuringly as Signor Speranza pushed his way into the butcher's shop.

Signor Maestro looked up and grunted. Three of his sons were behind the counter with him today, and they looked up and grunted also. Signor Speranza was temporarily mesmerized by the effect of it. It must be fascinating, he thought, to have offspring who looked and acted so much like oneself. It must be like having one of those mirrors that could be positioned so that one could see oneself reflected, over and over again, and into eternity. Or, he thought suddenly, recalling a television program he and Betta had once watched, it might be like synchronized swimming. In a flash, an image came to him of Signor Maestro and his fifteen identical sons all lining up alongside a swimming pool, and tucking their copious black locks into white lace bathing caps.

"What are you smiling about, Speranza?" growled Signor Maestro. "What do you want now?"

Signor Speranza shook the image from his head, and advanced toward the counter.

"Signore! You are a consummate businessman," he declared. "That is obvious to everyone."

The aproned pillars on either side of him did not budge, and Signor Speranza tried to suppress yet another unbidden image of the four of them joining hands and pirouetting into the deep end. He advanced closer, putting his elbows up on the counter, and clasping his hands. He lowered his voice to a conspiratorial whisper.

"Perhaps you have heard, signore, of Dante Rinaldi," he said, in thrilling tones. "Perhaps you have heard that he is coming to Prometto. To make a movie."

One of the sons' faces twitched, but Signor Maestro's expression did not change. He reached out, taking hold of Signor Speranza's jacket at the forearm and pulling it up, so that his elbow lifted off the counter.

"I just made chicken cutlets here," he said, pointing at the slime dripping from Signor Speranza's elbow patch. "I'm not responsible for dry cleaning."

"*Oddio.*" *Oh God*, Signor Speranza muttered, looking at the mess. He could feel it now, on both arms, the cold seeping through to his skin. Had they not just seen this man cleaning the counters?

"Never mind," he said firmly, wriggling out of the jacket and rolling it into a ball. "I'm here to let you in on an amazing opportunity. How would you like, signore, to see your name up in lights?"

Signor Maestro sprayed the counter and began to scrub it. "Not interested," he muttered.

Signor Speranza waved his hands. "Signore, it's an investment opportunity. You would put money into the movie, and then, when the movie is a hit, you make a killing." Signor Speranza flinched a little at his own choice of words, happening at that moment to notice the row of shiny knives mounted to a magnetic strip on the wall behind the counter.

Signor Maestro crossed his arms. "I am not interested in show business, Speranza. Now get the hell out of my shop."

Signor Speranza's shoulders slumped. His hopeless gaze roved over the four Maestro men. They were not a synchronized swimming team; they were a mountain range.

"Okay, signore," he said, despondent. "I understand. I'll go." He clutched his chicken-soaked jacket and turned toward the door.

But then one of the mountains spoke. It was the one directly to Signor Maestro's left. He broke ranks and turned toward his father.

"Papà," he said, and if Signor Speranza was not mistaken, there was something of a pleading note in the deep and sonorous voice.

Signor Speranza watched, spellbound. No other words passed between father and son. They only looked at each other. Mountains, it seemed, communicated by some other means than words. But, whatever transpired between them, Signor Maestro put down his cleaning rag.

"Come to the house tonight," he grunted. "We'll discuss it then."

8

Into the Lion's Den

$\mathcal{S}$milzo insisted on coming along, saying that he needed to get some footage. He ate dinner at home with his mother and met Signor Speranza at the shop at eight o'clock.

"I am making a documentary, boss. On the making of the movie. Is my big break." He hefted a canvas backpack stuffed with an array of audiovisual and lighting equipment onto Signor Speranza's desk. "I think, since Dante Rinaldi will be in it, I will have a chance of getting it into one of the big film festivals." He rummaged in the front pouch of the bag, withdrawing a black felt beret and placing it on top of his pointy little head.

Signor Speranza winced, and not only because of a slight burning sensation in his conscience because Smilzo was getting his hopes up about something that wasn't ever going to happen.

"Are you sure that is the *right* hat, Smilzo?" he asked, with uncharacteristic delicacy. Perhaps Smilzo was unaware that his haircut, which was freshened every three weeks or so by his mother with the aid of an upside-down bowl and a pair of kitchen shears, already looked remarkably like a black beret, and had the added benefit of being already attached to his head. "Do you not think it's perhaps a little . . . *redundant*?"

But Smilzo clutched at the hat protectively. "This is the look, boss," he said, in an injured tone. "This is the Hollywood look."

Despite the objectionable hat, Signor Speranza was secretly relieved that Smilzo was coming with him. It had struck him that Signor Maestro might want to ask a few questions about the inner workings of the movie business before agreeing to give him a pile of money, and on this topic he had no idea what he was talking about. As he and Smilzo trekked through the twilight to Signor Maestro's enormous house on the marina, he found himself in the novel and unnerving position of having to ask his assistant for professional advice.

"What will he want to know, Smilzo?" he asked as they shambled down the mountain toward the beach.

Smilzo's face lit up.

"Oh, a lot of things, boss. But mostly he will want to know about the back end."

Signor Speranza was alarmed. "The back end of *what*?"

Smilzo blinked. "Of the movie, boss. The back end is the money the movie makes. What percentage are you going to offer to Signor Maestro?"

"Oh, I don't know." Signor Speranza waved carelessly at the sky. "Fifty percent?"

Smilzo threw his hands up. "Fifty percent? Boss! Three percent! *Maybe* four."

"Okay, okay," said Signor Speranza. "Calm down. I will tell him three percent."

They trudged on in the watery moonlight, and Signor Speranza ran lines in his head, practicing. *So you see, signore, for the low, low cost of seventy thousand euros, you can receive three percent. This is a super-amazing deal. You can make —*

Signor Speranza paused, stopping in his tracks. "How much does a movie make, anyway?" he asked, suddenly curious.

Smilzo shrugged. "Oh, millions, boss. Could be hundreds of millions."

"Ha." Signor Speranza pulled a face and resumed walking. That was interesting. Too bad they were not really making a movie.

❈ ❈ ❈

They arrived at the Maestro estate. It was an acre plot near the beach, entirely encircled by a nine-foot wrought-iron fence.

"Who is he trying to keep out?" Signor Speranza grumbled.

"Maybe he is trying to keep someone in," Smilzo suggested brightly.

Signor Speranza, whose stomach was already in knots without the aid of ghoulish speculations, reached up and smacked his assistant on the back of the head, dislodging the beret. Then he pressed the buzzer to the left of the front gate.

There was a mechanical whirring sound, and a camera, secreted in the hedge behind the fence, panned back and forth, finally settling on Signor Speranza and Smilzo. A speaker, located above the buzzer, crackled.

"Speranza," came Signor Maestro's booming voice. "Who told you that you could invite company to my house?"

Signor Speranza looked sidelong at Smilzo. Then he leaned tentatively toward the speaker and spoke into it.

"It's just my assistant, signore."

"Tell him to wait outside," came the response.

Signor Speranza hesitated. "O-kaaaaaay," he called back. There was a buzzing sound, and the gate swung open. "Smilzo." He placed a heavy hand on his assistant's shoulder. "If I do not come out, tell Betta where to look for my body."

"Boss, wait!" Smilzo wriggled one arm out of his backpack and swung it up and around, blocking his face from Signor Maestro's prying camera. "I will follow you in, boss!" he whispered. "Maybe I can get some footage through a window or something."

Signor Speranza frowned. "What if someone sees you?"

Smilzo tussled with his backpack again, unzipping it and rummaging inside. "Here, boss. If you need to warn me that someone is coming, just press this." He thrust a remote control with a single button into Signor Speranza's hands.

Signor Speranza stiffened. He had seen this remote control before. His eyes flitted to Smilzo's formerly innocuous-seeming backpack.

Smilzo squirmed. "I wasn't going to use it, boss. Is actually in there by mistake. It looks just like the external hard drive for my computer."

They didn't have time to debate it. "Speranza!" roared Signor Maestro over the speaker. Signor Speranza stuffed the remote in his pocket. He waved one arm in an enormous half circle.

"Goodbye, Smilzo," he said loudly, taking care to enunciate each word. "I will see you tomorrow at the store where we both work." Then he turned, and, standing on tiptoe, he held one hand up to the camera, filling the lens. "Does this look like a splinter to you, signore?" he shouted. "I wonder if you have a pair of tweezers I can borrow when I get to the house?" Behind his back, he shooed Smilzo inside the gate.

"SPERANZA!" the speaker blared, and Signor Speranza took off toward the house, the gate clanging shut behind him.

❅ ❅ ❅

Signor Speranza and Smilzo proceeded to their destination, Signor Speranza by the main path, flanked by two lines of headless statues in the ancient style, like a moonlit walkway to hell, while Smilzo skirted along in the shadows in fits and starts, stopping at intervals to stand flush with the hedges, as if evading the sweeping beam of a searchlight. When Signor Speranza came finally to the massive front portico, Smilzo stole around the side of the building, and, except for the remote control in his pocket, Signor Speranza was alone.

He climbed the flagstone stairs. The entrance to the house was the size of a barn door, and there was a heavy silver knocker at its center, shaped like the roaring head of a lion. Signor Speranza had just lifted it when the door drew back, and a tiny, exhausted-looking woman, Signora Maestro, stood in the doorway.

"Welcome, signore," she said, ducking her head, her thin voice echoing in the cavernous foyer. "My husband and sons are waiting for you." She stepped back to admit him.

Signor Speranza balked, peering into the dim interior. He could just make out a grand staircase and a wide corridor, the walls red, and the floor a checkerboard of gray and silver marble. He thought also that he could detect the flicker of flames on the walls. That couldn't be right, could it?

"Uh, thank you, signora," he said, and fumbled in his pocket. He wanted one last assurance, before he went inside, that Smilzo was near. He pressed the button on the remote.

Signora Maestro frowned and glanced over Signor Speranza's shoulder.

"Did you hear something, signore?" she asked.

"No, no," said Signor Speranza, closing the door hurriedly behind him. "It's just the wind."

Signor Maestro's house looked exactly as Signor Speranza might have expected it would. It was like a cross between the catacombs and an IKEA catalog. The flames that he had spied from the front door turned out to be special LED lightbulbs manufactured to mimic medieval torches.

"It's remarkable, signora," said Signor Speranza, stopping to examine one of the flickering sconces. "How do they do it?"

"Oh, I am not clever enough to know that, signore," said Signora Maestro, ducking her head again. "I wanted white lights with linen shades, but Antonio insisted on these."

Signor Speranza suppressed a snort. Of course he did.

Signora Maestro led them deeper and deeper into the house. They passed rooms filled with gilt-framed photographs arranged on card tables, massive brocade couches in shiny plastic slipcoverings, and, by Signor Speranza's dizzying count, three grand pianos. They pursued a winding, circuitous route, but Signor Speranza sensed that they were nearly at their destination when they came upon an expanse of low-ceilinged hallway lined entirely with taxidermy animal heads, at the end of which there was a pair of swinging, stainless-steel doors, such as one might expect to see on an industrial kitchen, or a cruise ship.

Signora Maestro paused at the doors.

"You'll want to watch when we first go in, signore," she cautioned. Then she glanced at him and hesitated. "You don't have any meat or bacon in your pockets, do you?"

Signor Speranza's moustache quivered. "Signora?"

But she waved her hand. "It'll be fine. My husband will have dealt with them."

With this reassuring dictum, she pushed open the doors to a massive, velvet-carpeted dining room, and Signor Speranza, who had wildly assumed she was talking about her sons, saw immediately that he had been wrong. Lashed to Signor Maestro's enormous carved dining chair at the head of the table were three sleek Dobermans, each of whom, at Signor Speranza's entrance, leapt up snarling, showcasing each and every one of their gleaming white teeth.

"Don't worry about them," Signor Maestro grunted as Signor Speranza slid into an empty chair.

"Oh yes," said Signor Speranza, nodding knowingly. "These kinds of dogs, they look mean, but really, they are like kitty cats."

"No," said Signor Maestro, frowning. "They cannot chew through the chains."

"Oh," said Signor Speranza, his knees turning to jelly. "Ha-ha."

A mistake! he thought, panicking. *This is a huge mistake!* His eyes darted around the table. He was seated opposite Signor Maestro, mercifully twenty feet away from the dogs, and facing a bank of windows. The long sides of the table were lined with sons, seven on one side and eight on the other, all of them with their hands identically folded on the table. Like a mouse, their tiny mother scurried in and out among them, refilling water glasses and replenishing bowls of nuts. Signor Speranza noticed that she avoided the dogs, too, going three-quarters of the way around the room to get to the other side, rather than passing directly by them.

Signor Maestro leaned heavily forward on the table.

"How much?" he asked.

Signor Speranza was startled. He had expected to have to sell

Signor Maestro on the idea of investing in the movie in the first place. He hadn't planned to get around to talking numbers until the very end. Put on the spot like this, his sales pitch flew out of his head.

"Seventy thousand euros," he blurted.

"Mm," said Signor Maestro.

It was then that Signor Speranza first detected a small movement in the shrubbery outside the window behind Signor Maestro. It was followed—unmistakably—by Smilzo's pointy nose, pressed against the glass. Signor Speranza could not see much outside, with the dining room being so bright, but he could make out a pinpoint of red light, which must be Smilzo's camera. His pulse quickened, and his eyes flickered to the pack of dogs, roosting peacefully at their master's feet. How keen, he wondered, was the nose of a Doberman?

As if in answer to this unuttered question, one of the dogs, which had been dozing, stirred and stared up at the window, growling deep in its throat. In seconds, all three were on their feet, barking.

"*Basta!*" Signor Maestro shouted, and jerked the dogs' chains. He motioned to one of the sons. "Let them out," he said.

The son obliged, and the three dogs streaked out into the night.

Signor Speranza gripped his hair by the roots and yelped. *Run, Smilzo, run!* He craned his neck, trying to see.

Signor Maestro cracked his knuckles, and his diamond pinkie ring sparkled in the light of the chandelier. "I can give you sixty-eight thousand," he said.

Signor Speranza dropped back in his seat, all thoughts of Smilzos and marauding packs of dogs flying out of his head. "*Che?*" he said dazedly. "*Che,* signore?" In the anxiety of the last few moments, he had nearly forgotten why he was here in the first place, and now Maestro was simply offering to give him sixty-eight thousand euros! That was almost seventy thousand!

Signor Maestro narrowed his eyes. "But I want something for it, Speranza."

"Of course, signore." Signor Speranza's head bobbed up and down. "Maybe you know about a movie's backside—"

But Signor Maestro raised one hand. "My son is interested in show business," he said. "The handsome one."

Signor Speranza's eyes flitted up and down the double aisle of thick-jowled, low-browed Maestro men, and his soul quaked. Would he be expected to identify the handsome one?

"They are all very good-looking, signore," he stammered. "I cannot—"

Signor Maestro drew back, squinting. "Ernesto," he said. He pointed at the second son on the left. Signor Speranza thought, if he strained, that he could recognize this son as the mountain who had spoken up in the butcher's shop that afternoon.

"I want for you to find a part for my handsome son in this movie. You can do that, Speranza?"

Signor Speranza took a long draft of water and loosened his collar. It was exceedingly hot in here.

"Oh yes. Yes, signore. I am sure that can be arranged. I will have to talk to Signor Rinaldi, of course, but that will be a simple matter."

Signor Maestro frowned. "Ernesto wants this to be done properly, Speranza. Nothing handed to him. He expects to audition for a part. He has been preparing." He gestured at Ernesto. "Would you like to see something now?"

"No, no!" Signor Speranza flung his hands up in alarm, even as the second son on the left pushed back his chair. "That will not be necessary. We will be having formal auditions."

"When?" asked Signor Maestro.

"Oh!" Signor Speranza waved a vague hand. "That could be some time. Weeks . . . months . . ."

Sixteen pairs of beady eyes stared back at him.

Signor Speranza gulped.

"Two days, signore," he said. "The auditions will be two days from now."

Signor Speranza departed the front door of the Maestro home, relieved to be out of there, and giddy with victory. Easy! It had been easy to get the money out of Signor Maestro! So what if he needed to stage some bogus auditions? That would be easy, too. He was nearly at the gate, pondering where he was going to get the remaining two thousand euros, when he remembered Smilzo. He peered into the shadows, listening for the sound of dogs.

"Smilzo!" he whispered. *"Dove sei?"* Glancing over his shoulder and from left to right, he darted off the path, pressing the remote in his pocket three times in quick succession, and hastening toward the noise.

"Smilzo!" he called.

"Up here, boss!"

Signor Speranza halted and looked around, confused. He pressed the remote one more time, to get his bearings, and followed the sound up and into the branches of a chestnut tree.

"I got all of it until the dogs came out, boss," said Smilzo, beaming and patting his backpack. "Wait until you see it. Is really good stuff."

9

The Auditions

$\mathcal{T}$he exchange of the money was to take place outside Speranza and Son's at dawn, as though they were in a spy movie. Signor Speranza and Smilzo stood on their side of the street and waited. They could not see into the butcher's shop, as the blinds were tightly shut.

Signor Speranza crunched on a mouthful of indigestion tablets and fidgeted. After his first flush of triumph had faded, his conscience had caught up with him in the night and lodged itself in his stomach. Smilzo, by contrast, was annoyingly effervescent, in his ridiculous beret and a white T-shirt with the sleeves rolled up, scribbling notes for his documentary project into a tiny spiral notepad. His obvious joy gave Signor Speranza's moral sense a fresh jolt.

"Why do you like this movie business so much, Smilzo?" he asked, sounding more irritable than he intended. "What's wrong with vacuum cleaners?"

Smilzo looked up, his eyes bright. "Nothing is wrong with vacuum cleaners, boss. Is just, I want to be somebody. I want to go somewhere."

Signor Speranza opened his mouth to tell Smilzo that he was an idiot, but he was halted by a sudden image he had of himself at around the same age, helping his cousin Paolo load his luggage onto the train.

"Two weeks," he heard his younger self saying, and laughing. "Two weeks, and you'll be back."

He had stood there, on the platform, and waved Paolo into the distance, waved until the train had traveled far enough away that his cousin decided he didn't need to wave back anymore, and ducked his head back inside the carriage. And even though Signor Speranza hadn't wanted to go—had never wanted to be anywhere but his own village, and his own father's shop—he had felt the tiniest pang of regret. What would have happened if he had gone somewhere? Tried to be somebody, as Smilzo said?

He would never know. His chance for *something else* had passed.

Across the street, one of the blinds twitched, and Signor Speranza fancied he saw a sliver of Signor Maestro's swarthy face peeping out. Then the door opened, and two Maestro brothers emerged, bearing between them a bulky nylon pouch, which they marched across the street. When they came face-to-face with Signor Speranza and Smilzo, they halted.

"My father would like us to accompany you to the safe, signore," said the brother on the left.

They all went inside then and huddled over the safe as Signor Speranza counted out the bills, the breath of one of the butcher's offspring hot on his neck. When it was confirmed that all sixty-eight thousand euros were accounted for, he stowed the money in the safe, and everyone straightened up again.

The mouth-breather shook his hand. "I'll see you tomorrow, signore, for the audition."

"Ah yes. Ernesto," said Signor Speranza weakly. "I'll see you then."

The son shook his head. "He's Ernesto," he said, motioning to his brother. "I am Ivano. I am going to try out also." He flashed a sheepish grin.

"Oh . . . good," choked Signor Speranza. He saw the brothers out of the shop, and, when they had gone, he called to his assistant.

"Smilzo!" he said. "We're going to need name tags."

❄ ❄ ❄

The first thing Signor Speranza did, once the area was clear of Maestros, was to stretch the phone cord into the back room and call the Water Commission office. He informed them that he had sixty-eight thousand euros waiting in his safe at this very minute with their name on it.

"But I see here that your cost for repairs is seventy thousand euros, signore," said the toneless clerk. "I am afraid that in cases such as yours, the commission can only accept payment in full."

Signor Speranza was aghast. He did a quick calculation, tracing the numbers in the air. "But signore!" he cried. "We have over ninety-seven percent of the money!"

The clerk was implacable. "Then please ring us back when you have the other three percent. *Arrivederci*, signore. Have a nice day."

All regular shop business for the remainder of the day was laid aside in preparation for the auditions. Smilzo had never attended an actual professional audition, but he had at least seen one on television, and at his direction they pushed Signor Speranza's desk, all of the vacuum cleaners, and the revolving metal racks of vacuum bags against the walls, and, in the middle of the room, erected a card table and two folding chairs where Signor Speranza and Smilzo would sit with a pair of clipboards, two glasses, and a pitcher of water. A yard or two in front of the table, they rolled out an old square carpet sample to serve as a sort of stage for the auditionees. It was of vital importance that everything look authentic, as Signor Maestro had been spotted lurking in the vicinity of Speranza and Son's front window and had even once been seen to place his cupped hands against the glass and peer inside.

After things were set up, Signor Speranza was still antsy. "What will we have them do, Smilzo?" he asked. "When they come in here?"

Smilzo was surprised. "Don't you have a script for them to read, boss? Didn't Dante Rinaldi send something?"

Signor Speranza frowned. He wondered if Signor Maestro, having once ensured his son's rise to celebrity, might also expect him to come home with lines to practice.

"What about your scripts, Smilzo?" he asked cautiously. "Don't you have something?"

Smilzo's eyebrows shot up, almost into his beret. "Yes, boss!" The tip of his pointy pink nose was twitching, like a rabbit's. "Do you need a script, boss? You can have any of them! Any one you want!"

Signor Speranza crossed his arms, and his moustache rumpled. "What are they about?"

Smilzo counted off on his fingers. "One is about an alien spaceship. It comes to Los Angeles and—"

Signor Speranza put up his hand. "No. What else?"

"Period drama. Eighteenth-century London—"

"No."

Smilzo was on his feet now, and making sweeping gestures with his arms.

"Is Viking ship!" he said, flinging one hand out to the right. "Is modern-day New York!" He swung his other hand out to the left. "Is time travel!" He clapped his hands together. "Is huge crossover hit!"

Signor Speranza rolled his eyes to the ceiling and had a brief conversation with Saints John Bosco and Veronica, who, he had discovered in the *Compendium*, were the two long-suffering individuals doomed to an eternity of dealing with filmmakers.

But Smilzo wasn't finished.

"How about this one, boss?" He adopted a strange voice and hunched over, swaying back and forth, his hands held open on either side of his mouth. *"In a world where crime has taken over . . . where you can trust no one, and especially not the police . . . there is one man who fights back! Meet . . . Ratman!"* He dropped his hands and resumed his normal speaking voice. "Is kind of like Batman, boss, but he dresses like a muskrat."

Signor Speranza threw his hands in the air. "Smilzo! These are all terrible!"

Smilzo's exuberant balloon popped. His lower lip quivered. "Boss?"

"Aliens! Vikings! Muskrats!" Signor Speranza snorted, causing his moustache to blow outward, like a thick, black fan. "I want something simple. A love story. Something like that."

Smilzo pressed his lips together, concentrating. "I can do a love story, boss. I have a couple of scenes—"

"Perfect. You can go to Bisi's and make copies." Signor Speranza glanced around the shop and popped another Maalox. "What else do we need to do?"

"We should probably record the auditions, boss," said Smilzo. "Is called a screen test. Did Dante send a camera, or—"

"Ah!" said Signor Speranza, and he disappeared into the stockroom, emerging triumphant twenty minutes later, covered in dust and cobwebs, and bearing a 1984 Sony Betamax Betamovie BMC-220 Auto Focus Camcorder and accompanying tripod.

"We will have to put in a different tape," he said, blowing the dust out of his moustache. "This one is Gemma's christening, I think."

Smilzo wrinkled his nose. "Is very old."

Signor Speranza frowned. "Nothing wrong with old. Besides, it looks professional. Look at the tripod."

They both stood back and looked at it.

Smilzo shook his head. "I could shoot a higher-quality video on my phone, boss."

Signor Speranza pouted, his mouth drawing up and his eyebrows drawing down. He had about had it with this phone business.

"Won't we be getting new equipment, though?" said Smilzo, his brow furrowed. "All that money from Signor Maestro—"

Signor Speranza snapped out of his sulk in a second. "No, no," he said quickly. "That money is—is earmarked."

"For what, boss?" Smilzo was interested. "Costumes? Makeup? Special effects?"

Signor Speranza felt a now-familiar bubble of panic in his chest. "Movie theater!" he declared, with a flourish. One could not simply order a movie theater over the internet, could one? Neither could one expect a movie theater to be promptly built. "Dante says we need a movie theater. For the—the premiere. So the money from Signor Maestro—we cannot touch it."

Signor Speranza was quite pleased with his quick thinking, but he had not counted on his assistant's reaction. Smilzo was standing stock-still.

"A movie theater, boss?" he whispered. "Here? In Prometto?"

Signor Speranza's breath stopped in his chest. Something about Smilzo's awe-stricken tone reminded him suddenly of Carlotta, and the first Christmas morning she had been old enough to understand Santa Claus. "He brought something for me, Nonno?" she had asked, with that same echo of disbelief. "For *me*?"

Remembering that moment, Signor Speranza shuffled his feet. "It's not a big deal, Smilzo," he muttered, but when he looked sidelong at his assistant he was horrified to see that the young man was crying, large tears rolling silently down his thin cheeks and dripping off the end of his pointy nose. His skinny arms, sticking out of the armholes of his enormous white T-shirt, looked like scrawny chicken wings.

Signor Speranza panicked and made what he hoped was a soothing noise.

"I'm okay, boss," Smilzo choked. He sniffed and mopped his face with his rolled sleeve. "I just didn't know we could have a movie theater, that's all. I didn't know we were allowed."

Signor Speranza looked down at the floor. For the second time that day, he thought of his cousin Paolo, and the train station. "Don't you want to get out of here, Giovannino?" his cousin had said, standing there on the platform and staring into the distance. "Don't you want to get out of here before this place strangles you, too?"

Signor Speranza reached out to Smilzo and patted him awkwardly on the shoulder. "Of course we can have a movie theater, Smilzo," he lied, his conscience burning a hole in his stomach. "Who is there to tell us that we can't?"

✻ ✻ ✻

Signor Speranza picked at his dinner. His early triumph in securing nearly all the money they needed for the pipes had fizzled after his conversation with Smilzo. He pushed his peas around on his plate. Who did he think he was, anyway, lying to everyone like this? Some kind of big shot who didn't have to follow the rules?

Carlotta gave a happy shriek. Zio Franco was over for dinner again, and she was decorating his bald head with pieces of paper napkin.

"I heard you're holding auditions tomorrow, Papà," said Gemma. "For this movie of yours."

Signor Speranza looked up from his plate, surprised. His eyes met Betta's across the table. When was the last time their daughter had started a conversation?

"Where did you hear about that?" he asked, a little dazed.

Gemma waved her hand. "Around."

Signor Speranza and Betta exchanged glances again, Betta's eyes crinkling at the corners. What wonders had happened here? Gemma, talking to someone outside this house? Talking to someone who wasn't a world away, in Rome? And she wasn't even finished yet.

"I also heard there's going to be a movie theater," she continued, loading her fork with salad. "I was surprised to hear that."

Carlotta stopped sprinkling napkin bits onto Zio Franco's head.

"Can I go to the movie theater, Mamma? Can I?" she asked.

Gemma smiled. "Of course you can go, *cucuzza*. I'll take you, okay?"

Signor Speranza watched this conversation in disbelief, his

head swiveling back and forth between his daughter and his grand-daughter, a joyous ringing sound in his ears. What was happening here?

"Well, you must be careful about getting excited," he said cautiously, looking across at Betta and thinking of Smilzo. "Anything can happen. Projects like this get canceled all the time . . ."

Gemma shrugged. "Who cares? At least something is happening around here for a change. Don't you think, Papà?"

❖ ❖ ❖

By the following day, it was clear that word of the auditions had indeed spread like wildfire. Signor Speranza could not walk a step in town without people waving to him and calling out.

"I still don't understand, signore," said Don Rocco, frowning, as they stood on the step of Speranza and Son's. "Dante Rinaldi, a famous movie star, wants to come to our village and make a movie. But he wants *you* to raise the money. He wants *you* to pick the actors. It doesn't make any sense."

Signor Speranza avoided the priest's gaze. "Do you think it will rain today, Father?" he asked, shielding his eyes and peering up into the cloudless July sky. "I thought it was supposed to rain."

Don Rocco ignored this query. "And he has put *you* in charge, signore," he went on, his voice heavy with suspicion, "because you knew his father. *From the mines.*"

Signor Speranza's moustache twitched from side to side. Clearly, he was in a tricky situation. On one side, there was truth. There was truth, and there was also devastation. There was losing the village. There was losing Gemma and Carlotta. There was losing his father's shop. There was everyone he knew being chased out of their houses. On the other side? Yes, there was a lie, but there was also hope. Was hope not as important as truth?

He took a deep breath and met the priest's questioning stare.

"*Sì*, Father," he said, wide-eyed and innocent. "From the mines."

❖ ❖ ❖

By two thirty, everything was ready, and Signor Speranza and Smilzo were sitting at the card table, facing the front door and the carpet sample, and waiting. Their dispute over the suitability of the Betamovie had resulted in a compromise: they agreed to use the old camcorder and tripod for their imposing aesthetics, but they had taped Smilzo's phone over the lens cap.

A crowd formed outside.

"Look at that, Smilzo." Signor Speranza marveled. There had not been a throng like that outside Speranza and Son's since April of 1957, when Luigi Speranza had received a shipment of Hoover Constellations, the most wondrous vacuum cleaner ever manufactured, whose canister did not have wheels but instead relied on the power of its own exhaust to blast off the ground and float, like a spaceship, behind the operating technician.

"Maybe you should tell them to form a line, Smilzo," Signor Speranza suggested, recalling what his father had said about the rush of people when he opened for business that long-ago morning. "We do not want a stampede."

As Smilzo slipped out the front door, Gemma slipped in.

"Mamma made you artichokes, Papà," she said, placing a bowl covered by a steam-soaked tea towel on his desk. Usually, she would have whisked away again before Signor Speranza could even look up, but today she boosted herself onto the edge of the desk, the way she used to when she was little, and the way her daughter did now when she visited the shop.

Signor Speranza, who had long mourned his daughter's re-sistance to chitchat, found, now that she was here and apparently not in any hurry to go, that he had no idea what to say. He looked around for inspiration.

"You ate already?" he said finally.

But Gemma was gazing out of the window. "You have a lot of people here," she mused, and then she looked at him and flashed one of her rare, wistful smiles. "It's kind of cool, Papà."

Signor Speranza felt a painful tug in his heart. In a second, he was back in those early days, right after Carlotta was born, and the Ricci boy had left, when he and Betta had hovered and tiptoed out-side Gemma's bedroom door, desperate for any sign that their only daughter wasn't broken forever. A smile like this, back then, would have sent their hopes soaring.

"Yes," he said thickly, and cleared his throat. He looked out of the window also. "It is very cool."

❊ ❊ ❊

Signora Barbaro and Signora Pedulla, two widowed sisters, ages ninety-four and ninety-nine, respectively, were the first in line.

"Marianna does not want a part," said Signora Barbaro. "She's too shy. She's only here to use the bathroom." Signora Pedulla, who had been in the shop perhaps a hundred times, wandered into the stockroom and then the broom cupboard before arriving at the bath-room and closing the door behind her.

"That's no problem," said Signor Speranza. He handed one of Smilzo's photocopies across the card table. "Everyone will be reading from the same scene today, signora, even though this isn't the role you would be auditioning for. Smilzo here will read the part of Vincenzo, and you'll read the lines for Antonia."

Signora Barbaro accepted the script, and then squinted at Signor Speranza.

"I know you," she said, pointing at him. "You were the foreman at the factory where my father worked when I was a little girl." She shook her finger. "It was not nice that you made him work on Christmas Eve."

Signor Speranza, who had certainly not even been born when Signora Barbaro's father had walked this earth, considered his options.

"I'm very sorry about that, signora," he said, bowing his head. "I hope you can forgive me."

Signora Barbaro grunted and hobbled to the makeshift stage.

"This is a love story?" she asked, peering at him over the script, and then she shook her finger again. "I want you to know, young man, that I am not taking off my clothes."

Signor Speranza's cheeks burned, and Smilzo started to snicker. "No, no, signora," said Signor Speranza weakly. "Everyone is keeping their clothes on, I promise you."

Signora Barbaro sniffed, picking her way slowly to the stage. "*Vincenzo!*" she shouted at Smilzo, reading from the paper. "*I thought you would never ask me to dance!*"

It was fortunate that the audition was being recorded, because Signor Speranza missed the rest of it. He was distracted by a loud flush, and Signora Pedulla exiting the bathroom. Then, on finding herself face-to-face with a Dyson Ball Multi Floor, she promptly plugged it in and started vacuuming.

Signora Barbaro looked up from her script and shouted over the din. "You want for me to kiss him now, signore?"

❊ ❊ ❊

Antonella arrived for her audition in a skintight satin jumpsuit, a pair of gold hoop earrings embedded in her hair.

"Is Dante here, signore?" she asked, trying to peer around Signor Speranza into the back room.

Signor Speranza coughed. "Uh, no, signorina. Dante has asked us to begin without him."

Antonella frowned and put one hand on her hip. "Well, when is he coming, signore? He *is* coming, right?"

"Yes, boss, when?" asked Smilzo, whose eyes kept sliding to Antonella in her jumpsuit.

Signor Speranza waved his hand and poured a large glass of water from the pitcher. "Don't worry," he said, after a long drink. "He'll be here. He told me to get the ball rolling."

Antonella sighed. "It took a long time to do my hair, signore."

Signor Speranza nodded sympathetically. "Hair can be very difficult, signorina."

Antonella and Smilzo took their places on the stage, Antonella studying the scene and whispering the lines to herself, and Smilzo staring at the carpet.

"These two characters, signore," said Antonella, "they are the two leads, yes?"

"Uh, yes, signorina."

"So the man will be Dante?"

"Uh, yes."

Antonella pulled a face. "It's just, signore . . ." She looked at the ceiling and sighed. "I do not think I can perform the same with Smilzo as I can with Dante. They are worlds apart. It's not just in the face, either. Dante has an air of sophistication. Of confidence. Of charisma. You understand."

Signor Speranza shifted in his chair, his eyes flickering to his poor assistant, who looked very much as if he would like the floor to open and swallow him up.

"You'll have to make do, signorina. We have a lot of people to see."

Antonella brightened. "I know, signore!" She rummaged in her purse and extracted a glossy magazine, with Dante Rinaldi, in a lime-green tank top, smirking on the cover. "Maybe if Smilzo holds this up—"

"No," said Signor Speranza hurriedly. "That would not do at all." Then, a little desperate, he added, "You know, our Smilzo is the one who wrote this scene."

"Oh yes?" Antonella was surprised. She looked at Smilzo again, as if seeing him for the first time.

Smilzo flashed Signor Speranza a grateful look. "Is just a little scene," he mumbled, his cheeks pink. "Is no big deal."

Antonella frowned, peering at the paper again. "This character, she is called Antonia," she said. "That sounds almost like Antonella."

Smilzo stiffened.

"And Vincenzo." She frowned again. "Isn't that your first name, Smilzo? I remember that from school."

Signor Speranza groaned and put his hand over his face.

They began reading the scene, Smilzo standing on the far left of the carpet sample, and Antonella on the right. As they read, Signor Speranza noticed that they drifted closer and closer to each other, seemingly unaware that they were doing it. He found himself getting sort of interested in what was going to happen when they reached the end of the scene, and *Antonia kisses Vincenzo and folds him in a warm embrace*. It appeared Smilzo was wondering the same thing, his cheeks flaming pinker and pinker with each turn of the page.

But it was not to be. Just as they got to the end of the scene, just as they turned together to the final page, Antonella's phone emitted a sound like an air horn. She dropped the script on the floor and rummaged in her purse. When she looked at the incoming message, she gasped.

"Dante Rinaldi's official fan site is releasing a new line of pillow-cases with his face on them!"

She turned her phone around so Signor Speranza and Smilzo could both see, and sighed.

"Isn't he beautiful?"

※ ※ ※

It was nearing five o'clock by the time Ernesto Maestro and his band of brothers tromped in.

"You will have to wait outside, signore," Signor Speranza said to Signor Maestro, poking his head out of the door. "It's a professional audition. You understand."

Signor Maestro frowned and grumbled. "They will all get a part, Speranza?" he asked hopefully.

Signor Speranza grimaced. "I don't know. Do you have sixty-eight thousand euros fifteen times over?" Then, before Signor Maestro could work out what he had said, he whisked inside, whipping the door shut behind him.

Signor Speranza and Smilzo gazed at the invading throng, who were wandering about, examining the vacuum cleaners.

"We are surrounded, boss," Smilzo whispered, shuddering. "What are we going to do with all of them?"

Signor Speranza whispered back. "We could try the hokey-pokey," he said. "Might be fun to have that on video."

※ ※ ※

Ernesto was to go first. No Ernesto, no sixty-eight thousand euros. Ivano herded the rest of the brothers together, and they were sitting on the floor awaiting their turns, like cows in a pasture.

"Just stand on the carpet sample," Signor Speranza directed from his seat at the card table.

Ernesto started for the sample, but then stopped and hesitated. He turned around and strode instead toward Signor Speranza, twisting his hands.

"Signore," he said, in a low and trembling tone, "I want to be very clear about something. I have given this a lot of thought. I need you to know that I cannot accept a handout. Never mind my father's money—I have to *earn* whatever part I get."

Signor Speranza lifted his eyebrows. "Of course, Ernesto," he said. "Your father mentioned that to me already. But don't worry. I'm sure you will do very well."

Ernesto shook his head. "I will know, signore. I will know if you give me a part I do not deserve. I cannot accept that."

Signor Speranza nodded. "That is fair. Now, let us begin."

Ernesto advanced to the carpet sample. He took a deep breath and lifted the script. He raised his eyes to the camera, opened his mouth to speak—and ran out of the front door as if the devil was after him.

10

How to Run Like a Movie Star

The morning after the auditions, Signor Speranza was standing in the showroom of Speranza and Son's, winding a twenty-foot length of replacement cording around his left forearm, when he saw, through the front window, a group of teenagers meander by. What was remarkable about this particular group of teenagers was that he was quite certain he had never seen them before.

He gasped, dropped the cord, tripped, and then stumbled outside. Could this be it? Could this be the beginning of Prometto's own George Clooney–style miracle? Was the rumor of Dante Rinaldi's imminent arrival finally working its tank-top magic? For a few feverish seconds, he saw the village square teeming with tourists, the town coffers full, and Signor Maestro off his back forever.

When he got outside, however, his view and his path were both blocked by Signor Maestro himself, who had somehow sneaked across the street on little cat feet, and was now standing in front of

Speranza and Son's like an obelisk, his arms crossed over his gore-smeared apron.

"Speranza," he grunted. "What happened with Ernesto's audition? The boys will not tell me anything."

Signor Speranza cringed.

"I wonder, signore," he said delicately, "if you have not underestimated the talents of your son Ivano. His reading was . . ." Signor Speranza struggled for a moment, recalling Ivano wading stolidly through his lines like a human metronome. ". . . *competent*."

Signor Maestro shook his ponderous head. "It's Ernesto who is a star in the making. Did you ask him to sing? He has the voice of an angel."

Signor Speranza got a sudden, electrifying image of Ernesto Maestro in white robes and a halo, and shuddered.

"Signore?" he said.

Signor Maestro dug in, crossing his arms more tightly across his chest. "When will the list be up?"

"Yes, signore." Don Rocco, who was apparently a shameless eavesdropper, crossed the street and joined them on the step. "I'm sure everyone is very interested in the cast list. When can we expect to see it?"

Signor Speranza looked from one to the other of them, these dual harbingers of his physical and spiritual doom, and did the only thing he could do. He pulled an Ernesto.

"Rome was not built in a day, signori!" he shouted, and withdrew to the safety of his shop.

❄ ❄ ❄

Inside, Smilzo was sitting on yesterday's carpet sample and working on his script.

"Boss," he called, "what do you think if I have the hero rescue the girl from falling off the side of a cliff? He could be on a motorcycle, or in a helicopter, or something."

Signor Speranza's moustache bristled. His already-frayed nerves jangled.

"Why can you not just write a regular movie?" he snapped. "With normal people doing normal things?"

Smilzo shook his head. "I have to have a set piece. This is Hollywood we're talking about."

Signor Speranza sighed and looked around the battered old interior of Speranza and Son's. At least Smilzo's imagination was intact.

"What is a set piece?" he said wearily.

Smilzo's face lit up. "A set piece is the reason people go to see a movie, boss. Is Indiana Jones running away from a boulder. Is Tom Hanks dancing on a piano. Is the *wow* factor."

Signor Speranza wrinkled his nose. "And you don't think that, for our movie, we should go for fewer boulders and more dancing pianos?"

Smilzo pulled a face. "I don't know, boss. I think we should go big."

Signor Speranza rolled his eyes and glanced out the window again, hoping to spot more herds of unknown teenagers. Then he did a double take. Unless he was very much mistaken, Signor Maestro was standing at the window of the butcher's shop with a pair of binoculars trained squarely on Speranza and Son's.

Signor Speranza yelped and joined Smilzo on the carpet sample. Bogus auditions weren't going to be enough to keep Signor Maestro at bay. He was going to have to string the charade out a little longer.

"Listen," he said, "we need to talk about the cast list. I think we should have Ernesto Maestro for the role of Giorgio."

Smilzo's mouth dropped open. "Boss, what are you talking about? Giorgio is a big part. A lot of speaking lines. Ernesto did not even stay for the audition!"

Signor Speranza held up his hand. "An audition is not everything, Smilzo. It is not the only thing we have to consider." His eyes drifted to the safe, and Smilzo understood.

"But, boss," he said, his forehead rumpling, "Ernesto will not take the part. You heard him yesterday. He said he will not accept a role if he does not think he deserves it. What are we going to do about that?"

Signor Speranza's head pounded.

"Right," he said, rubbing his temples. "You are right. We are going to have to think of something."

❉ ❉ ❉

The next day was Sunday. It was nearly a week since Signor Speranza had started the rumor about Dante Rinaldi, and fifty-one days until the water was scheduled to be turned off. The safe at Speranza and Son's held 68,200 euros: sixty-eight thousand from Signor Maestro's Ernesto-contingent—and newly jeopardized—contribution, and two hundred from the Speranzas' own meager reserves, which left them eighteen hundred euros short. Signor Speranza awoke after a fitful night's sleep with his chest heavy and numbers swirling in his head.

"What's that?" he asked as he padded into the kitchen in his pajamas.

Gemma, who was already dressed and sitting at the table, looked at him over the top of an enormous wicker basket. "You're being wooed, Papà," she said, grinning.

Signor Speranza frowned. "What are you talking about?" he said. He padded closer and examined the contents of the basket. There were two glass jars of pickled eggplant, a wreath of dried tomatoes, and five brown hen's eggs in an old shoebox, nestled in shredded newspaper.

"There's a card," said Gemma, and she read it aloud. "'For Signor Speranza. We hope this basket finds you well as you work on casting the movie. Warm regards, the Trezza family.'" She looked up, eyes sparkling. "Wink-wink, right? They're trying to butter you up!"

Signor Speranza regarded his daughter in confusion. What was that supposed to mean? And what was she doing, smiling at him like that? He looked again at the Trezzas' basket with an uncomfortable feeling in his stomach. Was it possible he had taken this deception just a fraction too far?

The front door opened and then banged shut, and Carlotta streaked in, followed by Betta. "There is another one, Mamma, from the Bisis!" Carlotta crowed, brandishing a box of gold-wrapped Perugina chocolates. "Can I have one now? Please, please!"

Gemma shook her head. "Not until after church, *cara mia*."

Signor Speranza looked at Betta and raised his eyebrows. Then he cleared his throat.

"You, um, you are going to church with us?" he asked, trying to keep his voice light and casual.

Gemma opened one of the jars of eggplant and shrugged. "If everyone is going to be falling all over you, I want to see it."

Signor Speranza glanced at the ceiling and had a brief word with God.

I don't know what you are doing, Lord, but keep it up.

✳ ✳ ✳

They walked to church together in the morning heat, Signor Speranza, Betta, Gemma, and Carlotta, with Carlotta running out ahead of them, and then doubling back to check they were still coming. Three times along the way, Signor Speranza was stopped by some auditionee or auditionee's family member, to have his hand shaken and his shoulder thumped, and on each of these occasions Gemma snorted with suppressed laughter.

On their way into the church, Signor Speranza met Smilzo, and he hung back a moment as his family went ahead without him.

"I had an idea, boss, about the Ernesto situation," Smilzo whispered. He was wearing his church clothes, which were a collared shirt and khaki pants, but he also had on the black felt beret, and Signor Speranza's eyes kept drifting up of their own accord to look at it.

"I am going to try to sit near him," Smilzo went on, "so I can see what he thinks, and I will tell you after Mass is over."

They separated to find their seats, Smilzo removing his hat as he pelted down the aisle in quest of the Maestros, and Signor Speranza watching him go.

"Nino, over here!" Betta called from the left bank of pews.

Signor Speranza glanced around the congregation as he slid into his seat. "It's more crowded than usual, no?" he said. He ducked his head and pointed, trying to be discreet. "Those people over there—have you ever seen them before? Who are they?"

Betta looked, and shrugged, just as the organ struck up the processional hymn, and everyone stood for Mass to begin. Signor Speranza sang along, and went through the motions, but his thoughts wandered. He pondered this mysterious family at church. He recalled the teenagers he had glimpsed the day before outside his shop. He thought of Alberto, bouncing along in his Alfa Romeo down the streets of Oliveto, the cash flowing and the McDonald's cheeseburgers there for the taking. All of this gave him a warm, fizzy feeling of hope that continued through the first and second readings, the responsorial psalm and the Gospel, and only stopped when he sat down for the homily, and Don Rocco, standing at the lectern, adjusted his microphone, and found his eyes in the crowd.

"I want to talk to you today, my brothers and sisters," the priest began, his gaze locked on Signor Speranza, "about how much the Lord hates lying."

❊ ❊ ❊

It was the custom of the parishioners of Sant'Agata to gather on the church lawn for an hour of socializing following Sunday Mass. It was a custom in which, on this particular Sunday, Signor Speranza had no intention of partaking. If the pointed homily on the perils of deceit had not been enough to dissuade his attendance, the sight of Don Rocco during the recessional hymn, as he processed out of church, his step brisk and his robes flapping, like an avenging angel, was certainly enough to convince Signor Speranza that it was in his best interests to get the hell out of there.

However, he had no sooner shouted to Betta that he would see her at home, and fled out of a side door, than he ran into Zio Franco, who, like Signor Maestro the day before, was doing his best impression of a stone monument.

"Giovannino," he said, blocking the way, "I need to talk to you."

Signor Speranza squirmed. "What is it, Zio?" he said, craning to see over his uncle's shoulder. There was Don Rocco, perhaps five yards away, by the front door, shaking everyone's hands as they came out of the church. Signor Speranza figured he had maybe two minutes before everyone would have exited and Don Rocco would be at liberty to look around and find him. "Can it wait?" he pleaded. "Can you tell me later?"

Zio Franco crossed his arms and scowled. "I need to talk to you now."

Signor Speranza weighed up his options. He might not have time for a question, but he *really* didn't have time for a question *and* a tantrum. He sighed.

"All right, Zio. What is it?"

Zio Franco stuck out his jaw at a defiant angle.

"I want to go back to work," he said.

Signor Speranza spluttered. Back to work? Ninety-three, and twenty years retired? What was Zio thinking? He opened his mouth to say something to this effect when he thought of Giuseppe Ragosta, Prometto's current stonemason. He was a nice man. Most of his jobs were out of town now, of course, since no one in Prometto had built anything new for ages and ages, but maybe he could find a little throwaway job to keep Zio busy—patching a foundation or spackling a wall, maybe. It wasn't exactly masonry in a pure sense, but there might still be a trowel involved somewhere. That should be enough to keep Zio occupied and tire him out.

"Let me see if I can talk to Signor Ragosta and—"

"No," said Zio Franco, and he spat on the lawn.

Signor Speranza frowned. "Zio, I do not understand . . ." he began.

Zio Franco jabbed his own chest. "If I am going to work, then I am going to be the boss."

Signor Speranza rolled his eyes skyward. According to the *Compendium*, it was St. Anthony of Padua's unenviable job to look after old people. He sent up a quick petition, and took a deep breath. It didn't do to tangle with the elderly, he thought. They were just going to do what they wanted to do. A stubborn ninety-three-year-old was just an ordinary stubborn person who had been practicing being stubborn for nearly a hundred years. One had to pick one's battles, especially when, as Signor Speranza nervously observed, the line of people exiting the church had slowed to a trickle.

"All right, Zio," he said. "If that's what you want, then I'm happy."

"*Davvero?*" Zio Franco's face lit up with surprise, and he dropped his guarded stance. "You agree, then? You agree that I can be the boss?"

Signor Speranza was startled. "Of course. If that's what will make you happy—then that's what I want also."

Zio Franco threw his hands in the air. "You are my favorite nephew, do you know that?" he said joyfully, and shook Signor Speranza's hand. "Always my favorite. *Grazie!*"

He strode off then, and Signor Speranza was just reflecting that St. Anthony's response had been amazingly rapid, and perhaps even merited an asterisk and accompanying notation in the *Compendium* for future reference, when Don Rocco was upon him.

"Signore," he said, "if I could just have a moment of your time to discuss today's homily—" But he was interrupted by Smilzo hurtling into their midst, closely followed by Ernesto, Signor Maestro, and what appeared to be the entirety of Sant'Agata's congregation.

"Boss!" said Smilzo, his pointy face glowing. "Ernesto says he would like to do it!"

"Do what?" Signor Speranza asked, inwardly rejoicing at this last-second reprieve and inching away from Don Rocco.

"Be a stunt double!"

Ernesto nodded and beamed. "But I would have to try out, signore," he said firmly. "I do not want any special treatment."

Signor Maestro appeared to be working something out in his head, his brow furrowed. "But is this an important job?" he asked. "I want my son to have an important job."

Smilzo nodded. "Oh, yes, signore. Very important."

Signor Speranza had by now edged his way around the circle of people so that he was as far away from Don Rocco as he could get without leaving altogether.

"This sounds like a great idea," he declared. "I will talk to Smilzo. We will arrange something. Maybe we can hold a tryout over the next couple of days, and then—"

"How about now?" said Signor Maestro, drawing himself up to his full height and cracking his knuckles. "What do you say, Speranza?"

A murmur of approval for this suggestion went through the crowd.

Signor Speranza balked and scanned the surroundings, noting as he did the high prevalence of Maestro spawn.

"Wonderful," he said, his stomach dropping several inches. "How about now?"

❈ ❈ ❈

Signor Speranza made it very clear that, if people wanted to stay and watch, they were going to have to sit in prescribed areas on either side of the church lawn. Only those auditioning or intimately involved in the movie's production were to occupy the grassy area in the middle. By these means, he was able to hold Don Rocco at bay.

"I'm allowed to be in the middle because I will obviously be getting a part," said Antonella, tossing her hair. "Isn't that right, Smilzo?" she asked, looping her arm through his.

Smilzo opened his mouth and then closed it again, which Antonella took to mean yes, and she smirked at her friends on the sidelines.

Signor Speranza walked to the middle of the grass and addressed the crowd, which felt oddly surreal.

"Thank you all for coming," he shouted. He scanned the faces of his family and friends as they began to quiet down. There were Gemma and Betta with Carlotta, who was clapping her little hands. There were the Bisis, who ran the general store. There was Signora Catuzza, who had opened the café, and was walking around with a tray held over her head, passing out drinks and snacks. There was Signora Zamprogna, who had seven-year-old triplets, and who would not stop vacuuming up their Lego pieces no matter how many times he told her she had to stop, though at least she brought her vacuum in to be fixed each time instead of throwing it out and buying a new one. As Signor Speranza perused these familiar faces, his throat constricted. He did not look at Don Rocco, but lifted his face, ever so briefly, to the sky. *I know that I am lying, Lord*, he thought, his eyes stinging with tears, *but I am doing it for them. You have to understand, I am doing it for these people here.*

"Boss."

Smilzo was at his elbow now, his black felt beret freshly installed on top of his head.

"Do you want me to start now, boss?"

Signor Speranza looked at his assistant, and doing so steadied his nerves. He held his hands out. "Everyone, here is Smilzo," he announced. "Smilzo, take it away."

❉ ❉ ❉

Twenty people tried out, including the fifteen Maestro brothers. The crowd clapped and cheered as Smilzo, who had somehow acquired a silver whistle on a string, led them in a kind of bizarre aerobics class. They jumped, ducked, and rolled; they karate-chopped and kicked invisible opponents; they crawled on the ground using only their elbows, commando-style.

"Now," said Smilzo, as his students stood, panting and grass-stained. "The real test."

"What is it going to be, Speranza?" grunted Signor Maestro, who had refused to sit with the general populace and was pacing back and forth. "What kind of test?"

Signor Speranza shrugged. "I don't know. Smilzo is in charge."

"*Is* he, signore?" piped up Antonella, who was sitting cross-legged on the grass, recording it all for the documentary. "I didn't know that." She sounded impressed.

"Can anyone tell me," continued Smilzo, his hands clasped behind his back as he surveyed his students like a general inspecting the ranks, "the most important skill a stuntman can possess?"

A tentative hand went up. "Experience with explosives?"

Smilzo grinned indulgently. "A good guess, but no."

"Being able to jump from one building to another," called someone else.

Smilzo raised one finger. "You are very close. The single most important skill that a stuntman can possess is the ability to run like Tom Cruise. Allow me to demonstrate."

Smilzo jogged back twenty paces and faced the wooded area at the back of the church lot. He adopted a starting stance, one knee popped, and the other straight. Both elbows he bent at ninety-degree angles, the fingers of each hand rigidly straight. The right hand was up, near his face, the left, down at his side. He took a deep breath, and his chest rose and fell.

Then he was off. He sprinted, his knees pumping up and down like pistons, and his cocked arms cutting through the air like blades. Every three or four paces, he turned his head to peer over one shoulder, as if he were being pursued. He tagged a tree and stopped, and everyone cheered. Antonella stood and jumped up and down.

"Smilzo!" exclaimed Signor Speranza, when his assistant jogged over for a drink of water. "I didn't know you could do that. It's very impressive."

Smilzo beamed. "I watch a lot of movies, boss. I make it my job to study them."

Signor Speranza glanced dubiously at the mostly Maestro group on the grass, and whispered, "You think you can teach any of these *cafoni* to do that? You think Ernesto can?"

Smilzo shrugged. "Let's see."

He lined them up, like children in gym class, with Ernesto at the front.

"You're going to take turns," Smilzo told them. "When I blow this whistle, the first person in line will run all the way to that tree." Smilzo pointed to the chestnut tree he had tagged on his own run. "Touch the tree, then turn around and come back."

"This is it, Speranza," muttered Signor Maestro, his beady eyes focused on his son.

"This is it," repeated Signor Speranza. *Come on, Ernesto*, he thought, wishing he had the *Compendium* so that he could see if there was a patron saint of not messing up a sure thing.

Smilzo stopped in place, raising one arm. Then he lowered it with a flourish and blew a whistle blast.

Ernesto took off like a shot. He tried pumping his knees up and down like pistons, and made a valiant attempt at cutting his arms through the air like blades.

Signor Maestro frowned. "He is going off course every time he turns around," he said worriedly. "It looks as if he is weaving in and out."

Signor Speranza waved this aside. "He's doing fine. Maybe he's pretending to dodge bullets."

The Maestro siblings were following their brother's every move. Smilzo's organized line had given way to an excited knot. "Go, Ernesto!" one of them shouted, and then they all shouted it again, together.

Ernesto looked back over his shoulder one last time, perhaps at hearing his name, and ran smack into the chestnut tree. He bounced off of it and lay prostrate in the grass.

Everyone gasped.

Signor Speranza turned to Signor Maestro and blinked. "I think he did very well."

11

Tree Stumps Have Feelings, Too

$\mathcal{F}$ate. Chance. The Hand of God. Signor Speranza believed in the last of these, although over the next few days he did not recognize it when he saw it.

On Sunday night, he sat up late at the kitchen table with two pads of paper. On one, he scribbled the cast list, moving Ernesto Maestro's name from spot to spot and then crossing it out again. It wasn't likely that Ernesto, who had both run out of an audition and run into a tree, was going to feel he "deserved" any role he and Smilzo could dream up. Plus, it was both ridiculous and surreal having to go to all this trouble in the first place, when the movie was never actually going to exist.

Signor Speranza scowled. *Mannequin?* he scrawled in the margin, and then, *Ask Smilzo about this.* On the other pad, he had written at the top, *51 days/70,000 euros*, and circled it. Underneath this were two lonely figures: *68,000*, the amount Signor Maestro had contributed—the amount Signor Speranza very much feared might be rescinded if he did not find a satisfactory role for Ernesto—and *200*, the amount he and Betta had scraped together from their household funds. He sighed. Eighteen hundred euros left. He wrote this figure at the bottom of the page and drew a box around it. It might as well be a million.

"Papà? Are you in here?" came Gemma's voice from the hall.

Signor Speranza scrambled, shuffling his notepads together so that the one with the numbers was hidden from view. As Gemma came into the kitchen, he stretched his arms over his head and feigned a theatrical yawn.

"Papà, what are you doing up? I thought I heard a noise out here." Gemma looked over his shoulder at the notepad. "Oh, I see," she said. "You're trying to find a spot for poor Ernesto." She got a glass of water and sat down across from him. "I'm not surprised. He was always very quiet at school."

"Mm." Signor Speranza nodded. He had forgotten that Gemma and Ernesto had been at school together. It had always seemed to him that Gemma was somehow frozen at sixteen or seventeen years old, and everyone else had just grown up around her. Where had the time gone?

"You know," said Gemma, taking a sip of water, "he was always very good at singing. I remember that. Did you ask him to sing, Papà?"

Signor Speranza frowned. He recalled Signor Maestro saying something similar. "He has the voice of an angel." That was what he had said. Ernesto certainly did not look as if he had the voice of an angel. He looked as if he had the voice of a tree stump.

"Maybe I'll try that," Signor Speranza said. "Thank you for suggesting it."

They sat there for a few moments, Signor Speranza fiddling with his notepad and wishing he could think of something to say, and Gemma sipping her water.

Finally, he broke the silence.

"Everything is . . ." He hesitated. "Everything with you is going okay?"

He saw her stiffen, as she always did whenever he asked her questions like this, whenever he trespassed the borders of her private, closely held world. He ducked his head, waiting for the explosion—the shout, and the slam of a door.

But it didn't come.

"Yes, Papà," said Gemma, rolling her eyes. "Everything is going okay."

"Okay," said Signor Speranza, acting as though it was no big deal, but, as Gemma left to go back to bed, he snuck a quick glance at the ceiling and whispered, "Thank you."

❊ ❊ ❊

The next morning at seven, Signor Speranza crouched by the front window of Speranza and Son's and peered out into the square. It was too early for most people to be out and about, but he had darkened the lights in the showroom and posted the BACK IN 15 MINUTES sign on the front door, just in case, to discourage any unannounced visitors, and especially Don Rocco. He did not wish to discuss the state of his soul on an empty stomach, especially when he had an important errand to accomplish. Across the street, in the cracks around the blinds, he detected movement in the butcher's shop—the Maestro sons, no doubt, as Signor Maestro did not usually arrive on the premises until nine—and, diagonally, he saw Don Rocco waiting outside the church for the members of the Ladies' Rosary Circle. Once the ladies arrived, it would be safe for Signor Speranza to venture outside.

"GOOD MORNING, LADIES!" Don Rocco shouted as two of the members, Signora Barbaro and Signora Pedulla, approached. "DID YOU SLEEP WELL?"

The ladies hobbled closer, and Signor Speranza saw Signora Barbaro throw her hands in the air. "Marianna!" she cried. "Look who it is!"

"*Chi è?*" Signora Pedulla swiveled her head back and forth. "Who is it?"

"Jesus!" cried Signora Barbaro.

Signor Speranza bit his knuckle to stifle laughter as the two ladies converged on a very startled Don Rocco.

"*Che bello!*" Signora Barbaro pressed her hands to the priest's cheeks. "*Bello!*" She kissed him on either side of his face.

"Is He going to say the rosary with us?" asked Signora Pedulla.

"Marianna!" Signora Barbaro scolded. "It's Jesus! He's busy!"

"No, no, signora." Don Rocco's face burned red. "I am not Jesus. It's only me, Don Rocco. But I will be happy to say the rosary with you."

Signora Barbaro appeared to consider this.

"Come along, Jesus," she said, taking him by the hand. "Let's go and find a seat." And she and her sister dragged him into the church.

The coast clear, Signor Speranza gathered his courage and went across to the butcher's shop. The door jingled as he walked inside, and several Maestro sons looked up in surprise.

"Good morning, signore," said Ivano, who had paused in scrubbing the counter. "I'm sorry, but we are not open yet."

Signor Speranza held up one hand. "Is Ernesto here?" he asked.

The brothers murmured among themselves, and then Ernesto himself emerged from the back room.

"*Ciao,* signore," he said miserably, looking down at his feet, and Signor Speranza noted that he had a large, purplish goose egg in the center of his forehead.

Signor Speranza decided to get right down to business.

"I am here, Ernesto," he said, "because my daughter told me that you can sing."

Ernesto looked up, startled. "Gemma said that?"

Signor Speranza nodded. "She said it, and so did your father. Is this true?"

Ernesto frowned and gazed at the floor again, but Ivano spoke for him.

"It really is true, signore," he said earnestly. "He has the best singing voice I've ever heard. Sometimes, he sings the rest of us to sleep."

Signor Speranza's moustache quivered as he pondered this particular mental image, but he was able to maintain his composure.

"Well, then, Ernesto," he said, crossing his arms, "here is your second chance. Sing."

Ernesto looked up, panicked. "Signore," he pleaded. "I cannot . . ."

But this time, his brothers clustered around him, and Signor Speranza stood firm, blocking the door.

"Come on, Ernesto," coaxed Ivano. "We all know you can do it."

Ernesto glanced around helplessly, but there was no way out. Finally, he closed his eyes. He took a deep breath.

And he began to sing.

It was the "Ave Maria." As the first tremulous notes rang out, a chill went down Signor Speranza's spine. The song grew, and Ernesto's voice expanded, and the walls of the butcher's shop seemed to drop away. Signor Speranza closed his eyes, also, and found that he was at the church of Sant'Agata, sixty years ago. He saw himself, practically a baby. He saw his father. He saw a pine box covered in yellow flowers. Baby Giovannino reached out a chubby hand. "*Mamma!*"

Luigi Speranza caught the baby's hand and kissed it. "No, Giovannino," he said. "No."

The baby began to cry.

The song ended, and Signor Speranza was back at the butcher's shop. He opened his damp eyes and blinked.

"Thank you, Ernesto," he said, clearing his throat, and then he turned and left. He marched across the street, conscious that the eyes of the Maestro siblings followed him through the cracks in the blinds. When he opened the door of Speranza and Son's, he found his assistant, just arrived for work. "Good morning, Smilzo," he called. "I know what we are going to do with Ernesto Maestro."

❈ ❈ ❈

Signor Speranza, his conscience at the point of spontaneous combustion over the massive fraud he was about to commit against friend and neighbor, instructed Smilzo to text Antonella that the cast list would be posted that afternoon at two o'clock on the olive tree outside the café. So adept was Antonella in her self-appointed role as town crier that they did not need to tell anyone else, and practically the entire village was on hand when, at 1:57 p.m., employer and assistant emerged from Speranza and Son's, Signor Speranza in front, with the list held over his head, and Smilzo trailing after with a hammer and nail. Once the list was affixed to the tree's trunk, Signor

Speranza began to make a short speech, but he was soon engulfed by the crowd as they scrambled to see.

"Antonia!" crowed Antonella, raising her arms in the air in a double cascade of silver bangle bracelets. "I knew it!" Then she placed her finger on the spot where Dante Rinaldi's name was listed for the role of Vincenzo. "I'm right next to Dante because he is my *leading man*."

Signor Speranza heard this and glanced at Smilzo, who was filming the moment for his documentary, his face a delicate shade of purple.

Whoops went up from the Trezza family, and the Bisis, and the Zamprognas. Then a flock of Maestros fought their way over.

"Ernesto, look!" shouted Ivano, who had gotten there first.

Ernesto and his father made their way to the front, and Ernesto ran his finger down the list. "Marcello," he read aloud.

"It's a singing role," piped up Smilzo, who was still filming. "I have written the part just for you."

Ernesto looked at Smilzo and then back at the list, a dazed smile dawning on his face.

"This is good, Ernesto," Signor Maestro grunted, and he put his arm around his son's shoulder. Signor Speranza and Smilzo exchanged a triumphant look. *We did it!*

"So, Speranza." Signor Maestro turned around, his hands on his hips. "When does filming begin?"

Signor Speranza threw his hands in the air. *Oddio!* This man was never satisfied.

"I don't know, signore," he said sarcastically. "Why don't you tell me?"

Signor Maestro stroked his chin, considering. "I think Friday would be good."

Signor Speranza cast his eyes at the sky and sent up a petition to St. Monica, the patron saint of patience. Could he pretend to start filming? He supposed he could.

"But what about Dante, boss?" asked Smilzo, his forehead rumpled, after Signor Maestro had left. "And the crew, and the director? What if they are not here by Friday?"

Signor Speranza squirmed. "Dante—uh—Dante wants us to begin without them. He—he said that he trusts us." He flinched, waiting for Smilzo to question this ridiculous assertion, but his assistant merely turned a pleasant shade of pink and beamed.

The crowd dispersed soon after that, and Signor Speranza and Smilzo, having made their sensation, went back to the shop, Smilzo to finish his screenplay, and Signor Speranza to putter about and secretly obsess over the eighteen hundred euros they still needed to pay for the pipes. He had enjoyed the unveiling of the list quite a bit more than he had expected, but, now that it was over, he felt deflated.

"I'm going to wash the mat out front, Smilzo," he called to his assistant as he opened the front door, but Smilzo did not answer him. He was engrossed in his story, a world away. Signor Speranza sighed and went outside, and was just on the point of turning on the hose when he happened to glance up and perceive Don Rocco, whom, now that he thought of it, he had not seen earlier at the café, standing on the church lawn in the distance, and staring beadily at him across the square.

* * *

Betta unveiled a moneymaking idea that night at dinner.

"My mother's *crocchette di patate*, Nino," she announced, with an air of triumph. "That's the answer to your problem."

Signor Speranza squinted across the table at his wife. Stress had been gathering in his temples all afternoon, and this enigmatic suggestion gave his already-aching head a particularly vicious throb. He frowned.

"What are you talking about?"

Betta rolled her eyes, as if it were obvious.

"Come on, Nino. People would pay good money for those potato croquettes. They're delicious."

"I remember those," piped up Gemma. "Nonna used to hide them for me at parties so the grown-ups wouldn't eat them all." She glanced back and forth between her parents, her forehead creased. "Why do you need money, Papà?"

Betta intervened, waving her hand. "It's not Papà who needs money. It is the movie. The movie needs eighteen hundred euros."

Gemma's face cleared. "Oh, well, that's all right, then," she said, taking a bite of pasta. "How much would you charge, Mamma?"

Betta shrugged. "Maybe ten euros for a dozen."

"Mm," said Gemma. "That's not bad."

"I will make a batch of free samples tonight." Betta got up from the table and took down the big steel bowl from the top of the refrigerator. "Then, tomorrow, Nonno will go around the village with a notebook and take orders. Sell them door-to-door."

"I'm coming with you for that, Nonno," Carlotta announced firmly, twirling her spaghetti. "I want to go to all the doors."

"That's a good girl," said Betta, beaming. "You will help Nonno make sales. Who can say no to my little *cucuzza*?"

It was at this juncture that Signor Speranza attempted to regain control of his household.

"*Scusi*, but when did I say I am going anywhere?" he roared.

Betta scattered a handful of flour on the cutting board and pulled a face. "What, Signor Big Shot? You have a better idea?"

❀ ❀ ❀

Signor Speranza did not have a better idea, so the following morning he called Smilzo, asking him to mind the shop, and watched as Betta filled a basket with freshly fried croquettes, separated by layers of oil-soaked paper towels.

"Now, Nino," she said, wagging her finger, "Carlotta is going to be watching to be sure you don't eat all the samples. Isn't that right, *cara mia*?"

Carlotta answered by squealing, and jumping up and down.

Signor Speranza, who was affronted at his wife's suggestion that he might eat *all* the samples, crossed his arms and muttered darkly under his breath.

Betta followed them to the front door, rattling off instructions. "Gemma, make sure that Carlotta does not get too tired. If she does, you can bring her back early, and Papà will be fine on his own. Nino, make sure you get everyone's name down clearly and how many dozen they want. Oh, and be sure you tell everyone this is for the movie. Tell them that if they contribute they'll get their names in the credits. They'll like that."

As it turned out, Betta was right, and everyone did like that, very much. They also liked the free samples, and by noon, having canvassed most of the village, Signor Speranza had forty-nine orders recorded in his notebook, and four hundred and ninety euros lining his pockets.

They were just starting the walk up the mountain to call on the Rossis when Ernesto Maestro spotted them.

"Signore!" he called, waving.

Signor Speranza, who was hot and tired and not in the mood for Maestros, no matter how angelic their voices might be, angled sideways and tried to pretend he hadn't seen him, but Ernesto jogged cheerily over.

"Hello, Gemma," he said. "Carlotta." Then he turned to Signor Speranza and grinned. "I have been practicing my singing, signore."

"Oh?" said Signor Speranza vaguely. "That's nice." He tried steering Carlotta back on the path. "Come on, girls, we have to hurry. Nonna will be wanting us home soon."

Ernesto brightened. "Where are you going?"

Signor Speranza had been on the point of snapping that it was none of his business when Gemma beat him to the punch.

"We're going to see if the Rossis want to buy some of my mother's *crocchette di patate*," she said, lifting the basket of samples and giggling. "We're raising money for the movie."

"That's great!" said Ernesto. "Mind if I come with you? I could do with a walk."

And, before Signor Speranza could object, Ernesto had joined them, and the four of them were walking together up the mountain.

❃ ❃ ❃

Twenty minutes later, they were nearly at the Rossis'.

"What's in this bag?" Signor Speranza asked Carlotta crossly. He and his granddaughter were leading the little caravan, Gemma and Ernesto having lagged behind by several yards, talking. Signor Speranza was carrying Carlotta's sparkly pink backpack, which she had insisted on bringing with her and solemnly pledged she would carry herself. It weighed, according to Signor Speranza's conservative estimate, fifty pounds.

"Let's stop and wait for them to catch up," he said, dropping the bag onto the path. He unzipped it and peeped inside. Toys. It was stuffed to the brim with toys.

"Nonno, what is that?" Carlotta stood on her tiptoes and pointed.

Signor Speranza shielded his eyes. In the distance, on the Rossis' front lawn, he could just barely make out a puffy orange object with smaller black-and-white objects swarming over it.

He sighed. "That, *cara mia*, is a Bambolina." He watched the Rossis' front door open, and Signor Rossi come out, shouting at the pile of dogs and waving his arms.

Behind them, Gemma and Ernesto rounded a bend, and Signor Speranza caught a snatch of their conversation.

"I hope you don't mind," Ernesto was saying, "but I always thought Luca Ricci was a big jerk."

Signor Speranza stiffened. His heart thudded in his ears, and he waited for Gemma to shout or scream. Maybe she would even punch Ernesto in the face!

"Thank you, Ernesto," she said. "That's nice of you to say."

Signor Speranza's mouth dropped open. What?! Where was this *nice of you to say* when *he* had wanted to call Luca Ricci names? And much better, more elaborate names than *jerk*, too!

He was so stunned that Gemma and Ernesto overtook him on the path. He watched them go, Carlotta streaking out in front of them, until Gemma turned around.

"Come on, Papà!" she called. "What are you waiting for?"

❅ ❅ ❅

By the time they reached the house, Bambolina was safely inside and lounging on the front windowsill, her breath fogging up the glass.

The unattended schnauzers were bounding on the lawn in all directions, overjoyed at having company.

"Puppies!" Carlotta cried, and collapsed on the lawn amid them, elated at being a substitute Pomeranian.

"You should go in without us, Papà," said Gemma, laughing. "I think Carlotta is going to be a while."

The Rossis ordered a dozen.

"I don't know how we can thank you for this, signore," said Signor Rossi, pressing the bills into Signor Speranza's hand. "This movie business has made our Serena very happy."

"Yes," agreed Signora Rossi, who was knitting on the couch. "She's dancing, she's singing. You would not believe the change."

Maybe I would, thought Signor Speranza, his eyes drifting to the window. He could see Carlotta and Ernesto, both rolling on the ground with the herd of schnauzers, and Gemma, on the side, watching and laughing. Then he glanced around the humble Rossi house, which was so like the house in which he had grown up, and his conscience lurched.

"You know, signore," he said, lowering his voice, "I have not heard from this Dante Rinaldi. These movie stars—they have very busy schedules." He hesitated. "I worry if, for some reason, he were not able to come, or if he were somehow delayed—"

But Signor Rossi shook his head. "I don't care if he never gets here, signore," he declared. "Just the promise of him coming has been like a miracle."

Signor Speranza said his goodbyes then, patting the now-sleeping Bambolina on the head, and promising he would continue to contemplate her dilemma. When he went outside, he found all but one of the schnauzers gone.

"*Pleeeeeeeeeeeeeease, Nonno!*" said Carlotta, clasping her little hands.

"They said we could have one," said Gemma, nodding her head toward the neighbor's house. "Apparently eight schnauzers is too many even if you like schnauzers. But I told Carlotta she'd have to ask you first."

Ernesto scooped the remaining creature up and handed it over. Signor Speranza wasn't expecting it, and the puppy scrambled in his arms, tiny, silky, and probably ferocious, with its woolly white legs and a frizzled beard, like a scrubber brush.

Carlotta was jumping up and down. "I will take care of it myself, Nonno! I promise! I promise!"

Signor Speranza frowned up at the sky. *You did not think I was busy enough, Lord? Now you want to throw a puppy into the mix?*

12

Signor Speranza Steps in It

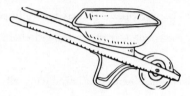

$\mathcal{F}$riday was the first day of filming, but Signor Speranza was late. At nine thirty he was still in his pajamas, his eyes bloodshot, his hair and moustache uncombed, and engaged in a battle of wills in the backyard with a schnauzer.

"It's up to you when we can go inside, my friend," he was saying, in a slightly hysterical tone. "All you have to do is the business God gave you to do, and then we can go inside."

This "business," as Signor Speranza had taken to calling it, had already been done over the last three days by this young schnauzer on the kitchen floor, the bathroom floor, the bedroom floor, and the insides of both his slippers. It was the slippers that made Signor Speranza think it was being done on purpose.

"Nino!" Betta called out the kitchen window. "Smilzo is on the phone."

"Okay," Signor Speranza called back, and then he pointed at the dog. "We are not done here."

Signor Speranza took the call in the kitchen, where Betta was mashing potatoes for croquettes on the counter.

"Boss?" Smilzo's voice was muffled and panicked. "I think I made a mistake, boss."

"What is it?" Signor Speranza was not fully paying attention. He was tracking the schnauzer around the kitchen, and waiting for it to strike.

"On Tuesday, boss. When I was here by myself. Signor Maestro asked if he could do craft services—that is the food for the cast and crew, you know—on the first day of filming, and I said yes."

Signor Speranza tucked the phone receiver between his ear and his shoulder and made an agitated grab for the schnauzer, who promptly darted under the table. "So what?"

Smilzo sighed. "So, right now, he is carving a roast on your desk under a heat lamp."

The image of this floated before Signor Speranza's eyes, and his temples throbbed. He thought for a moment of throwing a fit, but he was too tired. That was what happened to one's fighting spirit when one had had one's sleep murdered by a schnauzer.

"Just move the *Compendium*," he muttered, and hung up.

"Good morning, Papà," said Gemma, breezing past him on her way through the kitchen. She was tapping out a message on her phone.

"Good morning," Signor Speranza grumbled. When she was gone, he turned to Betta and frowned. "It's a little early for the king of Rome to be out of bed, isn't it?"

But Betta shook her head and smiled. "I don't think it's him," she whispered, as she smashed a potato with the back of a fork. "I think it's Ernesto Maestro."

Signor Speranza raised his eyebrows. Ernesto Maestro? Since when did Gemma —

"Nino." Betta stopped mashing and pointed her fork at a puddle on the floor. "You are taking that dog with you," she said.

Signor Speranza's moustache bristled. "*That dog* is Carlotta's responsibility!" he thundered. "You should tell her to take care of it."

Betta rolled her eyes and resumed mashing. "Oh yes," she said. "And maybe, after that, I'll have her clean the gutters, too."

❋ ❋ ❋

Smilzo had made another, much more serious mistake while Signor Speranza was out traipsing around Prometto with a basket of *crocchette di patate*, but it didn't come to light until later that day. When Signor Speranza and his furry charge arrived at Speranza and Son's at ten thirty, filming was nearly ready to begin. Antonella was standing head-to-head with Smilzo in front of a huge poster of the Colosseum, reviewing the script. Bella Bisi and Carmello Trezza were running lines as Bella's mother, Signora Bisi, knelt on the floor, pinning the hem of her daughter's dress. Ernesto Maestro was off by himself in a corner, his hands cupped around his ears, and singing softly.

Signor Speranza let the schnauzer down onto the floor and gazed around, blinking. *Out of control*, he thought bleakly. *This is now officially out of control.* He wondered if he could face an entire afternoon of lying to all these people.

"Smilzo!" he called.

Smilzo hastened over. "Yes, boss?"

"Smilzo, I'm putting you in charge," he said, nearly choking on the words. He had certainly never said them before. Of course, all this movie business being make-believe made it a little easier.

Smilzo just stared. "I'm in charge, boss?" he asked. "I am in charge of the movie now?"

The impudence of this suggestion rescued Signor Speranza, at least temporarily, from the iron grip of his conscience.

"Of course you're not in charge of the movie," he snapped. "But I'm going to let you oversee the shooting today. I am too tired."

Smilzo nodded, chastened, but by the time Signor Speranza had chased the schnauzer to the back of the shop, Smilzo was waving his script around and making an announcement as if he owned the place.

"All right, people!" he shouted. "We are going to begin now. There can be no noise. No cell phones. Nothing." He signaled to Ernesto, who pulled down the blinds for the front windows and switched off the overhead lights. Carmello Trezza dragged over a floor lamp whose shade had been removed and switched it on. Antonella stood in front of the giant poster and took a deep breath.

"On the count of three, I will say *action*," said Smilzo.

Signor Speranza, who had seen the schnauzer disappear under his desk, got down on his hands and knees and peered. "*Dog!*" he whispered. "*Come out of there, right now!*" He could see the tiny creature, sitting back on its haunches and staring up in the direction of the delicious smell wafting from Signor Maestro's carving board up above. Signor Speranza reached his arm under the desk and gave the dog a nudge. He was rewarded with a miniature growl. "*Oddio,*" he muttered, and stood up.

Signor Maestro gave him a curt nod over the heat lamp. "Speranza," he grunted.

"Maestro," sneered Signor Speranza.

"Action!" called Smilzo.

The filming started, and Signor Speranza and Signor Maestro

went quiet, both of them with their arms crossed and looking out at the showroom.

"Cut!" said Smilzo. "Let's try it again."

The scene played over and over, and soon Signor Speranza got bored. His eyes slid over the smorgasbord of meats ranged over every available inch of his desk. "Do you have any vegetables, signore?" he whispered, for a joke, but Signor Maestro did not react. His eyes did not even flicker.

Signor Speranza squirmed, and looked back at the filming, and only then did Signor Maestro speak.

"My Ernesto is very pleased with the role you gave him," he said. "We—my wife and I—had been getting a little worried. Nothing for him to do but cut meat. Now he is happy."

Signor Speranza looked at Signor Maestro, surprised. "Is that right, signore?" he said, but the butcher just kept staring ahead, like the stuffed boar over his shop.

Imagine that, thought Signor Speranza, and he recalled Signor Rossi, and what he had said about his daughter Serena. *A miracle, signore. It has been like a miracle.*

"And, Speranza?" Signor Maestro grunted.

"*Sì*, signore?"

"Your dog just pissed on my shoe."

* * *

Signor Speranza exited Speranza and Son's with the schnauzer held aloft over his head, hollering for everyone to get out of the way. When he reached the street, he scanned frantically for a patch of grass. If there was anything he had learned about infant dogs over the last three days, it was that where there were liquids, solids soon followed. His eyes lit on the church lawn, and, throwing caution to the wind, he sped there, but no sooner had he deposited the pup on the ground than Don Rocco emerged.

"Signore!" the priest called, bustling through the church doors and flagging him down.

Signor Speranza winced. He looked down at the dog and contemplated making a run for it, but for once in its life the creature was doing exactly what Signor Speranza had wanted it to do. There was no escape. The moment had arrived. Signor Speranza glanced at the sky. It was just as well. He could not avoid this priest forever.

He waved feebly back. "Hello, Father. You're looking well."

Don Rocco came nearer. "Signore, I want to talk to you."

Signor Speranza held up his hand. "I would not come any closer, Father," he warned. "He's a very big fan of shoes."

Don Rocco stopped abruptly and frowned at the silken-eared interloper at his feet. He pointed. "Is that a dog, signore? I didn't know you liked dogs."

Signor Speranza rolled his eyes. "Of course I don't like dogs, Father. Don't be ridiculous. Nobody likes dogs."

Don Rocco took this explanation in stride. "Signore," he said, "I have something important to discuss with you."

Signor Speranza took a deep breath. Here it was. Don Rocco was going to accuse him outright of lying. And then he, Signor Speranza, was going to—what was he going to do? He thought dizzily of Gemma, laughing at the dinner table. What was he going to do?

"I have heard from some of my parishioners, signore, that you are collecting money." Don Rocco peered keenly at Signor Speranza, seemingly unaware, or unperturbed, that there was a schnauzer climbing one of his socks. "I understand that you are trying to reach a total of seventy thousand euros for this movie project of yours."

Signor Speranza's moustache twitched. "It's not against the law to raise money for a movie, Father."

Don Rocco agreed. "No, it isn't."

Signor Speranza squirmed. He did not like the way Don Rocco was peering at him and being so polite.

"How much do you still need, signore?" the priest asked quietly. "To have your seventy thousand?"

Signor Speranza was startled. This was not how he had expected the conversation to go. "Thirteen hundred, Father," he said, without having to think.

Don Rocco withdrew a drawstring pouch from his pocket. Carefully, he counted out thirteen green bills. Then he looked directly into Signor Speranza's eyes and spoke in a clear, ringing voice.

"If what you say is true, signore—if you really do need this money to make a movie for Prometto—then I want you to have it."

The twelve o'clock sun hovered over the steeple of Sant'Agata, and a fiery beam of light refracted around the old spire and onto the sheaf of bills in Don Rocco's outstretched hand. Signor Speranza stared at them, and so did the errant schnauzer, who was, for the second time that day, sitting back on its haunches and paying attention.

Signor Speranza's heart pounded. A confession stuck in his throat. He swallowed.

"I—I do need the money, Father," he said. He forced himself to look back at the priest. He did not blink.

After what seemed an eternity, the priest nodded.

"Then I believe you, signore." He pressed the money into Signor Speranza's hand. "I want you to have it."

※ ※ ※

Signor Speranza watched Don Rocco go back into the church, and then, plucking the schnauzer off the ground, he whirled around, his mind already spinning the dial of the safe at Speranza and Son's.

He had not even crossed the street, however, when a scene at the café caught his eye.

"Signora!" he called to Signora Catuzza, who was bustling among the tables, a tray in one hand and a dishcloth over her shoulder. Signor Speranza hastened to meet her, the puppy squirming in his hands.

"What's happening here, signora?" he asked, looking around, agog. Every table at the café was occupied. There was a line, also, of people waiting to be seated. Signor Speranza scanned the faces and realized, with a sudden, effervescent thrill, that he did not recognize most of them.

Signora Catuzza dabbed her forehead with the back of her arm and beamed. "I have no idea, signore, but I hope it keeps up! You want me to get you something?"

"No, no!" Signor Speranza waved his hands. "Don't let me interrupt you." He looked around again at the tables full of young people and did a kind of jig. *"Mangia! Mangia!"* he encouraged them. *"Che bello!"*

His heart bursting, Signor Speranza glanced around the little square and noticed a pack of teenagers going into Bisi's Emporio. He dashed there also and ducked his head in at the door. Little Signor Bisi looked up from behind the register, dazed behind his rimless round glasses.

"Is it some kind of feast day, signore?" he called to Signor Speranza. He gestured around at all the young people perusing the shelves. "Where did they all come from?"

Signor Speranza stifled a whoop. "It's the feast of Dante Rinaldi, signore! *Santo Dante!*"

He spun again on his heel and raced back to Speranza and Son's, visions of shiny pipes and piles of money swirling in his head. When he got there, he nudged open the door and hissed.

"Smilzo! *Vieni!*"

Smilzo, who was sitting on the floor in the showroom, looked up from his copy of the script. At the back of the shop, Signor Speranza could see the actors on break, and milling around the meat table. The schnauzer, with a final squirm, jumped to the floor and sped there also.

"Boss, what is it?" Smilzo came over to the door.

Signor Speranza dropped his voice to an urgent whisper. "See if you can sneak back there and get me the money from the safe. Put it in the zip pouch. Make sure you count it. It's sixty-eight thousand, seven hundred." His head was swimming. There was a bank in Pardesca that did money orders. He would go there first, and then, if he hurried, he could deliver it in person to the Water Commission in Reggio before they closed, and then, after that—

"Is fifty-three."

Signor Speranza's mind went blank. *"Che?"*

"Is fifty-three, boss," said Smilzo again. "Well, fifty-three thousand, seven hundred."

Signor Speranza blinked. There was a strange buzzing sound in his ears.

"Smilzo," he said slowly. "It's sixty-eight thousand, seven hundred. I put it there myself."

Smilzo nodded. "I know. But on Tuesday, when you were out, I gave fifteen thousand to your *zio* Franco for building the movie theater. For the premiere. He told me he talked to you about it." Smilzo's ears turned pink. "Was I not supposed to do that, boss?"

❋ ❋ ❋

Signor Speranza sprinted to the flat field beyond the church where once there had been a shabby paddock for a pair of donkeys, and where lately there had been just overgrown grass, broken fencing, and trash.

"Zio!" he gasped as he arrived, halting abruptly and swaying on his feet.

Zio Franco was there, in his work clothes and cap, and smoking a cigarette. His shirtsleeves were rolled to the elbows, and he was supervising a team of men who were methodically removing the turf within the circumference of a large circle that had been marked off with pickets. He waved when he saw his nephew and strolled over.

"Pretty good, huh?" he said, glancing over his shoulder and waving his cigarette. "Tomorrow will be harder. We'll have to dig. It'll be tricky to get the slope right." He grinned, as if nothing in this world could delight him more.

Signor Speranza was speechless. Fifteen thousand euros. Fifteen thousand. That was—his head throbbed with the computational effort—over twenty-nine million lire! An image of Prometto, empty and deserted, drifted across his consciousness, followed quickly by one of Signor Maestro in a gore-smeared apron. He shuddered.

"Zio," he said weakly. "The money. Have you spent the money?"

Zio Franco frowned and crossed his arms. "Of course I've spent the money. What do you think this is?" He swung one arm out. "I have to pay the men." Then the other. "I have to buy supplies. Did my brother never teach you about money?"

Signor Speranza looked up at the blue July sky. *Lord!* he said simply, because all other words and thoughts failed him.

Then a funny thing happened. It was a thing that had happened only once before, fifty years ago, when Signor Speranza had heard that Goffredo Fraternità had been hanging around the hotel, running errands for Betta's father and charming her mother. Signor Speranza had heard that Goffredo was going to ask Betta to marry him. This thing had happened then, too, when Signor Speranza had been pacing the floor of his bedroom in the middle of the night, wringing his hands, and despairing of what to do.

He smelled roses. There weren't any roses for miles around, and yet he smelled them, then, in his bedroom, and now, here, in this pit, which only days ago had been filled with trash. The sweet fragrance bloomed all around him.

Mamma! he thought, with a sudden catch in his throat.

Zio Franco was tapping his foot now. He looked the same somehow, at ninety-three, out in this field and wearing his brown cap, as he had when Signor Speranza was a child.

"Can the grown-ups go back to work now, or what?" he asked, impatient.

"*Sì*, Zio," said Signor Speranza simply, and with a strange sense of calm. "Go back to work. You are doing a good job."

✾ ✾ ✾

Betta listened carefully to Signor Speranza's tale of what had happened to the fifteen thousand euros, and about going to get the money back from Zio, and, finally, about the sudden and engulfing fragrance of roses. She listened also to his story about the crowds he had seen at the café and the Emporio—encouraging, yes, but enough to save them in the next forty-six days? They were in bed, with a Dante Rinaldi DVD playing on the television set, and Betta was sitting up, her back against the headboard and the coverlet pulled up to her waist.

"Tickets, Nino. You will have to sell tickets," she said, crossing her arms. "And T-shirts. You can put this idiot's face on a T-shirt, and then you can sell that, too."

Signor Speranza and Betta both glared at the TV. Dante Rinaldi, his sun-kissed skin liberally oiled, was busily employed in wearing a white tank top and aiming a lazy grin at his costar. "I will meet you at the café at eight, *cara mia*," he drawled.

Signor Speranza rolled his eyes. "Why do we even own this movie?" he grumbled. "Why does *anyone* own this movie?"

Betta snapped pause on the remote. "Nino, pay attention!" she chided. "Here is the situation. Everyone is expecting for there to be a movie. Signor Maestro. Don Rocco. That assistant of yours. Now even Zio, with this outdoor movie theater. So . . ." She shrugged. ". . . give them what they want. Make a movie."

Signor Speranza frowned. "But—"

"But nothing!" Betta waved an airy hand. "Sell tickets. Pay for the pipes. Finish the movie. Simple. And, if there is actually a movie, you will not have to pay anyone back, either."

This last remark caused Signor Speranza's moustache to stand on end. Fix the pipes *and* not pay anyone back! That was an intoxicating thought.

Of course, reality immediately intruded.

"That won't work," he said, shaking his head. "Maestro only

gave the money because Dante Rinaldi was going to be in it. He would never have given it otherwise. He'll want his money back."

"Mm," said Betta. "Maybe there's a way to make it look as though Dante Rinaldi is in it even if he is not. I'll have a think about that."

Signor Speranza stared up at the ceiling and sighed. "I don't know if this can work. I would have to find someone to take Dante's role."

"What about Smilzo?" said Betta.

Signor Speranza snorted. "Can you imagine? Maybe we can make it 3D. People will pay lots of money to worry that Smilzo's nose is going to poke them in the face."

Betta stifled a giggle. "Don't be too hard on him, Nino. He wants this very badly." She switched off the lamp on her nightstand, and moonlight rushed in to fill the sudden darkness.

"I don't know," said Signor Speranza, thinking it over. "Smilzo is not exactly a matinee idol."

Betta shrugged and plumped up her pillow. "Maybe you just have to give him a chance. I think he looks a little like Humphrey Bogart."

Signor Speranza shook his head. "It's not possible — making a real movie. We don't even know what we are doing."

The bedroom door opened, spilling a crack of light from the hallway across the bed, and then Carlotta and the puppy scampered in and were upon them, Carlotta giving the puppy a boost onto the blankets, where it ran in joyous circles and licked everybody's faces. Through some alchemy of the light straining through the door, and the reflection of the TV on the window, the faint fragrance of Carlotta's strawberry shampoo and the velvety gloss of puppy fur, the moment collapsed in on itself, as some small, insignificant moments do, and Signor Speranza felt a strange sense of nostalgia even as he was in the midst of living it.

"There are no dogs allowed in this bed!" he cried, seizing the miscreant by the scruff of its silky neck and depositing it on the floor. "And no monkeys, either!" Now he grabbed Carlotta, who was shrieking happily, and turned her upside down by her ankles.

"Sorry, Papà," said Gemma, laughing, and standing halfway in the door. "They wanted to say good night."

Carlotta, who was right side up again, crossed her arms and glowered, like a miniature version of her grandmother. "This dog needs a name, Nonno. He is a Christian, and he needs a name. This has gone on too long now. It has been three days."

Signor Speranza blew upward, fanning his moustache out. "This dog is a Christian, huh? Has he been baptized? Is that what you are telling me, *cucuzza*?"

Carlotta, whose catechism was not so sturdy, faltered slightly and glanced at her mother for assistance. Gemma only laughed again.

"Tell Nonno your idea, *cara mia*."

Carlotta's eyes danced with mischief. "I think we should name him after your grandpa Guido, because they look as though they are twins."

Betta burst out laughing. "Oh my God, Nino! She's right! The same serious face. The same black-and-white beard. And the eyebrows!" She put her hands on her cheeks and shook her head. "This dog is the spitting image."

Now Signor Speranza crossed his arms. "And what do you know about my *nonno* Guido, *cucuzza*?"

Gemma grinned. "She saw him in the photo album on the mantel."

"I'm sure Nonno Guido would be honored if you named your little dog Guido," said Betta.

But Carlotta shook her head. "Not Guido, Nonna. Nonno Guido. That is his name."

Signor Speranza rolled his eyes. "Well, you had better get Nonno Guido out of here before he goes to the bathroom in my slippers. Now go to bed!"

Carlotta whooped and ran out of the room, and the tiny schnauzer streaked after her. Gemma made to close the door, and then paused, sticking her head back in.

"I was thinking, Papà," she said, her voice carefully casual. "Sometimes, in a movie, they have a makeup person. I was just thinking that if you need anybody . . ." She trailed off and shrugged.

Signor Speranza and Betta exchanged glances in the dark. Betta found her husband's hand and squeezed it.

"All right, Gemma," said Signor Speranza lightly. "Thank you for telling me."

Betta waited until Gemma had closed the door to squeal. "Did you hear that, Nino? She wants to help! Ha-ha!" She grabbed her husband's shoulder and shook it.

But Signor Speranza frowned. His exhausted conscience, which had been struggling along these past two weeks like an oil-clogged engine, now fully seized up. It was one thing, he thought, telling Smilzo that he was going to have his screenplay made into a real movie with a big-time movie star. That was bad enough. And it was bad enough telling Antonella Capra she was going to act alongside Dante Rinaldi. It was bad enough raising the hopes of Ernesto Maestro, and Serena Rossi, and the Trezzas, and the Bisis, and the Zamprognas, and everyone else. He wasn't going to do that to Gemma. He wasn't going to lie to his little girl; his little girl, who

"I'm going to try to do it, Betta," he said slowly and cautiously. "I'm going to try to make the movie for real. But I can't promise you how it's going to turn out."

Betta gasped and clapped and hugged him, and then they settled down, finally, to sleep. They turned off the DVD, which was paused on Dante Rinaldi's smarmy face, and Signor Speranza closed his eyes. For a while, his head swam with numbers, which was what always happened these days when he wasn't occupied with something else. Next came the parade of faces of all the people he was lying to. There was Don Rocco, pressing money into his hand. There was Ernesto Maestro, smiling dazedly at the cast list. There was Smilzo, his face glowing when he hit on the perfect act break for his screenplay. Then there was Signor Rossi—"I don't care if he never gets here, signore. Just the promise of him coming has been like a miracle." When they'd all passed by and had their say, Signor Speranza drifted off to sleep.

Ten minutes later, Betta poked him in the arm.

"Nino," she whispered excitedly. "What about a cardboard cutout?"

It took Signor Speranza a moment to wake up and realize what she was talking about.

"What do you think?" she asked. "Maybe we can borrow Don Rocco's Roomba and have him sail by in the background. I think they call it a *cameo appearance*."

"I'm sure Nonno Guido would be honored if you named your little dog Guido," said Betta.

But Carlotta shook her head. "Not Guido, Nonna. Nonno Guido. That is his name."

Signor Speranza rolled his eyes. "Well, you had better get Nonno Guido out of here before he goes to the bathroom in my slippers. Now go to bed!"

Carlotta whooped and ran out of the room, and the tiny schnauzer streaked after her. Gemma made to close the door, and then paused, sticking her head back in.

"I was thinking, Papà," she said, her voice carefully casual. "Sometimes, in a movie, they have a makeup person. I was just thinking that if you need anybody . . ." She trailed off and shrugged.

Signor Speranza and Betta exchanged glances in the dark. Betta found her husband's hand and squeezed it.

"All right, Gemma," said Signor Speranza lightly. "Thank you for telling me."

Betta waited until Gemma had closed the door to squeal. "Did you hear that, Nino? She wants to help! Ha-ha!" She grabbed her husband's shoulder and shook it.

But Signor Speranza frowned. His exhausted conscience, which had been struggling along these past two weeks like an oil-clogged engine, now fully seized up. It was one thing, he thought, telling Smilzo that he was going to have his screenplay made into a real movie with a big-time movie star. That was bad enough. And it was bad enough telling Antonella Capra she was going to act alongside Dante Rinaldi. It was bad enough raising the hopes of Ernesto Maestro, and Serena Rossi, and the Trezzas, and the Bisis, and the Zamprognas, and everyone else. He wasn't going to do that to Gemma. He wasn't going to lie to his little girl; his little girl, who had always been so sensitive and highly strung and hopeful. His little girl, who had, when she was six years old, entered a contest on the back of a box of cereal. Signor Speranza still thought of that box of cereal from time to time and cringed.

"The prize is a doll's house, Papà," she had told him. "When it comes, I am going to put it right next to my bed so I can keep track of it when I am sleeping." She had cut the picture out of the box and hung it on her wall, and she had told all her little dolls and bears that it was coming. Then she had cut stars and hearts out of foil because it was a very fancy house, and a fancy house needed fancy decorations.

"Can we buy the house ourselves, Betta?" Signor Speranza had whispered to his wife after Gemma went to bed, but when they found the house in a catalog it was more than they could afford.

"What about this house instead?" Betta had asked Gemma cheerily at breakfast the next morning, pointing out a smaller, cheaper house.

But Gemma had only shaken her head, and eaten her cereal with the big panel missing out of the back of the box. She had been so sure. So sure in her warm, fragile, big-dreaming heart that everything she wanted was coming to her. And when it didn't—when the days turned to weeks, and the weeks turned to months, and the prize still didn't come, when the little silver hearts and stars on her night table shriveled, and the picture of the house on her wall began to curl—she didn't say a word. Signor Speranza had just found them one afternoon in the trash can.

Here, now, he blinked at the dark ceiling. If Gemma wanted to be the makeup person for the movie—if that was something that would make her happy—then he was going to move heaven and earth to make it happen. No more lies. *We-ell . . .* he hesitated. Dante Rinaldi wasn't really coming, so maybe just the one lie?

Signor Maestro Calls in a Favor

$\mathcal{T}$ he next morning at work, Smilzo took the news in stride that Dante Rinaldi had been unavoidably detained. Movie stars, after all, were busy. He was more surprised to learn that he, Smilzo, was to succeed Dante in the leading role of Vincenzo.

"Me, boss?" Smilzo's mouth dropped open. "Are you sure you have got that right?"

Signor Speranza assured him that he had, and Smilzo began pacing the showroom floor, scribbling in his notebook, and thinking out loud.

"Dante will still have to have first billing, of course. I may have to rearrange the script to find somewhere new to put him that will not take very long to shoot. Maybe something like what Alfred Hitchcock did with Janet Leigh in *Psycho*. Have you seen that movie, boss?"

Signor Speranza wrinkled his nose. "Dante is *very* busy," he said. He recalled what Betta had said last night, about the cardboard cutout, and the Roomba. "Maybe you can find a place for him where he can just whiz by?" he asked hopefully. "Like on a skateboard?"

Smilzo was not listening. "I will have to put a hold on the documentary, of course. I will not have time for that now." He turned to Signor Speranza. "Is there an update on anyone besides Dante? The camera crew? The director?"

Signor Speranza's moustache twitched, and he threw an apologetic glance at the ceiling. How was it that the lies just kept piling up?

"He—he said that *I* will be the director."

Smilzo stopped pacing. He lifted his eyebrows. "You, boss?"

Signor Speranza nodded. "Yes. Me." There was a long silence, and he looked at Smilzo, his eyes narrowing. "Why? What do you want to say about it?"

Smilzo shrugged and shook his head. "Nothing, boss. Is just—when you were in the mines with Dante's father—was there some kind of collapse? Did you save his father's life or something?"

❋ ❋ ❋

Betta wasn't kidding about putting Dante Rinaldi's stupid face on a T-shirt. She was also putting it on water bottles, pillowcases, bumper stickers, and commemorative refrigerator magnets.

Signor Speranza nearly fell over when he got home from work and walked into the living room.

"What is all this?" he gasped. The place was stuffed with cardboard boxes, and there were T-shirts draped on every surface. A laser printer on the floor was spitting out glossy photos of Dante Rinaldi's face onto the rug. Betta was at the ironing board, Gemma was shrink-wrapping a photo to a water bottle with a hair dryer, Carlotta and Nonno Guido were running in circles, and the air held the faint, acrid smell of singed plastic.

Betta looked up and beamed. "Isn't it great? Me and the girls drove all the way to Cittanova this morning to get the stuff. Terrific deals. We only spent five hundred euros."

Five hundred euros? Signor Speranza choked. "What five hundred euros?" he asked, coughing.

Betta waved an airy hand. "I stopped by the shop before we left, but you were in the bathroom. Smilzo gave it to me from the safe. I told him I'd talked to you about it."

Signor Speranza gazed up at the ceiling. Forty-five days left, and now this. *Are you trying to kill me, Lord? Is that what this is? Death by Smilzo?*

"Can you take over the ironing, Nino?" asked Betta. "I want to call Antonella Capra about setting up a website to sell everything. She is very clever with computers."

Numbly, Signor Speranza took up the iron. "How many T-shirts are there?" he asked, eyeing the boxes.

"One hundred and fifty," said Betta, leaving the room for the phone.

One hundred and fifty. Signor Speranza ran the hot iron over the back of Dante Rinaldi's face as his well-practiced brain did some quick calculations. Following the fifteen-thousand-euro Zio catastrophe, the money for the pipes had dwindled from seventy thousand down to fifty-five thousand. Now Betta had taken another five hundred, leaving them at fifty-four thousand, five hundred. If she was right about these shirts, and if people would pay perhaps twenty euros apiece, they could add three thousand euros to that number, putting them at fifty-seven thousand, five hundred. The knots in his stomach loosened. That was not so bad. Plus, there was all this other stuff.

He glanced over at Gemma, who had just turned off the blow-dryer, and was examining the finished water bottle.

"What do you think?" she asked, holding up it. "Is this the face you want to see every time you have a drink of water?" She giggled.

Betta came back in.

"It's all set. Antonella is going to go to the shop tomorrow afternoon and help you design the website. She's very excited."

Signor Speranza frowned. "And how will people find this website? What if it gets lost in cyberspace?"

Gemma giggled again. "Nobody says *cyberspace*, Papà."

"Cyberspace!" shouted Carlotta, and she ran in faster and faster circles, Nonno Guido nipping joyfully at her heels.

"Antonella is going to take care of that also," said Betta. "She's going to send the link to her followers."

Signor Speranza rolled his eyes. There went the three thousand euros, then, unless Antonella's seventeen followers were going to buy a hundred and fifty T-shirts.

"She's going to add a feature for buying tickets, too. People will be able to purchase them and print them at home."

At this news, Signor Speranza experienced a simultaneous glug of hope and terror. Tickets. Tickets implied that the movie would someday be finished and ready to watch. Did he really believe they would be able to do that?

Nonno Guido stopped running in circles. He sat down and gave three sharp barks.

"I think he needs to go out, Carlotta," said Gemma, standing up from the couch. "Come on, *cucuzza*, you can help me."

Signor Speranza watched until the girls were safely out of earshot, and then he turned to his wife.

"Betta, do you think it's a good idea to have all these Dante Rinaldi faces around?" he asked, thinking of Antonella's obsession. He lowered his voice to a whisper. "We do not want Gemma getting . . . *attached*."

Betta threw her head back and let out a peal of laughter. "Nino! Come on. Gemma does not like Dante Rinaldi!"

Signor Speranza was relieved. "No?"

"Of course not." Betta took back the iron. "Any fool can see: she likes Ernesto Maestro."

* * *

Ernesto Maestro. Signor Speranza trudged to the shop on Sunday afternoon, his brow lowered darkly, and muttering under his breath. It was all very well for a son of Signor Maestro to sing the "Ave Maria" with the voice of an angel, but Signor Speranza was not fooled. The apple did not fall far from the tree. He recalled the night he had visited Signor Maestro's house, and Signora Maestro, who was not even allowed to pick out her own wall sconces, scurrying in and out of the dining room with those endless bowls of nuts. And the dogs. How would Gemma do with a pack of wild dogs for company? And the laundry! Signor Speranza shuddered. Who did Gemma think washed all those disgusting aprons?

"What do you make of this situation, Papà?" he asked out loud. It had been a long time since Signor Speranza had consulted with his father; his head had been so cluttered with numbers. Thankfully,

Luigi Speranza was still exactly where he was supposed to be, sitting on his bucket at the back of his son's mind, and stringing his bunches of peppers.

"I think you should think about something else, Giovannino," he said, nodding over his ball of string. "What about this movie now? I hear you are going to be a director?"

Signor Speranza drew himself up a little taller. "That's right, Papà. I am going to direct a movie. Are you surprised?"

Luigi cocked his head to one side. "I was thinking, if you're going to be in charge, maybe you'll need a hat, like Smilzo."

Signor Speranza snorted. The idea of a hat like Smilzo's was ridiculous. And yet, he thought, slowing in his stride, perhaps a different sort of hat might be appropriate. The right hat—worn by the right person, of course—might serve as a subtle signal of authority, and command respect. Not a black beret, obviously; Smilzo's instincts were seldom correct. Signor Speranza thought instead of a khaki explorer hat with a floppy brim. The kind that tied under the chin with a leather string. That might look imposing, especially if he were to pair it with a matching vest. It was worth looking into. If he was going to be the director, the village would expect him to look the part.

Cheered by thoughts of his new director's costume, Signor Speranza got to the shop and found Smilzo sitting on the floor, surrounded by scattered pages and his laptop, working on the screenplay.

"What are you doing here?" Signor Speranza asked, tossing his keys on the desk. "There is no work today."

"I know, boss," said Smilzo. "I could not concentrate at home."

Signor Speranza went into the stockroom and dragged out the old computer Gemma had used when she was at school, and which he had been storing in the shop ever since. "Antonella is coming to set up a website," he said.

Smilzo nodded. "She told me." He held up a page of script. "Boss, let me ask you something. At the end of the set piece, Antonia and Vincenzo are supposed to kiss."

Signor Speranza frowned. "So?"

"So . . ." Smilzo's face turned pink. "Now that I am playing Vincenzo, do you think maybe I should cut it?"

Signor Speranza was confused. "Why would you cut it? Don't you want to kiss Antonella?"

Smilzo blinked. "Of course I do. But that is exactly why I think I should cut it. I want her to *want* to kiss me, but if I put it in the script that she has to, it is as if I am cheating."

Signor Speranza had no time to contemplate this logic, because the bell over the door jingled, and Antonella arrived.

"*Ciao*, signore. Smilzo," she called, looking at her phone, but when they tried to return her greeting she held up a finger.

"One second. I just need to send Dante one more message."

Signor Speranza's eyebrows—and his blood pressure—shot up. "What?" He hastened from his desk to the front of the shop. "What do you mean, signorina?" he asked, a strange, skittering feeling coming over his chest. "What do you mean, you are sending *Dante* a message?"

Antonella did not look up from her speedy typing. "I told you, signore," she said, sounding a little exasperated. "It's social media. I can talk to everyone." She removed one hand from her phone to wave it in the general vicinity. "Did I tell you that I'm up to seven hundred followers now, signore? Did I tell you that?"

Signor Speranza's mouth went dry, and he licked his lips. "What did you say to him?" he managed to whisper.

Antonella shrugged. "I just told him we're all looking forward to him getting here. For the movie. And that we're disappointed it's taking so long."

"*And?*" Signor Speranza urged, his head threatening to burst. "Did he write back? Did Signor Rinaldi write back?"

Antonella finished typing and sighed. "Not yet, signore." Then she brightened. "But once he comes here, and I get to meet him, he'll always reply to my messages. It'll be different then."

"Yes," echoed Smilzo, staring at the litter of script pages on the floor. "Different."

Signor Speranza's heart began to return to its normal rhythm. Antonella was not talking to Dante. She was talking to the internet. That was almost the same as talking to herself. It was all make-believe. He threw a glance at the ceiling. *Thank you!*

"I still don't understand why you gave the main part to Smilzo, signore," Antonella said, frowning.

Smilzo's face turned pink to the tips of his ears.

"It doesn't make sense that Dante would not want that role for himself," she continued, puzzling it over. Then, suddenly, her face went white and she gasped. "It's not because of *me*, is it? You didn't send Dante a picture of me and then he backed out?" Her hands flew to her hair and picked at it, like two scrawny birds.

"Are you crazy?" cried Smilzo, indignant. "Of course that is not what happened. That would not be possible."

Antonella gave him a watery smile. "Thank you, Smilzo," she said. Then she turned to Signor Speranza, her chin still trembling. "That's not what happened, right, signore?"

"No, no, signorina." Signor Speranza held up his hands. "It's a scheduling problem, that's all. He could not commit to such a large part."

Antonella took a long, shaky breath. "Okay. That's good." She pointed at the computer at the back of the room. "Do you want me to get started?"

Smilzo scrambled to his feet. "Come on, you can use my laptop instead. We can take it to the café."

No sooner had the two of them left than the bell jingled again, and Signor Maestro stood in the door, his arms crossed and his face a thundercloud.

"Speranza," he said, his low and rumbling voice resonating through the very timbers of Speranza and Son's, and causing the floor to shake under Signor Speranza's feet. "A word."

✻ ✻ ✻

Signor Speranza's nerves had never performed at their level best in the company of the butcher, even under the most benign circumstances, but now, seeing that he was in debt to him to the tune of sixty-eight thousand euros, and living in a web of lies, he found the prospect of being alone with him at the shop, when all decent people were at home enjoying their Sunday lunch, petrifying. What could it be now? Signor Speranza racked his brains. Ernesto had been fine at the shoot on Friday, hadn't he? He squinted, trying to remember. He had seen him practicing his singing, and eating *bresaola*, and chatting with the other actors. He had *not* seen him running anywhere, or colliding with any trees.

"If you will just have a seat." Signor Speranza directed Signor Maestro to the folding chair next to his desk, and then bustled into the back room, calling over his shoulder, "How do you take your coffee, signore? For myself, I like to put milk and three sugars, but —"

"Black," Signor Maestro grunted.

Signor Speranza made the coffee, sloshing half of it on the counter, and put it on a tray with a plate of cookies.

"What can I do for you today, signore?" he asked heartily, as he bore the tray to his desk, where he found Signor Maestro sitting in his leather swivel chair and pawing casually through the contents of his drawers.

Signor Speranza's moustache stood on end. What if now, at this late hour, the butcher were to discover the water report? Signor Speranza could picture it now, folded crisply and tucked under the heavy walnut box that held his gavel.

He put the tray down with a clatter. "Very hot," he shouted. "Don't you think, signore? It's very hot today." In one movement, he deposited a coffee cup and saucer in front of Signor Maestro with one hand, and, with the other, snapped the desk drawer shut.

"Cookie?" he asked, sliding into the folding chair and waving the plate under Signor Maestro's nose. Signor Maestro batted the plate away like a bear with a bee. Signor Speranza took a too-large bite of cookie.

"Is this about Ernesto?" he asked thickly, spraying crumbs. "Is he not happy with the role after all?" For the second time that afternoon, his heart skittered. What if Ernesto wanted to quit the production? What if Signor Maestro had come to request a refund? Signor Speranza glanced at the safe and then at the ceiling. *If you are trying to kill me, Lord, you are taking the long way.*

But Signor Maestro shook his ponderous head. "No." He picked up his coffee and drained the entire cup in a single go. Then he leaned back in Signor Speranza's chair and crossed his arms over his chest. "I have come to ask a favor. I need Dante Rinaldi to do a commercial for my butcher's shop."

A muscle under Signor Speranza's left eye twitched.

"A commercial, signore?"

He squirmed and ate another cookie.

Signor Maestro swept his hands, palms out, in front of him. "Only the best shop at Maestro's!" He dropped his hands. "And then maybe a cartoon chicken or something could fly into Dante's mouth."

Signor Speranza choked on powdered sugar and pounded his chest with his fist. "A chicken, signore? You wish for a whole chicken to fly into Dante Rinaldi's mouth?"

Signor Maestro shrugged. "Could also be a chicken cutlet," he said, unconcerned. "That would also be all right."

"Uh . . ." Signor Speranza returned his eyes to the ceiling. He had of course consulted the *Compendium* already with regard to butchers, but he was still at odds over how to direct his prayers in this matter, especially after what had happened with St. Vincent Ferrer and the pipes. He was not going to appeal for help to a saint who, after all, might be biased in Signor Maestro's favor. He did not wish to pray *for* a butcher, which was probably what the makers of the *Compendium* supposed, but rather for deliverance *from* a butcher.

Seeing as this was an emergency, and he was pressed for time, with a butcher actually in his midst, and staring him down at this very moment, he sent up a quick petition to Our Lady, Comfort of the Afflicted, a handy catchall for situations such as these.

"I don't know, signore," he said slowly and delicately, when he was finished praying, "whether movie stars make commercials for butcher's shops. I do not think they do."

Signor Maestro puffed out his chest. "Then mine will be the first one."

Signor Speranza frowned. "I don't think Dante —" he began again.

"He'll do it," said Signor Maestro, standing up and rapping his knuckles on the desktop. "He owes me big, for the movie." He started toward the door, and pointed at Signor Speranza. "When he comes here, you get me a meeting, or maybe I want my money back. *Capisci?*"

Signor Speranza's heart fluttered.

"*Sì*, signore," he whimpered. "*Capisco.*"

14

Technology Is Hard

On learning of her husband's hankering for a special outfit to mark his directorial debut, Betta took a break from manufacturing T-shirts and went with Carlotta to the secondhand store in Scrisa on Sunday afternoon, coming back with two plastic bags filled with a khaki explorer hat that exactly matched his specifications, a vest with pockets, a pair of roomy cargo shorts, forest-green knee socks, and a megaphone.

"I thought you might have to shout at people from across a room," she explained.

Signor Speranza, who had never even considered the need for such equipment, was beguiled. Examining it, he was reminded of a documentary filmmaker he had seen on TV once, sitting at the top of a hydraulic lift on set in the Sahara. He described it now to his wife.

"Hydraulics?" She frowned, pondering it, and then her face

brightened. "I'll call Beppe Zello. Maybe he'll have a dentist's chair you can borrow."

❄ ❄ ❄

The new website launched first thing Monday morning, its birth heralded by a flurry of social media postings from Antonella. By two o'clock they were sold out of T-shirts, and by five the only unclaimed item was a magnet of Dante Rinaldi's smiling face, which Carlotta took and stuck to the front of the refrigerator.

"Maybe Antonella *is* talking to everyone," said Signor Speranza, a bit dizzy, as he sat at the kitchen table reviewing the receipts. They'd made three thousand euros on the T-shirts, five hundred on water bottles, seventy-five on magnets, and three hundred and twenty-five on pillowcases. Additionally, they'd sold two hundred and fifty-one tickets for the premiere at seven euros a ticket, for a total of one thousand, seven hundred and fifty-seven euros. With forty-three days to go until the Water Commission cut the water, they were at sixty thousand, one hundred and fifty-seven euros.

"We're going to have to set a date for the premiere, Nino," said Betta, who was looking at the calendar on the fridge. "I cannot keep telling everyone *TBD*."

Signor Speranza frowned and shuffled his feet. Having once declared that he would make the movie, he was now having serious doubts that he was up for the challenge.

"I don't know about saying a specific date," he said, evasive. "That's a very final decision. Maybe we'll have to cancel after all."

Betta's eyebrows shot up. "What, and pay everyone back for the tickets?" She shook her head and turned to the August page.

"They're shutting the water off on a Monday, right? We will do the Friday before that."

Signor Speranza looked up at the ceiling and groaned. How was he going to shoot an entire movie that fast? How?

But Betta wasn't having it. "You need to snap out of it, Nino," she said sharply, hands on hips.

❊ ❊ ❊

On Tuesday, which was to be the second day of filming, and Signor Speranza's first official day as director, he lunched early with Don Rocco at the café. The priest frowned over his plate of *pane pazzo*. Signora Catuzza, who was still trying to adjust the scale of her cooking to the sudden influx of patrons at the café, had overbaked for the week, and now she had turned her stale leftovers into a dish of old bread soaked until softened in a simmering slurry of olives, scallions, and thinned tomato sauce. But Don Rocco was not frowning about the food.

"There's going to be a premiere?" he said incredulously. "Here? In Prometto? And *in less than six weeks?*"

Signor Speranza, who was garbed in his new outfit, shuddered on the inside at these words, but on the outside, he managed to maintain a calm expression. He cut a chunk of *pane pazzo* with the side of his fork, and waved an airy hand. "You know how it is, Father," he said. "The wheels turn more quickly when one is unfettered by the studio system." He found it was easier to lie to the priest if he used industry terms, like Antonella. Was it really lying if he did not totally understand what he was saying?

Don Rocco laid down his fork. "And Dante Rinaldi is coming? Or he is not coming? I do not understand that situation."

Signor Speranza took a hasty gulp of iced water and then a large bite of food. "A cameo," he said, looking at his plate. "He will only have time for a cameo." It was not necessary for Don Rocco to know the means by which Betta was planning for this cameo to be accomplished. A priest did not need to know *everything*.

Don Rocco's forehead creased. "But what about the butcher? I've heard he has big plans for a commercial."

Signor Speranza winced. He had not, since Signor Maestro's visit to the shop two days ago, even allowed his mind to wander in that direction. There was not enough space in his brain. He would have to deal with it later.

He wiped his mouth with his napkin. "Dante's people are handling it," he said, and found that just saying these words out loud sparked an idea. He would not have to turn Signor Maestro down—he would have Dante Rinaldi's people do it instead. Yes! A letter. A letter was the answer. Something on nice stationery. *Dear sir, Although we admire your business acumen, and have no doubt as to the quality of your fine meats and poultry, we regret to inform you that Dante Rinaldi would never, not in a thousand years, do a commercial for a great big dope like you.* Signor Speranza suppressed a smile at this thought. Well, it would go something like that, anyway. He could even drive, under cover of darkness, to Rome, so that the letter might have an authentic postmark. What was a thirteen-hour drive when a butcher with fifteen sons was breathing down one's neck? Nothing!

Don Rocco was frowning again. "And what kind of movie is it?"

Signor Speranza relaxed. This he could talk about all day long. He picked up his butter knife to assist his fork, and eagerly sawed at his lunch. "It's great, Father," he enthused. "Smilzo is putting in everything we like. Romance. Action. Spies. Musical comedy."

Don Rocco looked appropriately amazed. "He's putting in all those things, signore? I don't think I've ever seen a movie like that. What's it called?"

Signor Speranza swept out his hand. "*Giovannino Speranza's Great Italian Movie.*" He waited for a reaction.

Don Rocco blinked.

Signor Speranza flushed. "It's a working title," he muttered, spearing a large chunk of sodden bread with his fork. "But trust me, Father. It's going to knock your socks off."

"Speaking of socks . . ." said the priest, peering over the side of the table.

Signor Speranza looked down. Something was tugging on his sock with its tiny, needling teeth. "Nonno Guido," he grumbled. Then he turned to Don Rocco.

"Father," he said, keeping very still. "Are you finished with that?" He indicated the small can of *aranciata* next to the priest's plate.

"This can?" said Don Rocco, picking it up, puzzled. "It's empty. Why?"

Signor Speranza did not have time to explain. Even now, the tensile strength of his new forest-green knee sock was being sorely tested. "Listen to me," he hissed. "I need you to throw that can at the ground, directly next to my foot."

Don Rocco glanced at the can, and then under the table, where Nonno Guido, his teeth firmly attached to his master's sock, was doing his best to rip it clean in two.

"THROW THE CAN, FATHER!" Signor Speranza roared.

Whether Don Rocco threw the can or it jumped out of his hands, it hit the ground with a crack and a burst of orange-scented droplets, and Nonno Guido, startled out of his wits, let loose the sock, which puckered damply at Signor Speranza's ankle, and took off like a shot for Speranza and Son's.

❈ ❈ ❈

Signor Speranza returned to the shop after lunch to find Beppe Zello's second-best hydraulic dental chair installed next to the stockroom. He inspected it, his mood rising. Maybe things were not so bad. He was excited to test out this chair, and the megaphone, which lay ready on his desk. He was also excited to say *Action!*, and had practiced it this morning in the mirror. The Maestro problem was as good as dealt with, and then there was this business with Nonno Guido and the *aranciata* can. There was no denying that had been a huge success.

As if he didn't have enough to think about with the movie, Signor Speranza was struggling to turn Nonno Guido into a functioning member of society. He had spent an hour last night looking for solutions on the internet after discovering the young vagabond in the backyard, licking slugs, and had finally stumbled upon the tip about the tin can.

"Your dog is not complicated," said the stern bald man in the video, who was standing in a large, barnlike enclosure with an unsuspecting Labrador. "If he's looking at a squirrel, he's thinking about a squirrel. If he's chasing a ball, it's because he wants to catch it."

Signor Speranza had sat up a little straighter. Here was a man with confidence. Here was a man who would not allow a schnauzer to ruin his life. The man had gone on to explain and demonstrate that if a dog was engaged in some negative activity, such as the chewing of one's sneaker, then all one needed to do was to throw a tin can, perhaps with a couple of pennies inside it, next to whatever it was the dog was doing.

"The dog will be so focused, he'll think it's the sneaker that has produced the sound, and will quickly learn to leave it alone."

Signor Speranza had been dubious, but now he had seen the theory in action. Don Rocco had thrown the orange juice can, and Nonno Guido had stopped chewing on his sock. If that was not a miracle, it was at least miracle-adjacent.

❋ ❋ ❋

The cast and crew began arriving at twelve thirty.

"Hi, Papà!" called Gemma, with a nervous smile, as she came in carrying her little bag of makeup and brushes.

Signor Speranza waved.

"Nice chair, signore," said Antonella, and Signor Speranza was on the point of showing her how to work the pedal that operated the hydraulics when she hopped into the chair without permission, fluffed her hair, and snapped a selfie.

At one o'clock, Signor Speranza availed himself of the megaphone, and ordered everyone to be quiet. Two of the Maestro brothers brought in a table and chairs borrowed from the café and arranged them on the showroom floor. Smilzo and Antonella, as Vincenzo and Antonia, took their seats. Carmello Trezza, who had proved he had a steady hand on Friday, once again held the shadeless lamp, dragging it over on its cord. Pietro Maestro took over camera duties, while Gemma put the finishing touches on Antonella's lipstick and a last dusting of powder on Smilzo's pointy nose. Signor Speranza, his dental chair cranked to its maximum height, raised his megaphone and called, "Action!"

Antonella crossed her arms. "I do not care about the war, Vincenzo. Or the spies at the Pentagon, or MI6. I only care if you love me."

Smilzo produced a cigarette and tucked it into the corner of his mouth. "Whatever you say, doll. If you want to escape with me, I'm all for it."

"Oh, Vincenzo!" Antonella leapt to her feet and held the back of her wrist to her forehead. "If there is any way for us to escape, then we will have to steal the president's Ferrari, the one with the fuel-injected carburetor. It's the only car in the world that is fast enough for us to get away!"

Smilzo jumped to his feet also and grabbed Antonella's hands. "Then we will steal it, babe! You can count on me."

They both continued to stand there, each holding their poses, until Smilzo turned his head.

"I think you should say *Cut* now, boss," he said, in a stage whisper.

Signor Speranza, who, in the excitement, had forgotten that he was supposed to do this, scowled, and allowed a few more seconds to pass so that it would be clear to everyone who was in charge, before lifting the megaphone.

"Cut!"

❊ ❊ ❊

They took a break at three, and everyone wandered around the shop, chatting. Signor Speranza was just coming out of the bathroom when he spotted Ernesto Maestro sitting in Gemma's makeup chair next to the rack of vacuum cleaner bags. Gemma was applying makeup to Ernesto's face with a sponge, and laughing, while Nonno

Guido lay under the chair, contentedly chewing the shop's phone book to pulpy shreds.

Signor Speranza drew his mouth up into his moustache. "Mmm," he grumbled, and stalked back to his desk. "How long has he been here?" he whispered to Smilzo, throwing his thumb over his shoulder in Ernesto's direction. "He isn't on the call sheet for today."

Smilzo, who was sitting on a vacuum canister beside the desk, his black felt beret askew, was absorbed in putting the finishing touches on the next scene. He looked up, as if surfacing from underwater, his eyes glazed. "Who is here, boss?"

Signor Speranza rolled his eyes, but, before he could continue, the telephone rang. He sat down at his desk and picked it up without thinking, so busy was he staring beadily at Ernesto, who had probably three inches of pancake makeup on his face and the personality of a boulder, but who was, nonetheless, somehow making Gemma laugh until she snorted.

"*Pronto*," he grumbled into the receiver. "Speranza and Son's."

"Hello," said a quavering voice. "Can I speak to Dante, please?" Then the voice broke into a giggle, and there were giggles in the background also.

Signor Speranza took the receiver away from his ear and frowned at it. "Who is this?" he barked. "What do you want?"

The giggles increased in both volume and pitch, and then there was a clattering sound, like the phone dropping, and then the muffled sound of the receiver being dragged over fabric, and, finally, whoever it was rang off.

Signor Speranza was indignant. He swept his eyes around the shop. "I think Antonella is making prank calls!" he said, hanging up the phone. "Laughing and laughing and asking to talk to Dante."

"No, boss." Smilzo shook his head. "It's not Antonella. Look." Smilzo produced the pad on which all messages for Speranza and Son's were to be recorded. He flipped through three densely written pages. "Has been happening all morning when you were out. Once when Antonella was standing right next to me."

"Give me that!" Signor Speranza snatched the pad and pored over the messages, all of which were written in Smilzo's peculiar back-slanting hand.

Is Dante there?

When will Dante be arriving?

Can you please tell me Dante's favorite color? I am knitting him a scarf.

And so on and so forth.

"What does this mean?" said Signor Speranza, dazed. "How do they know to call here?"

Smilzo shrugged. "Antonella has been posting about the movie a lot. She's up to one thousand followers, you know. I think one of the pictures might have had the shop in the background."

Signor Speranza frowned. And yet there had been no calls regarding vacuum cleaner repair. Wasn't that typical of the current generation? All flash, no substance.

"What did you tell them?" he asked, agitated.

"I just said he isn't here yet, boss," said Smilzo. "Mostly they were nice about it. There was only one who yelled at me."

Signor Speranza pulled a face. "Yelled at you? For what?"

"I don't know, boss. She was crazy. She was pretending to be Dante's agent. She was very rude. I had to hang up."

Signor Speranza was startled. Dante's agent? That was a very strange angle for some young girl to pursue in a prank call.

Gemma's voice carried from the front of the shop. "Let's go outside and see how it looks in natural light." Then she, Ernesto, and

Nonno Guido, who had tired of phone books, exited the shop, the bell jingling behind them.

Signor Speranza watched them go, and, once they had strolled out of sight, he leapt from his chair.

"Smilzo, quick!" he whispered. "That blinking box of yours, with the button! You have it with you?"

Smilzo was mystified, but he retrieved his backpack and rooted in it, producing the box and the matching remote. "This, boss?" he asked.

"Tape it to the chair!" Signor Speranza gestured wildly at Ernesto's abandoned seat in the showroom. "Underneath! Tape it underneath!"

Smilzo accomplished this nefarious task, flitting among the mingling cast and crew, pink in the face, and stubbing his toe twice on a Hoover upright, and when he was finished, his nerves shot, he fled to the back room to splash water on his face.

Signor Speranza, for his part, hunched at his desk, ignoring the chatter around him, his eyes focused on the front door and the remote clenched in his fist. The bell jingled, and Nonno Guido streaked in first, darting under the desk and romping at his master's feet, but Signor Speranza paid him no attention. He concentrated on Gemma and Ernesto, who were oblivious to everyone around them. He waited for the perfect moment, when Ernesto had sat down, and Gemma had turned her back to him to peruse her little pots of makeup. He opened his hand, spun the volume dial on the remote all the way up, and pressed the red button.

PBBBBBBBBBBBT!

Everyone turned and stared at Signor Speranza.

Signor Speranza's mouth dropped open.

Nonno Guido yelped, and dashed into the stockroom.

"Ha!" said Ernesto Maestro.

"*Pa-PÀ!!!*" said Gemma, and then everyone burst out laughing.

"Oh," said Smilzo, who had sidled out from the back room, his face a nauseating shade of purplish green. He reached into his backpack, which was still open on Signor Speranza's desk, and fished out the correct blinking black box, the one that was a remote-controlled farting machine, and not, like the device that was currently taped to the underside of Ernesto Maestro's chair, a convenient and compact external hard drive.

"Sorry, boss," he mumbled.

15

Signor Speranza Prepares for Battle

$\mathcal{S}$ignor Speranza sulked through dinner.

"Tell it again, Mamma!" cried Carlotta, clapping her hands at Gemma.

Signor Speranza crossed his arms. "It wasn't real," he said flatly. "It was pretend. Make-believe. A *machine*."

Gemma sighed happily and began clearing plates from the table. "You should have seen his face, Mamma! Priceless. It was priceless."

"It sounds like it," said Betta, chuckling. Then, to her husband, "Nino, you have a little something here." She pointed to her own chin.

Signor Speranza didn't budge, but only glowered at her. Betta rolled her eyes and threw her hands up in the air. "Girls, you go," she said. "Take the dog for a walk. I want to talk to Grandpa."

When Gemma and Carlotta had gone out, she reached across the table and swatted her husband on the shoulder.

"*Che fai?*" cried Signor Speranza.

Betta leaned back in her chair and narrowed her eyes.

"Do I look like an idiot to you, Nino? You think I don't know that you were up to something today with Ernesto Maestro?"

Signor Speranza's mouth disappeared into his moustache, and his brows lowered over his eyes like a hedgerow.

"That's what I thought," Betta snapped. "*Disgraziata!* You should be happy she's interested in someone new! Look at her this evening—she's coming out of herself again."

"A *Maestro*?" Signor Speranza burst out. "You want me to be happy she's interested in a *Maestro*? Maybe next she can go out with a plumber!"

"Hush!" Betta held up one hand and jerked her head at the open window. "I don't know what your problem is. Give him a chance! He seems like a perfectly nice boy. Gemma says he has a beautiful voice, too."

Signor Speranza rolled his eyes. "And the neck of a plow horse."

"Enough!" said Betta, whisking the rest of the plates off the table. "You do not get involved. You let her make her own decisions. Do you understand?"

Signor Speranza retreated then, muttering under his breath and twitching his moustache from side to side, which was his preeminent strategy whenever Betta dug her heels in. He continued the argument in his own mind, which was hugely satisfactory, as he found his wife to be much more cooperative there. *Don't you remember the last time?* he demanded. *Don't you remember how she wouldn't get out of bed? Don't you remember how she cried?*

Oh, yes, Nino, imaginary Betta answered meekly. *I cannot watch her go through that again. I know you're right.*

Signor Speranza sat back in his chair and blew a puff of air out his nose. *Of course I'm right.*

❈ ❈ ❈

Over the next few weeks, shooting on the movie progressed rapidly, as did Betta's online merchandising efforts, which now included limited-edition Dante Rinaldi plates, teacups, earrings, aprons, pot holders, key chains, and Christmas ornaments.

"I could put this man's face on a toilet seat cover and people would buy it," she marveled one evening as she was going over the receipts. Then she looked thoughtful. "I wonder how much they would cost to make?"

Thanks to Betta's efforts—and Antonella's relentless postings— the money in the safe at Speranza and Son's had swelled to sixty-eight thousand, seven hundred and seventy-five euros, only one thousand, two hundred and twenty-five euros short of what they needed. With nineteen days to go until the premiere, and twenty-two until the Water Commission's deadline, Signor Speranza felt almost as if he might dare take a breath.

He and Betta were sitting at the kitchen table after dinner, try-ing to determine how much profit they could turn on Dante Rinaldi lunch boxes, when the doorbell rang, and they looked at each other in confusion. There had not been an unexpected guest at the hotel for at least a year.

"Who is it?" wondered Betta. "Is it the girls?"

Signor Speranza shook his head. "I just heard them in the back-yard with Nonno Guido." He grinned. "Maybe it's Dante Rinaldi."

Betta snorted and went to answer the door.

"*Scusi*, signora," said Signor Rossi, coming into the foyer. "I am so sorry to bother you. I hope I did not catch you at dinner." He glanced anxiously over her shoulder.

"No, no," said Betta, ushering him into the parlor. "Please do not worry."

"What can we do for you, signore?" asked Signor Speranza, joining them. "I hope everything is all right."

"Oh, things are very bad," said Signor Rossi, taking a seat on the couch and wringing his hands. "It's Bambolina. I've brought her with me, outside. I hate to tell you that she's not eating."

Betta gasped. "She is not eating, signore?"

"It's those schnauzers," said Signor Rossi. He clenched his hands into fists, and the knuckles turned white. "Our Bambolina cannot find a moment's peace. Now they've started barking at night, and howling at the moon, and it startles her in her crib." His eyes glistened with tears.

Signor Speranza perked up. "Did you say she sleeps in a *crib*, signore?"

Betta elbowed him in the ribs and smiled at Signor Rossi. "How is it that we can help?" she asked.

The screen door at the back of the house banged open, and Gemma, Carlotta, and Nonno Guido came clattering in.

"*Papà!*" called Gemma. "Carlotta says she saw an enormous orange puffball in a wagon out front. Nonno Guido was going crazy."

Signor Rossi jumped to his feet. "Bambolina!" he cried.

Signor Speranza scrambled to intercept Nonno Guido, who was running in frantic laps and yapping. "Don't worry, signore," he said, scooping up the furred demon. "This animal is being rehabilitated." He handed the dog off to Gemma. "Upstairs," he hissed, and she took him away.

Signor Rossi was at the window. He had yanked back the curtains, and was craning his head to see.

"She is fine, signore," soothed Signor Speranza, pointing. "See?"

Signor Rossi sighed with relief and sank back onto the couch. "My wife and I were thinking," he began, glancing at the stairs up which Nonno Guido had just been ushered, "that perhaps what Bambolina needs is a couple of weeks away to recuperate. I know this is a hotel for people, but . . ." He stopped, hesitating.

"But," Betta encouraged him, "maybe it could also be a hotel for dogs?"

"Yes!" said Signor Rossi. "We would pay you, of course. Just a couple of weeks. A vacation! So she can regain her strength, signora. Get her appetite back. She would not be any trouble. I—I had not thought of . . ." He trailed off, his eyes drifting again to the stairs.

Signor Speranza put up his hands, thinking that even if they were to charge a reduced rate for a non-human guest—say ten euros a night, or something like that—it was nothing to sneeze at when they had one thousand, two hundred and twenty-five euros to go. "It will be no trouble, believe me," he said. "The animal you have just seen will be sequestered in his room. Bambolina will be perfectly safe."

Signor Rossi beamed. "*Mille grazie,* signore! I'll go now and get her."

❊ ❊ ❊

Two hours later, Signor Speranza was in the living room, talking on the phone to Smilzo. Nonno Guido was locked in his room upstairs, loudly protesting his incarceration, and Carlotta was sitting on the carpet, trying to make sense of their new hotel guest.

"I have checked the weather, boss," Smilzo was saying. "Is supposed to be nice tomorrow, but then nothing but rain, rain all week. Maybe even two weeks."

Signor Speranza frowned, adjusting his reading glasses and flipping through his photocopied script. Interior scenes were marked in yellow, exterior in blue. Those that had already been shot were struck through with red pen. It was clear to Signor Speranza what Smilzo was getting at.

"Is time, boss," Smilzo continued. "Is time to shoot the set piece."

Signor Speranza sighed, taking off his glasses and staring up at the ceiling. There was no patron saint of movie set pieces; he had checked. He had also, in a moment of frustration, begun drafting a letter to the editors of the *Compendium*, cc Pope Francis, c/o the Vatican, protesting the lack of diversification and specialization among its entries. Now that he was really in the thick of things, it seemed patently preposterous to have to rely, for a minutely specific problem, on a generalist like St. John Bosco, who, in addition to overseeing the entirety of the motion picture industry, was also in charge of apprentices, laborers, students, Mexican youth, editors, and magicians. It was like finding out that one's surgeon was also a mechanic. Signor Speranza had been so aggravated, he had spent an entire afternoon paging grimly through the *Compendium* in quest of saints who were more likely to have spare time on their hands, finally emerging, triumphant, with St. Barbara, the patron saint of death by cannonball, who must really be sitting on her hands these days, and St. Magnus of Fussen, patron of reptiles. Signor Speranza thought it distinctly unlikely, however much a person might admire and respect a reptile, that it might occur to them to pray for it.

Whoever it was up there who was lending assistance, Signor Speranza had at least managed to persuade Smilzo that they could not safely or convincingly portray his original set piece idea—a dramatic cliffside rescue on the back of a motorcycle. Not only was it dangerous, but Smilzo did not know how to ride a motorcycle, and they didn't even have a motorcycle to begin with.

"Perhaps there is some room in the budget—" Smilzo had said, hopeful.

"No," Signor Speranza had said, in so forceful a tone that Smilzo had gone back to the drawing board.

So there had been that improvement. Even so, the alternative scene that Smilzo had come up with was still complicated, and required shooting all the way up a mountain, in the Bosco di Rudina, which would be difficult. Signor Speranza was dreading it.

"Okay," he said finally, still staring at the ceiling. "I'll work out the shots tonight. Tell everyone we will meet on the northern side of the forest tomorrow morning at eight thirty. I'll stop by the church on my way to get the fireworks we need from Don Rocco." His fate sealed, he hung up the phone.

"*Nonno*, look!" said Carlotta from where she sat on the floor.

Signor Speranza looked. Bambolina lay in the middle of the carpet, dressed from top to tail in baby-doll clothes, her pink tongue lolling out the side of her mouth, gently panting. Her little foxlike face peeped out from a lace-trimmed bonnet.

Signor Speranza rolled his eyes. *"Mamma mia."*

❊ ❊ ❊

"I can't put her in a room by herself, Nino," Betta scolded as they climbed into bed. "What if she needs something in the middle of the night?"

Signor Speranza glared across his bedroom at Bambolina, who

was ensconced in Carlotta's old playpen, which Gemma had dragged down from the attic. The girls had made her a nest of blankets, and Carlotta, on saying good night, had kissed her tenderly on her fluffy orange head. All this after they had fed her an elaborate three-course dinner directly from the table on a tiny silver spoon, such as one might use to feed a royal infant, following the strict instructions Signor Rossi had left them.

Signor Speranza's moustache twitched, and he fussed with his blankets. "At least she is quiet," he grumbled. He was sitting up, his back against the headboard, and his photocopied script on his lap.

Betta plumped her pillow. "You're not going to use that searchlight again, are you, Nino? I'm so tired."

Signor Speranza was affronted. "It's not a searchlight! It's a book light!" This was not technically true. On finding that he needed to work at night over the last week, Signor Speranza, unwilling to make any new purchases after the outlay for the khaki outfit and megaphone, had devised his own manner of portable lighting, composed of the disembodied headlight of a car connected by a thin red wire to a rechargeable battery he parked next to his slippers on his side of the bed, and which emitted only a slight humming noise and an awful lot of light.

"I'll angle it this way and block it with my pillow," he said, by way of compromise, but Betta was already asleep.

Signor Speranza sighed and paged through the script until he came to Smilzo's famous set piece. He had discovered, over the past few weeks of shooting, that making certain decisions regarding angles and shots before actually arriving on set cut shooting times in half. The only thing to even come close to that with regard to increasing efficiency had been confiscating Antonella's phone whenever it was her turn to be on-screen.

EXT. WOODED AREA

Antonia is stranded up a tree. She is trying to rescue her neighbor's cat. Below, several heavily armed men are trying to catch her.

But hark! Our hero enters, swinging from another tree on a vine.

Signor Speranza groaned. Was it possible, he wondered, for a saint to adopt the patronage of a single, particular person? Might not St. Barbara, for example, idle as she was, be prevailed upon to take a special interest in Smilzo? Signor Speranza wondered how many of the cannonball cases had been accidentally self-inflicted. Smilzo might be exactly the sort of person she was accustomed to dealing with. Unbidden, an image came to his mind of his assistant, in the military garb of some bygone era, circling to the front of a cannon he was manning. *Just a second, boss*, the imaginary Smilzo called to his superior. *I think it might be clogged.*

Boom!

Signor Speranza chuckled and clicked the top of his pen, ready to write, when a terrible odor reached his nostrils.

"*Oddio!*" he gasped. He covered his nose and rousted his wife. "Betta!" he cried. "Do you smell that?"

Betta burrowed farther under the blanket. "Leave me alone, Nino!" she grumbled. "I am sleeping."

"*Ma*, Betta! Can you not—"

Signor Speranza was interrupted by a noise so loud, it forced him to sit bolt upright. Smilzo's remote-controlled contraption had nothing on Bambolina.

Through the wall, there was giggling from Gemma and Carlotta's room.

"Is that you again, Papà?" called Gemma.

"*Nonno!*" said Carlotta. "I think it's time to go to the doctor!"

Signor Speranza's moustache bristled. Of all the things to bring his family closer together. "Go to sleep!" he shouted. Then he jiggled his wife's shoulder. "Betta! I cannot work in these conditions!"

Betta didn't open her eyes. "It's a hotel! There are other rooms. Go upstairs!"

Signor Speranza collected his things, holding his nose and gagging. *God help us!* he thought, peering in at Bambolina on his way out and seeing that she was sleeping peacefully on her back, fat paws in the air, and perfectly happy. *What wonders God hath wrought!*

He padded up to the second floor, his pillow and his notebook under his arm, petulant and sulky. He didn't like sleeping in a strange bed. He most especially didn't like sleeping in a strange bed because his bedroom had been usurped by a flatulent Pomeranian. *That* he objected to on principle alone. He stalked into the first bedroom, the "green room" as they called it because of its grass-green carpeting, and flipped on the lights, squinting in the sudden brightness. Directly opposite him, with his lazy grin and wearing a tank top and shorts, was the life-size cardboard cutout Betta had ordered of Dante Rinaldi.

"Oh, great," said Signor Speranza sourly, tossing his things on the bed. "It's you."

❋ ❋ ❋

At two o'clock in the morning, Signor Speranza couldn't stand Dante Rinaldi staring at him any longer, and he turned the cardboard cutout around. At four, he fell asleep, sitting up, and with the lights still on. At eight forty-five, he woke to open curtains, streaming sunlight, and Nonno Guido licking his nose.

"*Mamma mia!*" he spluttered, swatting at his own face.

"Good morning, Nonno!" crowed Carlotta.

Signor Speranza drew his mouth up into his moustache. "*Che fai,* signorina?" he demanded. "Are you and this creature in cahoots?" He pointed at the back half of Nonno Guido. The front half had insinuated itself inside a pillowcase.

Carlotta giggled. "Nonna says you are late. Smilzo is calling and calling. Mamma already left."

Signor Speranza glanced at the clock on the bedside table and groaned. He asked Carlotta to fetch the cordless telephone and called Smilzo back.

"I'm going to be an hour late," he announced. "I need you to keep everyone in order."

"Maybe we can do a dry run, boss," said Smilzo. "I can get a couple of the Maestros to boost Antonella into one of the trees, and then—"

"Absolutely not," Signor Speranza snapped. "Everyone stays on the ground until I get there." If anyone was going to break a leg today, as he very much feared they would, then it was just going to have to be while the camera was rolling.

Fifteen minutes later, garbed in his khaki outfit and green knee socks, a canteen of fresh water banging around his neck on a cord, and clutching a large, plastic-wrapped egg-and-potato sandwich, Signor Speranza raced over to the church of Sant'Agata. It was going to be hot today, very hot. He hurtled through the church doors, finding it cool and dim, with scraps of colored light on the floor from the stained-glass window, and Don Rocco kneeling in silent prayer. Signor Speranza ducked his head, made a hasty sign of the cross, and slid, canteen banging, into one of the nearby pews. When Don Rocco failed to look up, or in any other way acknowledge his presence, he cleared his throat.

Don Rocco did not move. "I'm in the middle of a conversation, signore," he whispered.

"Of course, Father," Signor Speranza whispered back. "Sorry. So sorry." With a clatter, he dropped his own kneeler and attempted to pray also, his eyes screwed tightly shut. It was very quiet. "It's just . . ." Signor Speranza began again, cracking one eye open. ". . . Smilzo is in charge until I get there, Father. I don't want to say that the thought of this exactly chills the bones, but . . ."

Don Rocco sighed. He opened his eyes and gazed at the ceiling.

Signor Speranza followed his gaze. "Is there a problem with the roof, Father?"

Don Rocco did not lower his eyes from the rafters. "Members of my congregation have asked me to pray for their intentions. That's what I'm doing, signore. It's very important."

Signor Speranza pondered this for a moment. "Did they tell you what the intentions are, Father?"

Don Rocco shook his head. "That's not how it works."

Signor Speranza lifted his eyebrows. "Do you mean to say that you pray for the prayers of others, without first knowing what they are?"

Don Rocco looked at Signor Speranza now, narrowing his eyes. "It is customary for a priest to pray for the petitions of his congregation, signore. If you do not trust their intentions—"

"*If!*" Signor Speranza exploded, sending his canteen flying. "Do you have any idea what some people pray for, Father? You don't! Once, Giosuè Pergola ate the last *mozzarella en carozza* at the café, and I prayed that . . ." He stopped here, realizing that what he was about to say would not be protected by the seal of the confessional.

Don Rocco crossed his arms. "Yes, signore?"

"Actually, Father, I think that's a story for another time," said

Signor Speranza sweetly. "My point is, I don't think you should be blindly praying for someone else's intentions. Anyone's."

Don Rocco sighed. "If someone is praying for something . . ." He struggled to find the appropriate word. ". . . *unwise*, then my prayer may help him to see a better path. If a man prays for self-advancement to the disadvantage of another, my prayer may help him to see that he should not beg from Peter to pay Paul."

It was Signor Speranza's turn to narrow his eyes. What was this scenario Don Rocco was floating here? Was Signor Maestro supposed to be Peter and the Water Commission Paul?

He frowned. "I'm not sure I know what you're referring to, Father."

Don Rocco gave up altogether and sat down. "What can I do for you, signore?" he snapped.

Relieved that they were down to brass tacks, Signor Speranza sketched out the requirements for the set piece. "Twenty or thirty pounds of fireworks ought to do it, Father," he concluded. "We will replace them before the next feast day, I promise."

❊ ❊ ❊

There was a small lean-to shed with a simple metal padlock at the side of Sant'Agata where Don Rocco stored all the things critical to the maintenance of a small country parish, but which clashed with the sacred environment—gardening shears, a small rotary lawn mower, a bucket of plaster of Paris, purchased in the 1970s by Don Rocco's predecessor twice removed to repair the hands of a statue some errant youth had smashed on an immoral dare, and, finally, an enormous, watertight chest of fireworks for the celebration of important feast days.

"You're not going to allow Smilzo to light these himself, are you?" Don Rocco asked, hesitating over the chest.

"Father!" Signor Speranza gave him a meaningful look.

Don Rocco backtracked, putting up his hands. "I'm not saying he cannot manage it, you understand. It's just—"

"It's just he is Smilzo," Signor Speranza finished for him, thinking again of St. Barbara and the cannon.

They finished picking over the fireworks, and Signor Speranza stowed them in a bag.

"I wanted to ask you, signore," said Don Rocco, his face serious as he secured the padlock. "I have been getting strange calls at the rectory. One lady in particular has been leaving messages saying that she is Dante Rinaldi's agent."

A prickle of fear started at the back of Signor Speranza's neck. "Uh—prank call, Father," he said, his eyes darting across the street to Speranza and Son's.

Don Rocco frowned. "Yes, but—"

Signor Speranza searched the square and spotted Signora Barbaro and Signora Pedulla walking together, in matching Dante Rinaldi T-shirts, and carrying Dante Rinaldi water bottles. He brightened. "Look who it is," he said, waving them over.

"Oh!" said Don Rocco, ducking behind a shrub. "It's not necessary to bother them, signore."

But Signora Barbaro and Signora Pedulla weren't bothered at all.

"Marianna!" cried Signora Barbaro, pointing. "Look who it is!"

"*Chi è?*" said Signora Pedulla, in her wispy, tissue-paper voice. "Who is it?"

"It's Jesus! Jesus is here!"

"Ah! *Che bello!*"

The two ladies descended on Don Rocco in the shrubbery, and Signor Speranza, free from this uncomfortable line of questioning, and with the bag of fireworks on his back, escaped.

❖ ❖ ❖

How much of a problem was this prank caller? Signor Speranza frowned as he picked his way through the grass and rocks behind the church on his way up the mountain. He didn't like to admit it, even to himself, but Don Rocco's report of the phone call made him very uneasy. It wasn't the legions of giggling girls calling the shop that bothered him—they were harmless enough. It was this woman pretending to be Dante's agent—she was another matter altogether.

Signor Speranza had instructed Smilzo to stop answering the office telephone, and so this person had taken to leaving recorded messages, and Signor Speranza had played them back a number of times. She was clearly an older woman. Could an older woman possibly be so infatuated with a pup like Dante Rinaldi as to spend her days impersonating his agent? It seemed inconceivable. And yet the alternative, that she actually *was* his agent, was ridiculous. The odds that the actual agent of the actual Dante Rinaldi had not only stumbled upon Antonella's gushing social media posts but had also taken them seriously were, in his opinion, infinitesimal.

In any case, just suppose she actually was his agent? Signor Speranza entertained the notion theoretically. What could she do to them? If she threatened them with a lawsuit, or some other unpleasantness, he could simply issue a statement of some kind, couldn't he? That was what people did these days. It had all been a misunderstanding, he could say. They had never intended to suggest that

Dante Rinaldi was going to be *personally* involved in their movie. They had merely endeavored to produce a project *inspired* by him, or in his honor.

This explanation would not please Signor Maestro, of course. Signor Speranza frowned, a queasy feeling coming over him. And then there were the T-shirts, he reminded himself, the bottom dropping out of his stomach altogether. And the water bottles. And the commemorative dinnerware. There was such a thing as licensing.

"Focus!" he said aloud, and smacked his own cheek. There wasn't going to be any problem. The woman who kept calling was just a fan, like the rest of them. What had she said in her last message? He wrinkled his nose, trying to remember. Oh yes: she had said that he had better call her back because Dante's mother had gotten wind of what was going on, and was quite upset about it. *Tuh!* Was it really likely that some high-powered talent agent would be going on about her client's mother? No, it was not.

Just to be on the safe side, though, he would tell Betta to put the brakes on new orders. It was time to quit while they were ahead. Maybe another couple of rounds of potato croquettes could get them to the top instead. In a little over two weeks, the people who had paid good money to see the premiere would come and go, and then the whole project would fade into comfortable obscurity. The pipes would be fixed, Signor Speranza would go back to restoring vacuum cleaners, and everything would return to how it was supposed to be. Yes. That was it, then. He sealed up his worries like an envelope. Everything was settled.

Signor Speranza came now to the crest of the hill behind the church, to the old donkey paddock and the location of Zio Franco's ambitious new outdoor amphitheater. Signor Speranza had not visited the construction site in over two weeks, and, when he glimpsed it now, he gasped. What had Zio done? Where just a fortnight ago there had been nothing but a hollowed-out pit of dirt, there was now a flat circle, fifty feet across, of smooth bricks. Curved banks of stone seating rose out from it in graduated semicircles, like ripples in a pond. Everywhere that was not brick or stone was covered in fresh green turf, like soft velvet, as if the whole thing were the interior of some enormous jewelry box.

Signor Speranza gazed in wonder. How many people would fit here? Three hundred? Maybe four? He felt again that strange feeling of calm he had felt on the day he had first learned that Zio Franco was building this place. *Perfect*, he thought. It was perfect to the last brick, perfect to the last blade of grass.

"Zio!" he called, scrambling closer, and flagging down his uncle. "Look at this, huh? *Che bello!*"

Zio Franco looked over and rolled his eyes. "Let me see what this *chiacchierone* wants," he muttered to his men, and stalked over.

Signor Speranza smiled to himself. Zio Franco, tough guy. He glanced at the crew. These men respected his uncle, he could see that. That had to be a satisfying experience for a man who had been the youngest of five brothers.

Now, from somewhere at the back of Signor Speranza's mind, Luigi Speranza, who had been so quiet lately, stirred. "Will you look at my baby brother?" he said, smiling as he strung his peppers. "He always liked to make things. Thank you, Giovannino."

Signor Speranza had not been expecting to hear this, and a sudden lump formed in his throat. Imagine, he thought, this cranky ninety-three-year-old man being anybody's baby brother!

He was still choking on this particular emotion when his uncle reached him.

"Eh," said Zio Franco, standing beside his nephew and looking out over the amphitheater as well. He lit a cigarette and drew on it. "Turned out okay," he said, shrugging.

Signor Speranza laughed. "Yes, *Zio*, I'd say it's okay. Emperor Vespasian would say it was okay."

Zio Franco made a sort of barking sound that was the closest thing to a laugh he had uttered since his wife died twenty years ago. "Yeah, I guess it's pretty good," he muttered, his wrinkled face cracking into a crooked smile.

"Just think," said Signor Speranza, gazing around again in wonderment. "You did all this for only fifteen thousand euros."

And *that* was when Zio Franco laughed for real.

16

Smilzo's Spectacular Set Piece

$\mathcal{Z}$io Franco was laughing so hard, he was wheezing.

"What's the matter with you?" he asked. "Haven't you ever hired a contractor before? Half up front, half when the job is done. That is how it works." He leaned over and knocked on the side of his nephew's head. "Hello! Anybody home?"

Signor Speranza just stared. The breath had gone out of him.

Zio Franco clapped him on the shoulder. "Come on, Giovannino. No one has died. The bill's all paid. Smilzo gave me the rest of it yesterday."

Signor Speranza's mouth opened and closed. He tried to speak, but the words would not come.

"Franco!" called one of the men. *"Vieni!"*

Zio Franco drifted away, leaving Signor Speranza standing alone.

He looked up. *Why have you done this to me, Lord?* he asked, his eyes searching the empty sky. *You know I have worked so hard. You know that.* His tired brain did the calculation automatically, without his permission. The one thousand, two hundred and twenty-five euros he had needed this morning had swollen in an instant to sixteen thousand, two hundred and twenty-five. He thought of all he had done to raise that money—humbling himself to Signor Maestro, going door-to-door in the hot sun with a basket of croquettes, turning his business into some kind of three-ring Hollywood circus— and now this?

A surge of anger filled up his chest. *This is funny to you, Lord?* he asked, with a bitterness he had never felt before. *My life to you is some kind of joke?*

God didn't answer.

Signor Speranza crashed onto set twenty minutes later, a raving, sweating madman.

"Boss!" called Smilzo, waving him over. "Boss, look!"

Signor Speranza raked his eyes over the landscape—the uneven ground, with its rocks and weeds, and the dark outer fringe of the forest. There were Gemma and Antonella in Gemma's makeup tent, which was really just a billowing bedsheet tacked to a flimsy aluminum laundry rack. He saw a blue-and-white cooler, with a herd of Maestros clustered around it, and Pietro Maestro training the Betamovie on his brothers' antics. Finally, he spotted Smilzo, who was off by himself, pointing excitedly at what appeared to be an enormous, pink, slumping stuffed animal.

"Is for you, boss!" he cried, as Signor Speranza came closer. "My mother has made it for you!"

Signor Speranza had been to Smilzo's house exactly one time, and he had happened, on that occasion, to use the bathroom. There he had discovered, perched upon the toilet tank, a garish, staring doll that had been handmade by Smilzo's mother and stretched over a roll of toilet paper.

It would seem she had set her ambitions higher this time.

"There's toilet paper in here?" Signor Speranza whispered cautiously to Smilzo.

"Bo-oss!" said Smilzo. "Is a chair! Is a director's chair. Look!"

Smilzo's mother had employed the tried-and-true methods that had served her so well in the fashioning of toilet paper cozies. She had crocheted an enormous pink slipcover, which she had then stretched over a simple folding chair.

"Oh," said Signor Speranza. He walked in a dizzy circle, his brain still flooded with anger and despair, and regarded the chair from all angles. God, it was ugly, he thought with a shudder. It was impractical, too—how did Smilzo's mother expect wool yarn might fare on location? What if it rained? What if it was muddy? Imagine what it would look like next to a real director's chair! It was not just ugly—it was the dumbest thing he had ever seen.

"And look, boss!" Smilzo pointed to the back. REGISTA, it said, in wobbly white embroidery.

Director, Signor Speranza thought, lingering on the word, and running his fingers over the bumpy letters. Whatever one might say about Smilzo's mother's aesthetic sense, she had gotten that part of it just right. He looked up at Smilzo, who was waiting for his reaction, so hopeful, so proud—so anxious that he should like it. His eyes wandered around the set, at all the other young people who had joined up with him to make this movie, and who were all trying so hard.

"Great," he declared, swallowing his anger and his pettiness. "This is so great. Tell your mother that I love it."

Smilzo beamed. "Thank you, boss."

❊ ❊ ❊

Sitting in a woolen chair, on the top of a mountain, in the middle of August, a scant twenty-seven-hundred miles away from the equator, was a singular experience, and one which Signor Speranza felt confident he would remember until the day he died. The worst of it was the backs of his knees, which, given the cargo shorts, were exposed, and by noon had broken out in a wool rash. This was not the only problem, either. There had been a small, equipment-related debacle after Signor Speranza spotted Ivano Maestro smoking on set.

"What is he doing?" Signor Speranza had muttered, training his binoculars on him. Then he stood up, a cool breeze striking the mottled backs of his knees, and shouted through his megaphone. "NO SMOKING!"

Unfortunately for Ivano, Signor Speranza had been peering through the wrong end of the binoculars, which had made it appear that his quarry was quite far away, when in reality, he was mere inches from the mouth of the megaphone.

"*CHE*, SIGNORE?" Ivano shouted back, unable to hear himself above the ringing in his ears. "WHAT DID YOU SAY?"

From Signor Speranza's itchy perch, he grumpily laid out the game plan. Antonella was to be boosted onto the sturdiest-looking branch they could find among the chestnut trees at the outer perimeter of the forest for maximum light. They had scrapped the idea of her being stranded there in order to rescue a fictional neighbor's cat, as Signora Bisi's cat, which they had counted on borrowing for the occasion, had taken an instant dislike to Antonella on meeting her, and had done its very best to swipe her across the face with its sharp-clawed paw.

"Why is she up the tree, then, boss?" asked Smilzo, frowning worriedly.

Antonella rolled her eyes. "Maybe she's looking for cell reception," she said, holding her own phone over her head and squinting at the screen. "It's as though we're in the Amazon," she muttered.

"Don't worry about that," said Signor Speranza, waving his hand. "It's not important. We can go back and plant something." This so-called "planting" was another screenwriting trick Signor Speranza had picked up from Smilzo over the last couple of weeks. An audience could be made to accept anything, absolutely anything, his assistant had said, provided the screenwriter sprinkled enough hints along the way. "Maybe we say at the beginning that she wants to build a tree house, or that she's friends with a bird."

"This girl is becoming very weird, signore," complained Antonella. Script changes over the past week had necessitated that her character speak Mandarin, suffer from short-term amnesia, and have a long-lost twin.

"Never mind," blustered Signor Speranza. "Now. Lorenzo. Ignacio." He looked around for the two Maestro brothers in question, located them, and flinched. "Did you go already to the makeup tent?" he asked cautiously.

"Yes, signore."

Signor Speranza frowned and addressed Pietro out of the corner of his mouth.

"It's not necessary to get close-ups of these two, you understand. It's just meant to be a vague presence of danger."

Signor Speranza showed them the field to the right of the forest, and the large boulders, behind which Smilzo would crouch until he heard the call for *Action!* Smilzo would then run—in the manner of Tom Cruise, obviously—across the field, vaulting over roots and rocks, and eluding the grasp of both Lorenzo and Ignacio. Then he would grab hold of the sturdy rope that Ivano had spent the morning adorning with leaves and securing to a nearby tree. He was to swing over to Antonella's branch, grab her about the waist, and scoop her to safety.

"Then I will blow everything up, boss."

Signor Speranza fixed his eyes on the heavens. Smilzo had been adamant, from the beginning, that any proper movie included a scene in which the hero blew something up and then casually walked away from it, not looking back.

Signor Speranza had been perplexed. "He doesn't even look back to see if the fire is closer to him than he thinks?"

"No, boss. Watch." Smilzo had acted it out on the showroom floor, tossing an imaginary match carelessly over one shoulder and adopting an expression of complete unconcern. "You will want to switch to slow motion, of course." This Smilzo had done, moving with exaggerated motions, until his foot caught on the carpet, and he went sprawling, head over heels.

"No, Smilzo," said Signor Speranza through gritted teeth. "You will not, as you say, blow everything up. Fireworks will do perfectly well."

Antonella giggled, and Smilzo pouted, and Ivano Maestro was dispatched to the far reaches of the field to shoo away a few errant goats who had wandered into the picture, and were utterly wrecking the illusion that they were in the immediate suburbs of Los Angeles. Signor Speranza called for a break of five minutes before they were to begin shooting, and during which he personally intended to hobble to the cooler and pour two bottles of cold water down the backs of his welted knees.

"Boss," said Smilzo, following him. "Boss, what about the end of the scene?"

"What about it?" Signor Speranza opened the cooler and combed irritably through the mounds of crushed ice. Not a single bottle left! They had all been guzzled, no doubt, by the Maestros. He muttered darkly and grabbed handfuls of ice, stuffing them into his knee socks.

Smilzo continued to hover. "Boss, is just . . ." He lowered his voice to a whisper. "*I am supposed to kiss her at the end. Remember?*" His pointy face was a picture of pink-and-white agony.

"Ah," said Signor Speranza, understanding. "I see. It's no big deal, Smilzo. If the moment is upon you, and you do not feel you can do it, then you just angle this way and press your cheek against her cheek." Signor Speranza demonstrated by flattening his own cheek with the heel of his hand. "No one will know the difference." He shrugged. "It's movie magic."

"Okay," said Smilzo, taking a deep breath and letting it out slowly. "Thanks, boss."

"Anytime," said Signor Speranza.

Smilzo trotted off to practice running and looking over his shoulder, and Signor Speranza, on bending to retrieve another handful of ice, happened to glance up.

"*Che fai?*" he yelped. *What are you doing?*

Gemma and Ernesto Maestro, with no help from movie magic whatsoever, were kissing in the makeup tent.

❊ ❊ ❊

Signor Speranza was still standing at the cooler and gaping at Gemma and Ernesto when the set piece scene got underway without him. In fact, no one was expecting for it to begin, and it was an act of God that Pietro Maestro had the camera running.

Smilzo was pacing, preparing for his big moment. Ivano, Lorenzo, and Ignacio were talking together, and throwing a ball back and forth. Antonella had wandered off, looking for cell reception, and was now attempting to scale one of the boulders behind which Smilzo was shortly to crouch, holding her phone in the air and waving it. Pietro was sweeping his camera back and forth, getting ready to film, and it was he who first saw it. He gave a kind of strangled yell, and pointed, and everyone except Antonella, who was too far away to hear, spun around to see what was the matter.

Signor Speranza shielded his eyes and scanned the horizon. Then he gasped.

A goat!

One of the goats Ivano had shooed away earlier had come back. It was a ragged brown-and-white goat with a broken horn, and something about it was not right. It was skittering closer and closer to the oblivious Antonella, tossing its head, eyes rolling.

Signor Speranza bit his knuckle. He had seen a goat act like that one other time, fifty-five years ago, when the village schoolmaster had been nearly gored to death in the village square.

Now the goat bucked, and reared up on its hind legs, and Antonella finally noticed it. She gave a thin cry and tried to scramble up the boulder.

Whoosh!

Smilzo streaked across the field, his legs pumping like pistons and his arms cutting through the air like blades. Twice, he looked back over his shoulder at Pietro, who was running after him with the camera.

"Stay back!" he yelled.

Pietro, who wasn't about to give up, only slowed down.

Smilzo pelted up to the mountain goat, hollering and waving his arms. Then, when the goat hesitated, just for a second, he turned, scooping up Antonella, her cell phone flung to one side, and ran back toward the encampment, the furious goat now at his heels.

"Run! Run!" Pietro shouted, and then took his own advice, the camera still going.

The following thirty seconds of footage, when they watched it later, over and over again, was a confusing mélange of earth and sky and snippets of people running, and then, cutting across it all, the sudden screech of a megaphone being switched on.

"IVANO!" Signor Speranza's voice boomed, startling even the goat. "DON'T!"

He was, however, too late. As the footage showed, Ivano had failed to hear either Signor Speranza's warning or the impending goat stampede. He had also, so it would seem, missed out on the intel that the fireworks were being stored in a metal trash can on loan from the Rossis, from which they would later be safely deployed. He had, somewhat understandably, mistaken this for an *actual* trash can in good standing, and had flung into it a match.

A stray Maestro leapt into the frame, tackling a cheerfully unsuspecting Ivano to the ground. A second later, there were a series of frightening bangs. The goat, having gotten more than it bargained for, fled. Then the fireworks burst into glorious, cacophonous bloom, and in the foreground of the shot, as if on cue, Antonella, who had no godly idea of where her cell phone was, and who for once in her life didn't care, tipped her head forty-five degrees so as to avoid Smilzo's pointy nose, and kissed him square on the lips.

❋ ❋ ❋

The crocheted chair emerged a casualty of the shoot.

"She was a beautiful chair, Smilzo," Signor Speranza said in an appropriately mournful tone.

"Is all right, boss," said Smilzo, prodding the pink husk with the toe of his shoe. Smilzo probably wouldn't have minded at that moment if the chair had been blasted to kingdom come. Antonella, who had watched the video of her harrowing rescue three times now, was clinging to his arm and was also gently applying ice to his left temple, which had been somewhat abraded in the scuffle.

"All it took was a goat," Signor Speranza muttered.

There was a general sense of jubilation at having captured the set piece, and everyone except Signor Speranza was in an effervescent mood. He, too, had been quite pleased until he'd recalled what had happened that morning with Zio Franco, and his extra fifteen-thousand-euro problem. Now it was seven forty-five, and dusk was falling. Signor Speranza's large egg-and-potato sandwich was a distant memory, and he had managed to step into a rabbit hole, wrenching his ankle. It was time to go home. A conscientious Maestro checked the forest one last time for lingering embers or smoke, another hefted the cooler onto his back, and Signor Speranza gingerly tested his ankle.

"If you need to lean on me, signore—" Ernesto began, with every show of quiet gallantry, but Signor Speranza rebuffed him.

"This ankle is sixty-two years old, young man," he said icily, straightening to his full height. "It is perfectly capable of walking home."

Smilzo, whose arm was entwined with Antonella's, blinked. "Bones do not get stronger as they get older, boss. I think that you have that backward," he said, and Signor Speranza was obliged to reach up and smack him on the back of the head.

They wended their way back to the village as a sort of informal caravan, Signor Speranza, whenever he detected any twinge of weakness in his ankle, hissing to Smilzo out of the corner of his mouth so as not to alert Ernesto. "Smilzo!" he'd say, and Smilzo would hurry over to lend support, dragging Antonella with him.

"WE WILL GO WITH YOU ALL THE WAY TO THE HOTEL, SIGNORE," shouted Ivano, whose hearing, after a trash can full of exploding and ricocheting fireworks, was still not at its best. "WE WILL SEE YOU HOME SAFELY."

Signor Speranza demurred, but Ivano couldn't hear him, and the other Maestros insisted, too. Not to be outdone in the way of solicitousness for his boss's welfare, Smilzo said he would accompany him also. They were nearly there, and about to round the embankment that would reveal the front of the hotel, when Signor Speranza detected the sound of voices up ahead.

"What is going on there?" he mumbled, and then his cell phone, which had rung only twice before, began to buzz in one of the copious pockets of the khaki cargo shorts.

"Betta, what is it?" he answered, frowning. The sun had sunk below the horizon over the past couple of minutes, and now the first twinklings of stars began showing in the sky. He was hot and hungry and sore, and he had that uniquely irritable feeling begotten of dried sweat and dirt. What was it now? Some fresh problem that would interfere with his dinner and his shower, no doubt.

"Nino." Betta's voice coming over the line was muffled, even though he knew she was probably less than a hundred yards away. "Nino, there are all these people outside. I don't know—"

Signor Speranza quickened his pace and winced at the stab of pain in his ankle. "What is it?" he asked, trying to get there faster, trying to see. "Carlotta's all right?"

"Yes, yes."

Signor Speranza was toward the back of the little caravan. He attempted to cut ahead now, trying to push his way through the pack, but he could not get through. That was why he heard before he saw.

"Oh!" said Gemma, clearly startled, and then there was a "Ha!" from Ernesto.

Antonella, who was not hampered by a twisted ankle, and who was also thin enough to slip more easily through the crowd, dropped Smilzo's hand and fought her way to the front.

"*Aaaaaaaaiiiii!*" she screamed, and pointed.

When Signor Speranza finally broke free of the crushing throng, and could actually see what was happening, his stomach dropped out from under him.

There were two lights on in the hotel, two lights behind un-covered windows. In the newly fallen darkness, this illumination allowed passersby to see directly into the rooms beyond. On the ground floor, there was the living room, with Carlotta playing jacks, Bambolina asleep beside her on a velvet cushion. Then, higher up, on the second floor . . .

Signor Speranza froze. He gaped. His phone slipped from his fingers, and he scrambled to recover it.

"Betta! Betta! The green room! Turn out the light!" he said— because he had neglected to extinguish it in his rush that morning. Because Betta had not thought to check that it was switched off, either. Because Betta never checked the lights on the second floor anymore. Because the green room had not had a visitor in over a year, save for a life-size cardboard cutout of Dante Rinaldi, which, despite being in an awkward location, was visible from the road.

Antonella screamed again. "He's here!"

"Boss? What is happening?" asked Smilzo, panicking, and looking back and forth.

Betta made it to the second floor in what was probably record time, and the light was snuffed out. The green room was plunged into impregnable darkness.

But it was too late. The damage was already done.

17

The Guest

The occupancy of the Speranzas' hotel, excepting its owners and one rate-paying Pomeranian, held steady at zero. The short pathway in front of the hotel, however, was a different matter. Smilzo's forecast rain never materialized, and this sunny, inauspicious patch of pavement was transformed overnight into a gathering place for all the young ladies from miles around who were both idle enough and infatuated enough to devote hours of their precious time on this planet to the standing upon of pavements and the hopeful gazing upon of blank windows. Antonella emerged as the gathering's de facto leader, and Signor Speranza, clutching his porridge bowl, and with his moustache twitching, watched her pointing to the sacred spot from a crack in the living room curtains.

"Nino, don't spill!" Betta scolded.

"You would think it was the second coming of Christ," Signor

Speranza grumbled, and despite his wife's warning he dribbled some of the porridge off his spoon and onto the back of the couch, but in one quick bound Nonno Guido was there, lapping it up. Nonno Guido was learning quickly. For one thing, he had discovered that it was in his best interests to tolerate Bambolina, and not only because failing to do so meant being relegated to his room. The main reason was that Bambolina was also prone to dribbling. All an enterprising young schnauzer had to do, then, was to wait, quietly, as his new houseguest was eating, which she was once more doing upward of six times per day, and he was sure to be rewarded for his troubles.

The phone rang.

"It's for you, Nino," Betta called. "It's Smilzo."

Signor Speranza accepted the receiver.

"What?" he barked.

"Is he there, boss?" Smilzo whispered, as if someone might be listening. "He is there with you now?"

Signor Speranza rolled his eyes to the ceiling. As far as he knew, there were no saints who had been allocated to dealing with situations such as the one in which he now found himself. It appeared he would have to forge ahead on his own.

"Listen, Smilzo," he said. "Take it easy, okay? Everything is going to be fine."

There was a long silence.

"She is there, boss?" Smilzo asked flatly. "Antonella? She is there also?"

Signor Speranza pretended he had just been called away. "Oh yes! I'm coming!" he shouted over his shoulder. Then, into the receiver, "I'm sorry, Smilzo. I have to go now. *Ciao.*"

Not thirty seconds later, Signor Maestro phoned.

"Nino!" hissed Betta, holding the phone. "Talk to him!"

Signor Speranza waved his arms, frantic. "Absolutely not!"

So Betta stood in the living room doorway and talked to him herself. "My husband is busy at the moment, signore . . . Yes, signore . . . No, signore . . . Of course, signore . . ." Her forehead creased. "I don't think that's a good idea." She stood there awhile, nodding and murmuring. "Okay," she said finally. "I'll give him the message."

She hung up and turned to her husband.

"*Well?*" said Signor Speranza, half-wild.

Betta shrugged. "You have a problem there, Nino."

There was one more phone call before Signor Speranza ripped the cord out of the wall.

"Signore!" came Don Rocco's hearty and cheerful voice. "I heard that Dante Rinaldi is there. I am calling to apologize. You know, I never really believed that he was coming."

❋ ❋ ❋

Signor Speranza did not go into the office. Neither, apparently, did the fifteen Maestro brothers report for work at the butcher's shop. Instead, at around eleven thirty, and to the decided interest of the bored-looking girls on the pavement, they appeared in front of the hotel, wearing matching khaki pants, black shirts and hats, and complicated-looking earpieces. At some sort of signal from Ivano, they fanned out around the perimeter.

Signor Speranza, who heretofore had pursued a lie-low policy, threw open the living room window.

"What the hell do you think you're doing?" he called, sticking his head out.

Ivano, who had regained his hearing, shouted back.

"We thought you might need security, signore. Signor Rinaldi is precious cargo."

Gemma and Carlotta, who were sitting at the window, waved and giggled, and Signor Speranza gave up and went upstairs.

Around noon, the chanting started. At two thirty, Signor Maestro, who must have shuttered the butcher's shop to come, showed up, prowling like a menace, and asking questions in so distinct a basso profundo that Signor Speranza could discern his words even from the green room on the second floor, which was where he was crouching, looking down, flinching, on the knot of people below.

"No one has seen anything?" Signor Maestro growled, and "There has been no light on?" and "He has not even poked his head out of the window?" When he did not receive any satisfactory answers to his questions, he parked himself perhaps fifteen feet back from the front of the hotel, feet apart and arms crossed. "Maybe he's not really in there!" he bellowed. "It seems to me a movie star would say hello to his fans!"

There was silence, and then a murmur of agreement from the girls on the pavement, and then the chanting started again.

"We want Dan-te! We want Dan-te!"

Signor Speranza glanced desperately around the room. How could he make it look as though Dante was really here? In a flash of inspiration, he crawled along the floor, reaching up, on his knees, and switching on the floor lamp. Then he crawled over to the cutout of Dante and dragged it at an awkward angle in front of the lamp, where he allowed it to cast a Dante-shaped shadow on the tightly drawn curtains.

A collective gasp and cheer went up from the crowd below, and Signor Speranza experienced a tiny thrill of triumph.

Of course, in the next second, the door to the green room burst open, and Smilzo spilled inside, Betta at his heels.

"I'm sorry, Nino!" Betta cried, wringing her hands. "I couldn't stop him! Carlotta let him in the back."

Smilzo, who had come here to confront Dante Rinaldi and—and—well, he hadn't quite worked out what, looked around, blinking in bewilderment.

"Boss?" he yelped.

❋ ❋ ❋

Smilzo was ushered into the green room's most comfortable chair, and brought bracing cups of sweet coffee on a tray. The lamp had been switched off, and a second chair wedged under the doorknob to prevent further intrusion.

"You mean *none* of it was real, boss?" Smilzo asked, dazed. Despite the heat, he had a knitted blanket around his shoulders, and his teeth were chattering.

"Shhhh," warned Signor Speranza, motioning to the door. "The girls don't know." He looked at Smilzo, and how miserable he was, and his spirits sank ever lower. Oh, Smilzo. He had never meant for him to find out this way. "*Some* of it was real," he mumbled.

Smilzo shook his head. He was staring at some spot on the wall.

"Dante Rinaldi never liked my screenplay," he said, his voice hollow.

"Hey, now!" Signor Speranza's moustache bristled. "*I* liked your screenplay. *I* thought it was good. Who is Dante Rinaldi, anyway? *Tuh!*" He leaned over and flicked the cardboard cutout, which wobbled and fell over.

Smilzo's face cracked into a crooked smile. "He's terrible, isn't he?"

Signor Speranza threw his hands in the air. "He is okay, maybe, if you are advertising a tanning salon."

Smilzo's smile widened. "Tank tops."

"Yes!" said Signor Speranza. "Maybe a hair tonic."

They both laughed, but when the laughter subsided Smilzo was morose again. "She likes him, though, boss," he said, his face darkening. "It is him who she likes."

Signor Speranza frowned. There was little sense in denying this statement, when Antonella was parked twenty feet away on the pavement in a Dante T-shirt and matching earrings. "He's make-believe, Smilzo," he said instead. "He's just an idea. Even Dante Rinaldi is not *Dante Rinaldi.*"

"Mm," said Smilzo, looking somewhat baffled by this theory, and unwilling to commit either way.

The whole story poured out then, about the junior plumbing inspector and the pipes ("It *was* Hubba Bubba, boss," said Smilzo, smiling faintly at the memory. "Strawberry, I think."), the trip to Alberto's, and the rumor of George Clooney's house hunt. Smilzo listened to it all, laughing and wincing in all the right places.

"But what are we going to do now, boss?" he asked, when Signor Speranza came to the end.

"We will say he came and went." Signor Speranza was resolute. "That is what we will have to do. Tomorrow, we will say he sneaked out in the middle of the night. We cannot have these lunatics camping here." He gestured at the window.

Smilzo bit his lip. "I don't know, boss. Signor Maestro—"

"Ancora!" Signor Speranza snorted. "Again with Signor Maestro? The devil can take Signor Maestro." Despite this show of bluster, however, he peeked uneasily through the crack in the curtains. The girls were still there, sitting cross-legged on the pavement now and styling one another's hair, and the Maestro brothers, posted every three yards or so, on sentry duty. And then there was Signor Maestro, standing just where he had been before, his feet still planted, and his arms still crossed, glowering into the distance, with all the timeless tenacity of a stuffed boar.

"I think, boss . . ." said Smilzo, hesitating, ". . . I think we have to make it look as though Dante is really here. At least for a couple of days. Just to be on the safe side. What do you think?"

Signor Speranza looked at the ceiling and sighed.

"Maybe you're right. Where do we start?"

❧ ❧ ❧

They took a dim Polaroid of Smilzo beaming alongside the cardboard cutout.

"We need more light, boss," said Smilzo critically, examining the result. "In this one, the flash is bouncing off his tank top."

After some trial and error, and barricading of the entranceway to the second floor, they found the perfect combination of lighting and distance—four floor lamps, stretched into the hallway on their cords, and approximately twenty paces—to produce a convincing shot.

Signor Speranza squinted at the finished print. "I can tell it is you and Dante," he said. "If I look very hard."

"Maybe I should be holding up today's newspaper," suggested Smilzo.

Signor Speranza considered this, wrinkling his nose. "You are thinking of a hostage situation, Smilzo. It's not necessary except for in a hostage situation."

Smilzo was not convinced. "I don't know, boss," he said, dubious. "I still think it would be better . . ."

Signor Speranza rolled his eyes, and shouted down to Betta to bring up the paper.

At four o'clock, Gemma and Carlotta were dispatched from the premises to stay with Zio Franco. Signor Speranza and Smilzo watched their departure, kneeling by the window and peeping over the sill. Mother and daughter were mobbed as they left the front door.

"Where is he?"

"Did you see him?"

"Did you talk to him?"

"Why won't he come outside?"

Gemma tried to wave them all quiet. "I don't know! I don't know!" she said. "It's very hush-hush. My mother said he checked in wearing a disguise, and that he wants privacy. I have seen nothing!" She shrugged. "Maybe he has a pimple or something."

Far from evincing laughter, as Signor Speranza might have expected, this offhand suggestion of Gemma's gave rise to serious debate among the girls on the pavement, who, after conferring for some time, came to the sober agreement that that was, in all likelihood, *exactly* the situation. One brave soul even rummaged in her handbag and produced a tube of concealer, shouting up at the window that she would be quite happy to part with it, if only Dante were to lower a small basket on a string.

Phase one completed, Signor Speranza sent Betta out around five, ostensibly to sweep the porch and driveway.

"I can tell you nothing!" she shouted, and she mimed zipping her mouth shut, locking it, and throwing away the key. Then, without another word to anyone, she vigorously brandished her broom, sending the pavement dwellers dancing out of her way. When she was quite finished, and had kicked up satisfying clouds of dust, she passed by Signor Maestro and at the crucial moment let drop the Polaroid of Smilzo and the cardboard cutout, so that it fluttered gently to the ground at his feet. She was already back inside and beyond the reach of questioning by the time he bent to pick it up.

Signor Speranza and Smilzo watched with bated breath.

Signor Maestro studied the photograph. Then he grunted and called one of his sons over. They contemplated it together and then beckoned a second son.

Signor Speranza rolled his eyes. "Maybe we should have labeled it," he muttered.

But then one of the girls insinuated herself into the Maestro huddle. Shortly thereafter, she shrieked, nearly causing a stampede, and the picture was passed from hand to hand, like a hot potato.

"That is Smilzo!" Antonella gasped, disbelieving at first, and then, as she recovered her equanimity, she repeated herself with a smug toss of the head. "That is Smilzo with him, you know. They are friends. He will introduce me later." Then she made a show of yawning—that was how bored she was with it all.

It was at this moment that Signor Speranza threw open the window of the green room and stuck his head outside.

"You there! Ivano!" he shouted, his moustache fanning outward, like a party horn.

Everyone froze and looked up, and then there was a surging forward.

"Can you see him?" someone screamed.

"Is he there, signore?"

The clamor was terrible.

Signor Speranza ignored all this and addressed himself only to Ivano.

"What kind of operation is this?" he asked, scowling. "Dante is trying to rest, but now he has called me here to say there is nothing but chaos."

The crowd fell silent at this insight into Dante Rinaldi's current mood, and all heads swiveled to regard the instantly miserable Ivano. He turned bright red and stammered.

"I'm so sorry, signore," he said, taking off his hat and twisting it. "Maybe I can come in and talk to Signor Rinaldi—"

Signor Speranza cut him off. "I am afraid that is impossible. He says . . ." Here, Signor Speranza broke off theatrically and inclined his head, ducking back inside the window. For the ensuing seconds, the spellbound crowd below could see only Signor Speranza's profile, and the enveloping curtain on either side of him, but they were able to fill in the blanks.

"He is talking to Dante!" said someone, with a slightly hysterical tinge to their tone.

Signor Speranza stuck his head back out. "He says if this situation does not improve, he will be forced to call in his own people. He says . . ." Signor Speranza broke off again, repeating his earlier performance. "He says he wants this place cleared out. He cannot hear himself think. He says . . ." Signor Speranza drew back again.

"I think is going on a little long, boss," whispered Smilzo, who was monitoring the situation from the other end of the curtain.

"Okay, okay," said Signor Speranza, impatient. He leaned outside a final time. "Dante also asks me to say," he called, "that the guy in the front, with the arms crossed . . ."

The crowd below the window turned inward, so that everyone was looking, curious, at Signor Maestro. Signor Maestro himself perked up expectantly.

Signor Speranza finished with a bang.

"Dante says he looks like a side of beef."

Smilzo yanked his employer back inside then for his own good, and the window crashed shut of its own accord.

18

Signor Speranza Pushes His Luck

Ivano Maestro took his job as head of the security detail very seriously after that. No one other than the security team members were permitted on the property save Signor Speranza, Betta, and Smilzo, who were all issued special clearance badges that had to be presented each time they arrived at or departed from the premises.

"I do not understand," Signor Speranza had said, "why I need a badge in the first place. You know who I am. I've known you since you were a baby."

Ivano shook his head. "I'm sorry, signore. It's protocol. As soon as one abandons protocol, one allows things to devolve into chaos."

Yes, Signor Speranza thought, frowning at the sky. He himself had abandoned God's protocol for truthfulness, and look how things were turning out. He had a cardboard cutout booked into the second floor of his hotel, and he needed to display a security badge to make a trip to the mailbox. That was what violating protocol had gotten him.

Gemma and Carlotta were still staying with Zio Franco, and calling at all hours to check on Nonno Guido and Bambolina, and Smilzo was now a regular fixture at the hotel in their place. It was his job to turn the lights in the green room on and off at various intervals, and to occasionally whisk past the curtain, so that the Maestro brothers, watching avidly down below, would perceive occasional signs of life. On the second day, in the interests of verisimilitude, Signor Speranza placed an order for an enormous, expensive lunch from a nearby town, under the name D. Rinaldi. It arrived via courier, and was subjected to Ivano's rigorous inspection. "May be poison, signore," he said, holding out his arm to prevent Signor Speranza from bringing the food into the house straightaway. A sheaf of spoons was fetched, and Ivano sampled each dish, while Signor Speranza gazed up at the blue sky and beseeched Saints Gervase and Protase, patron saints of high blood pressure, to prevent the Maestro brothers from driving his so high that the last thing he ever did was to watch Ivano Maestro shift a mouthful of broccoli rabe with hot peppers and slivered almonds from one side of his mouth to the other.

Once Ivano had waited fifteen minutes and still hadn't died, he released the bag of now-cold food from confiscation, and Signor Speranza, Betta, and Smilzo ate it at the kitchen table and discussed what to do next.

"The cameo with the cardboard cutout is not going to work anymore," Signor Speranza pronounced, twirling his poison-free spaghetti Bolognese on a fork. "Everyone has seen the Polaroid with Smilzo."

"I think you're right," said Betta. "Besides, when everyone

thinks he's here at the hotel for days on end, how do we explain that he only had time to glide by in the background? I don't think people will accept that." She glanced toward the front door and shuddered. "I don't think *Signor Maestro* will accept that."

Signor Speranza sighed. Dante Rinaldi's sudden supposed arrival had thrown quite a wrench into his plan to deal with Signor Maestro via a well-timed, forged letter. Now Signor Speranza was like a farmer in one of the old stories, with a wolf at his door.

"I think I might have something, boss," said Smilzo. "You know I have been watching a lot of movies upstairs."

Signor Speranza nodded. Smilzo had been so bored just sitting in the green room all day, turning the lights on and off and rustling the curtains, that Betta had suggested moving the TV and DVD player from their bedroom for him to watch.

"So," Smilzo continued, "I was watching the Dante Rinaldi movie you have yesterday, and—"

Signor Speranza interrupted. "Why would you watch that idiot's movie?"

Smilzo lifted his eyebrows. "Is called hate-watching, boss."

Signor Speranza considered, recalling the time he and Betta had tried watching it also. He waved his hand. "Continue."

"I was thinking . . ." Smilzo hesitated. "What if we don't need Dante's face? What if all we need is his voice?"

Signor Speranza frowned. "What does that mean?"

Smilzo explained that he could copy the audio from Dante's earlier movie and splice it into their own.

"Will be simple, boss," he said, his enthusiasm growing as he described the plan and helped himself to salad, dropping half of it on the table. "I can cut words and phrases together. He can be our narrator."

"A narrator," Signor Speranza muttered, thinking it over.

"I have all the equipment I need, boss," said Smilzo. "I can start working on the sound files today."

Signor Speranza caught Betta's eye across the table and shrugged. "Signor Maestro might not like that," he said.

Betta crossed her arms, her eyes flashing. "Well, he's going to have to."

❊ ❊ ❊

Smilzo spent the rest of that day and night working on the audio, and the next day he and Signor Speranza were obliged to leave the house to go to the shop. There was one final scene to shoot, in which Smilzo's character proposed marriage to Antonella's character as Ernesto serenaded them with a guitar.

Signor Speranza felt an overwhelming sense of foreboding as he departed the property.

"Don't go out. And don't let anyone in! And don't talk to those idiots!" he told Betta as he was leaving.

"Everything is locked up tight, signore," said Ivano, with a jaunty salute, and, indeed, it seemed to be. Signor Speranza's eye roved over the bleak environs of the hotel, dotted as it was with uniformed Maestros. The brothers had worked out a schedule, seven on and seven off, twenty-four hours a day.

This is what I have done, Signor Speranza thought grimly. *These are the consequences of my actions. A cavalcade of Maestros.* He glanced at the sky. *I hope you are happy now.*

He and Smilzo flashed their badges at Ivano, and they waved goodbye to the troops.

Once at the shop, and with the door safely locked behind him,

Signor Speranza was supposed to be thinking about two things: the final scene for the movie, and the sixteen-thousand-two-hundred-and-twenty-five-euro deficit for the pipes, which was due in seventeen days, and of which he had not thought once in almost seventy-two hours. Too much! This fake Dante Rinaldi situation was too much. There was no room to think—there was not even room to breathe.

Signor Speranza fidgeted with the *Compendium* and glanced out of the window. He could see Don Rocco, the great Doubting Thomas, across the way, waiting for the Rosary Circle to arrive. And, oh, great—there was Signor Maestro. He was pacing up and down in front of the butcher's shop and glaring into the distance, in the direction of the hotel. Now, as Signor Speranza watched, he crossed the street and came right up to the window of Speranza and Son's, cupping his hands around his face and placing his forehead on the glass. He banged on the window with his fist.

"Speranza! I want to talk to you!"

Ernesto, who was tuning his guitar, glanced up at Signor Speranza and cringed. "I'm sorry, signore," he said, ducking out of his guitar strap. "Let me take care of it." He unlocked the front door and poked his head out. "Papà, please. You have to be quiet now. It's time for my song."

Signor Maestro threw his hands in the air and gurgled, his face a peculiar shade of purple, but he stormed back across the street.

"A flying chicken cutlet," Signor Speranza muttered, flicking through the *Compendium* again. *Do you see what I am dealing with, Lord? A man who is angry because he wants to fly an animated chicken cutlet into a famous movie star's mouth.* He glanced up at the ceiling. *And you made this man! You are the one!* Signor Speranza did not often take his Heavenly Father to task, but there was such a thing as quality control.

Gemma arrived at nine o'clock to do the makeup, and Ernesto let her in.

"Hello, handsome," she said, and stood on her tiptoes to give him a kiss.

Signor Speranza, watching from his desk, rolled his eyes.

Carlotta dashed in around her mother's legs, talking a mile a minute. "Ernesto!" she shouted. "Look at what my mother got me from Signor Bisi's store. It's a yo-yo. I know how to do a trick." She stuck her finger in the loop of string at the top of the yo-yo and swung it around in a wild circle, nearly whapping Ernesto in the face with it.

"Wow, that's very cool," said Ernesto. "Here, let me show you something." He took the yo-yo, wound it up, and then let it go. He flicked his wrist, giving the string a little bounce, and the yo-yo rolled gently forward on the floor, like a dog on a leash.

Carlotta's face lit up. "You are going to teach me that!" she announced.

Signor Speranza cleared his throat, and Gemma looked up. "Oh, hi, Papà," she called. Then she bent down and whispered to Carlotta, who looked up also, and waved.

"Hi, Nonno."

Signor Speranza waved back and grumbled under his breath. Who needed grandpas anymore when there were Ernestos wandering around, with angel voices and a waiting repertoire of yo-yo tricks? *I am like Bambolina now*, he thought. *Old. Forgotten. Yesterday's news*. Any day now he might be expected to be lying on a lawn somewhere, helpless, and swarmed by schnauzers.

The morning wore on. It took longer than usual to get things going because Antonella had to keep stopping every thirty seconds to refresh her phone, which had survived its tumble on the boulders with only a few dings and scratches.

"I'm sure Dante is going to post something soon about arriving in Prometto," she fretted, her brow furrowing each time there was no news. "I don't want to miss it." She turned to Smilzo. "Did you get to talk to him yet? Has he said anything about me?"

Smilzo's eyes flickered. "I—I have not talked to him," he mumbled, glancing at Signor Speranza. "He—he stays in his room."

Signor Speranza took out the megaphone after that and got everyone to focus.

It was just after one o'clock that the emergency struck. Smilzo was wrapping up his proposal for the tenth time, Antonella was dosing her eyes yet again with Visine tears, and Ernesto's *serenata* was swelling to its *decimo* crescendo, when Signor Speranza happened to glance up at the window and perceive Signor Maestro storm out the front of his shop, throw off his apron, swing his fist at Speranza and Son's, and leave, most definitely pointed in the direction of the hotel.

"*Scostumato!*" Signor Speranza gasped, and without even yelling *Cut!* he ran right through the scene in progress to get to the front door.

"What's happening, boss?" squeaked Smilzo, but Signor Speranza was already gone.

He raced down Via Sant'Agata, and then plunged left, down the little-traveled shortcut that he had used to take years ago, when he was a boy going to see Betta at her parents' hotel. He waded, calf-deep in yellow licorice plants. Had there been this many of them when he was young? He didn't remember it being this difficult to get through.

He arrived just before Signor Maestro, disheveled, and with a sprig of licorice somehow stuck in his hair, and his moustache askew.

"Signore," said Ivano, blocking the way with the angle of his substantial person. "I was not expecting you. Do you have your badge?"

Signor Speranza, who was gasping for breath, opened his mouth and closed it, like a fish. In another second, his advantage was lost, as Signor Maestro careened onto the scene, followed by Smilzo, Antonella, Ernesto, Gemma, and Carlotta.

"What is going on here?" asked Ivano, tapping his earpiece and then spreading his arms out.

"I LIVE HERE!" Signor Speranza roared.

"Not so fast, Speranza!" bellowed Signor Maestro, pushing his way toward Signor Speranza and standing directly in front of him, nose to nose. "The jig is up."

Signor Speranza looked sidelong at Ivano. "A little help here?" he said. "He does not have a badge!"

But Ivano took one look at his father and turned red to the tips of his ears. "Sorry, signore," he mumbled.

Signor Speranza rolled his eyes, but he did not have time for praying.

"You listen here, Speranza." Signor Maestro poked his finger in Signor Speranza's chest. "My boys have been here for three days. Seventy-two hours. I know you don't have air-conditioning in this dump, and that window"—here, Signor Maestro swung his enormous paw, pointing toward the green room on the second floor— "has not been open one *crack*! And do you know why?"

Signor Speranza squirmed. "Some guests enjoy a balmy temperature, signore—" he began, but Signor Maestro cut him off.

"I'll tell you why! Because he is not in there. That is what I think. He is not in there, but you are telling us all that he is."

A bank of silence met this proclamation. When Signor Speranza regained the ability to speak, his voice was shaking.

"Signore, I'm sorry you feel that way. If I could prove it to you—"

"Yes." Signor Maestro crossed his arms. "Yes, you can prove it to me. I want a meeting with Dante Rinaldi. Tonight."

Signor Speranza shrugged, helpless. "I can ask him, signore, but—"

"No." Signor Maestro shook his head. "None of this go-between. For sixty-eight thousand euros, I will ask him myself." He rolled up his sleeves. "Now." He shifted Ivano to one side and marched toward the hotel.

"Signore!" yelped Signor Speranza, scurrying after him.

Everyone followed then, because protocol had just gone to hell and security badges had lost all meaning. Only Smilzo broke off from the group.

"Don't worry, boss!" he whispered, as he slipped away, his cell phone pressed to his ear. "I have an idea."

Signor Maestro did not go to the door. Instead, he bent over and retrieved a handful of pebbles from the ground. Straightening, he threw them, like scattershot, at the green room's window.

Nothing happened.

Signor Speranza could hear his heart pounding in his ears.

Signor Maestro put his hands on his hips.

"Signor Rinaldi!" he called. "You think you are a big shot? Well, maybe I am a big shot, too!"

There was no answer, only the distant chatter of birds in the trees.

"Knock, knock!" Signor Maestro tried again. "Who is there?"

This time, there was a rustling behind the curtains. Antonella cried out, but Signor Speranza waved for her to hush.

"It's just the wife," muttered Signor Maestro, crossing his arms and throwing Signor Speranza a contemptuous glance.

Slowly, the window opened, perhaps six inches, and a white handkerchief was bobbed up and down from a hand barely visible.

Signor Speranza rolled his eyes. Was this Smilzo's big idea?

Signor Maestro snorted, but he made his voice pleasant now, wheedling, just in case he was wrong. "Allow me to introduce myself, Signor Rinaldi. I am Antonio Maestro, a very successful butcher and the financial backer of your new project."

There was silence for a moment, and then, crisp and clipped, "*Ciao.*"

Antonella gasped. "That's him!" she said. "I know Dante Rinaldi's voice—that is him!"

There was a stir of excitement among the Maestro brothers, and Carlotta squeaked and jumped up and down.

"I told you so, Papà," said Ivano, grinning, and adjusting his earpiece. "I told you he was really here."

Signor Maestro looked like a man who had just had the wind properly knocked out of his sails, and Signor Speranza thoroughly enjoyed it. But Signor Maestro recovered his wits. He gripped his thick paws together and scampered closer.

"Please, Signor Rinaldi. I have a business proposition I would like to discuss with you. Would be very lucrative. If you can meet in person . . ." Signor Maestro let the question dwindle, half-spoken.

Signor Speranza held his breath. There was a pause. It was rather a longer pause than one might expect to occur in normal conversation, but he had to hope that Signor Maestro imagined it was his own feelings of anticipation that lengthened the seconds.

"Sure," said Dante finally, in a lazy, absent drawl. "I will meet you at the café at eight."

The window snapped shut then, signaling the end of the conversation, and the Maestros sent up a collective whoop of celebration.

Smilzo slid back into the picture.

"Pretty good, huh, boss?" he whispered, grinning.

Signor Speranza, who had just found himself suddenly robbed of the will to live, did the only thing he could do under the circumstances, which was to reach up and smack his assistant on the back of the head.

19

Incognito

$\mathcal{S}$ignor Speranza, Betta, and Smilzo gathered in the green room to reckon with the aftermath of what had just transpired.

"Smilzo did the best he could," Betta maintained. It was she who had been his accomplice on the inside. She had run up the stairs from the kitchen when he called her, racing to power up the laptop onto which he had copied and categorized all the sound clips he'd ripped from the DVD of Dante's movie. The handkerchief had been a stalling tactic, improvised on the spot when the sound program had failed to load.

"He was very clever. I could not have done it without him," she continued, smiling encouragement at Smilzo. "He knew by heart exactly which number went with which recording."

Signor Speranza grunted, crossing his arms and glaring at his assistant. "So it was premeditated, then," he said acidly, and Smilzo's face, which had brightened at Betta's lavish praise, dissolved again into abject misery.

"I'm sorry, boss," Smilzo said for the hundredth time. "I—I didn't think things through."

Betta snorted. "*Please*, Smilzo! Your boss never thinks things through. He is the *patron saint* of not thinking things through! Stop apologizing, and let's all think what to do next."

They discussed their options in hushed voices, the clock on the night table ticking ever closer to eight o'clock, and the looming specter of the newly invigorated Maestro Brothers Security Squad, Ltd., just outside the window, a grim reminder of what was at stake.

"We have to cancel," Signor Speranza said, throwing his hands up. "That's it. I don't see any other way."

Betta winced. "I don't know, Nino. You couldn't see Signor Maestro's face from where you were standing." She shivered. "I wouldn't like to be the one to tell him he's not getting his meeting. It would be like trying to tell a wolf I'm going to take back its dinner."

Signor Speranza frowned, recalling that he had thought of Signor Maestro as a wolf only yesterday.

The three of them all lay back on the bed and stared at the ceiling, thinking it over.

"What about a phone call?" said Betta. "We could use the sound clips again."

Smilzo shook his head. "I don't know, signora. I have not finished scrubbing most of the clips yet. They still have background noise, music. Would sound very strange, I think."

"Probably you don't have any sound clips of Dante saying *flying chicken cutlet*, either," pointed out Signor Speranza.

They went around and around in circles, until, finally, inspiration struck. Signor Speranza sat up. He knew *exactly* what they were going to do. He laid out the plan in meticulous detail, garnering Smilzo's instant and enthusiastic support, and a reluctant vote of confidence from his wife.

"All right, Nino, I'll help you," she said, a worried crease in the middle of her forehead. "But I told you before, and I'll tell you again—if this goes bust and they want to take you to jail, I know *nothing.*"

❀ ❀ ❀

For Signor Speranza, the relentless march of time had brought with it many indignities. First, there had been the slow slide into long-sightedness, followed by a newfound aversion to spicy food. The last decade had seen an embarrassing reliance on fiber drinks and supplements. Recently—and to his great surprise, given his family history—there had even come a lamentable, but as yet scarcely detectable, thinning around the crown of his magnificent helmet of hair. But through all of this, one thing had remained sacred.

"No." Signor Speranza stuck his lip out. "I am not shaving it. And if that means Antonio Maestro murders me in cold blood, then so be it."

Betta rolled her eyes. "Nino, will you stay still and try not to be so dramatic? Maybe there's a way to cover it up or something." She wielded the tiny silver moustache comb, combing her husband's moustache this way and that, and finally giving it up in despair. "You'll just have to zip the jacket up to your nose."

Logistically speaking, this would not be a problem. The enormous velour tracksuit Signor Speranza was wearing would more than accommodate such an arrangement. Burgundy velour up to his nose, or, even better, past it, and a pair of aviator sunglasses, and his identity would be fully hidden. Betta covered the gray in his hair with black shoe polish.

Smilzo called ahead to the café and booked the table with Signora Catuzza for eight o'clock, letting her know that Signor Maestro could be expected to arrive first.

"But I wonder, signora," he said, "if you would mind turning off the twinkle lights on the trees outside the restaurant? Is just that Signor Rinaldi prefers to be inconspicuous, and—"

Signora Catuzza interrupted, her voice crackling over the receiver. "I understand completely, Smilzo. I have experience catering to elite clientele."

"Who do you think she meant, boss?" asked Smilzo, bewildered, as he hung up the phone. "Maybe is Don Rocco?"

It was tricky working out what to do with the Maestro brothers. When Signor Speranza got the idea, it was so like a flash of divine inspiration that he made the sign of the cross. On a slip of paper, he wrote the names of the brothers who were part of the security squad in two columns, pairing them off. One pair was to clear the square by the café. The rest of them were to act as decoys.

"This is a very popular technique with the American CIA," Signor Speranza told them. "It's cutting-edge."

One brother in each pair was to dress in his security uniform, while the other was to disguise himself as Dante, by which arrangement they would deflect and confuse anyone wishing to lay harm to the real Dante. That none of the brothers was assigned to the "real Dante" was a fact that was easily concealed via the declaration of a solemn oath that no one was to reveal whether he was guarding the genuine article or a copy. Every single brother on the squad was dazzled by the sheer brilliance of this plan, and only one unanimous question emerged: What did Dante Rinaldi wear?

Signor Speranza was well prepared for this.

"I know in movies you see him always with the tank top, tank top," he said deviously. "But in his downtime, when he is not filming, he prefers a velour tracksuit."

❊ ❊ ❊

At seven forty-five p.m., Signor Speranza and Smilzo watched from the second-floor window as the decoy Maestro pairs fanned out from the hotel grounds, like seven khaki-and-velour vectors, into the night. They themselves would not leave until it was actually eight o'clock, so as to ensure Signor Maestro's arrival at the café first.

"Well, that's done," said Signor Speranza, relieved, after they had gone. He was wearing the tracksuit, which was zipped to the bridge of his nose, plus the aviators. Now, he stood alongside the cardboard cutout of Dante Rinaldi and struck a pose.

"How do I look?"

Smilzo looked, his eyes darting back and forth. "I don't know, boss," he said slowly.

Signor Speranza threw up his hands. "Of course we will not look exactly the same," he said, impatient, his voice muffled inside the jacket. "What do you think? He's a piece of paper."

Smilzo hesitated. "Ye-es, boss. That is one of the differences." He considered some more. "Are you sure you do not have a tank top?"

Signor Speranza frowned. "Why—do you think that would make it more convincing?"

Smilzo's ears turned pink. "On second thought, boss, maybe the tracksuit is a better idea. It covers up that there is *more* of you than there is of Dante."

Before Signor Speranza could post a rejoinder to this remark, there was a noise at the window. Then a voice called softly, "Hello? Hello, are you there?"

Smilzo peeked out the side of the curtain and gasped. "Is Antonella, boss! She must have seen there was a light and no guard."

Signor Speranza rolled his eyes and made a shooing gesture with his hands. "Make her get out of here. We have to go!"

Smilzo clamped his mouth shut, and shook his head. "Uh-uh. No, boss," he said. "I don't want to."

Signor Speranza groaned. He unzipped his jacket, flung the aviators on the bed, and threw open the window, sending Smilzo skittering into the corner.

"Signorina!" he called, agitated. "What are you doing here?"

Antonella tipped her head back and squinted up at Signor Speranza, scrunching her nose.

"Did you dye your hair, signore?" she asked.

Signor Speranza gazed up at the night sky, at the vast lake of stars, and asked God if there wasn't any other way he could get his kicks than this.

"Is there something you need, signorina? I'm very busy."

Antonella stood on tiptoe, craning her head and looking wistfully over Signor Speranza's shoulder. She looked very like her younger self just then, ten-year-old Antonella, with her gawky knees and elbows, and her wobbly chin, and the constant look of anxiety.

"I guess that Dante isn't here, signore," she said, despondent. "I know he has the meeting with Signor Maestro, but I saw the light and thought—"

"That's right. He's not here," said Signor Speranza, glancing behind him, at the clock on the wall. Seven fifty-eight. Two minutes. They needed to get going.

"Did he say anything, though?" Antonella was looking hopeful again. "Has he watched any of my scenes yet? Does he think they're good?"

Signor Speranza did not have the opportunity to reply. Suddenly, Smilzo was at his elbow, and then he was jockeying past him and leaning over the windowsill.

"I talked to him, Nella," he said, using her nickname from when they were at school together. "He said you are . . ." He broke off, scanning the sky, as if expecting to see the word written there. "Amazing! He said you are amazing."

Antonella gasped, and scurried a little closer. "Did he, Smilzo? Did he really say that?"

Smilzo nodded. "He did. He said he was impressed that you'd never acted before. He said lots of professional actresses would be jealous."

"*Jealous?*" Antonella squealed. "Smilzo, you're lying now!" she said, swatting her hand at the idea, but she was grinning from ear to ear.

Signor Speranza spent the next fifty-nine seconds, by the clock, listening to Smilzo enumerate to Antonella the manifest virtues of her acting abilities, as had been supposedly relayed to him by Dante Rinaldi, internationally renowned movie-star-turned-cardboard-cutout. There was her grace. Her poise. Her diction. Her attention to detail. Her impeccable comedic timing. The particular way in which she had delivered a line in Act Two, Scene Three, the one right after the guy in the bar told her he liked her dress, and —

Signor Speranza had a sudden vision of himself in a doctor's office, having his blood pressure taken. *My, my*, said the doctor, squeezing the inflation bulb and peering over his half-moon spectacles at the needle gauge. *You will want to be careful, signore, or your head will explode,* and right as he said it, that was precisely what happened.

Boom!

"Smilzo!" Signor Speranza cried. "Wrap it up!"

Smilzo halted his recitation of Antonella's flawless line delivery and glanced back at his employer. "Sorry, boss," he said, his cheeks pinkening. He turned back to Antonella. "I have to go now," he said sheepishly. Then, with an impulsive gulp, he blurted, "He also said you are very pretty."

Signor Speranza had happened to glance over Smilzo's shoulder just then, as he uttered the word *pretty*, and so he was able to catch the expression of undiluted astonishment that flashed across Antonella's long, thin face. It gave him an unexpected pang. Hadn't anyone ever told her that before?

There wasn't any need to shoo Antonella off the property after that. She went of her own accord, hands clasped, and whispering, as if she were in church. "Thank you, Smilzo," she said, awe-stricken. "Thank you for telling me that."

Signor Speranza and his assistant watched her go from the window, until she was out of sight, Smilzo beaming.

"I am happy I finally said all of that, boss," he said. "I have been wanting to for a long time."

❊ ❊ ❊

They arrived within sight of the dimly lit café, approaching via the untraveled licorice patch. Smilzo was sulking, because he had realized on the way over that his little speech had probably made Antonella like Dante even more. Signor Speranza was ignoring him.

He held back, scanning the darkness, and spotted Signor Maestro, seated already at the table Smilzo had stipulated over the phone. Signora Catuzza was there also, in high heels and a beaded flamenco skirt.

Signor Speranza caught at Smilzo's arm.

"You are ready, right?" he asked urgently. "You know what to do?" Now that the moment was upon them, his own heart was fluttering in his chest like a bird.

Smilzo shrugged. "Sure, boss."

Signor Speranza stiffened. This kind of listless attitude was not going to cut it.

"Listen to me." He stopped walking and took Smilzo by the shoulders. "This Dante stuff is nonsense. It is only nonsense. Antonella is never going to meet him. He's make-believe, you understand? It was your words that made Antonella happy. *Yours*, Smilzo. And when all this is over I will help you win her back. *Va bene?*"

Smilzo perked up. "You will help me, boss?" he asked. "You will really do that?"

Signor Speranza straightened up. "I will do that, Smilzo. You have my word of honor." He glanced at the café and then put on his sunglasses. "Now let's do this right, or that maniac over there is going to turn me into *fileto di* Speranza. If you want me to be able to help you, you need me whole and functioning."

❊ ❊ ❊

Signor Maestro stood up as they approached, leaning forward to shake hands, but Smilzo was ready.

"I am so sorry, signore, but Signor Rinaldi prefers not to shake hands."

At this cue, Signor Speranza made his hands into a steeple and gave a gentle bow, which evidently impressed Signor Maestro.

"I have seen that in movies," he muttered, almost giddy, as he retook his seat.

Smilzo shuffled around the chairs. His own he placed closest to Signor Maestro, and Signor Speranza's he shunted back slightly, into the inky shadows of the olive tree. "Nothing for me, signora," he said to Signora Catuzza when she approached for the orders. She glanced, hopeful, at her most esteemed guest, but Smilzo intervened again. "Nothing for Signor Rinaldi, either. He is on a very strict Hollywood diet." To Signor Maestro, he added, "That is also why he looks bulkier than you may have expected, signore. He is wearing ten layers of sweat suit. Is an old Hollywood weight-loss technique."

"Ah!" said Signor Maestro.

Signor Speranza, who had been unprepared for this ad-libbed line, nearly choked. Ten layers of sweat suit. Ten!

But Smilzo was already forging ahead, just as they had rehearsed. Quick and painless, that was what they had decided on. Get out of there as fast as possible.

"I have told Signor Rinaldi all about your very successful business, signore," Smilzo began smoothly. "He was very interested to hear of your wide range of products. He is a big supporter of meat, you know. Cutlet. Pork chop. Any kind of meatball."

Signor Speranza, who could scarcely see anything through his tinted lenses, could as yet discern Signor Maestro's eager, greedy face. *He is so sure*, he thought contemptuously. *He is so sure everything is going to go the way he wants it to go.* Well, if there was anyone who could say no to Signor Maestro, it was a movie star.

Signor Maestro scooched his chair closer. He strained to peer at the shadowy occupant of the chair next to the olive tree.

"I'm so happy to hear you say that, signore," he said. "I am a fan of you, and you are a fan of me. That's a very good start."

Signor Speranza rolled his eyes behind his glasses. Dante Rinaldi, number one fan of Signor Maestro's butcher's shop! *Are you seeing this, Papà?* he asked, checking in with his father, who was sitting at the back of his mind on the upturned bucket and had keeled over laughing.

Signor Maestro scooched his chair again, putting distance between himself and Smilzo.

"I have a big idea for a television commercial," Signor Maestro continued, edging closer to Signor Speranza with each word. "Big idea. Big. Would be a big deal for me, and a big deal for you, too."

"About that," said Smilzo, poking his pointy nose in. "I have spoken to Signor Rinaldi about this commercial of yours already, signore, and I am afraid—"

"No offense," Signor Maestro snapped, swiveling his ponderous head to glare at Smilzo, "but this is business. *Real* business. No playtime here. It's time for you to get lost." He turned back toward the olive tree then, as if everything was taken care of.

He is not used to anyone telling him no, thought Signor Speranza, smirking behind his thick layer of velour. This was amazing. He wished he had thought to get it on video! Signor Maestro, the big, dumb dope who was so gullible that he could believe a sixty-two-year-old man he had known his entire life was a twenty-five-year-old movie star in a tracksuit.

Smilzo insinuated himself again, just as they'd practiced.

"Signor Rinaldi has asked me to act as his spokesperson this evening, signore," he said briskly, extracting from his inside jacket pocket a folded letter and pushing it across the table toward Signor Maestro. "He is not currently able to speak for himself. His acting coach has put him on complete vocal rest for at least three days."

Signor Maestro's forehead rumpled. "Vocal rest?" he grunted, suspicious.

"*Sì*, signore," Smilzo bobbed his head. "An actor's voice is his instrument, you know."

Signor Maestro looked from Smilzo on his right to the velour-covered monument on his left, digesting what he had just heard. His mouth puckered.

"I heard him talk this afternoon!" he burst out. "He sounded fine to me!"

Smilzo gave him an indulgent smile. "That is because you have an untrained ear, signore," he said, tugging cheerily on his own ear-lobe for emphasis.

Signor Speranza had to pinch himself to stop from giggling when Signor Maestro's mouth dropped open. If it had ever occurred to him to think that it might be possible to turn Antonio Maestro into a laughingstock simply by going undercover as Dante Rinaldi, he would have done it years ago!

"Then you will have him read the letter, Smilzo," Signor Speranza had instructed his assistant when they were planning the stunt. The letter, which had been designed with a professional-looking letterhead from a fictional law firm in Rome—Signor Maestro wouldn't know what an agent was, but he would understand lawyers—stated verbosely, but unequivocally, even for a butcher of very little brain, that Dante Rinaldi *could* not, and *would* not, be appearing in any butchery commercials, in this life or the next, for-ever and ever amen. "We will be perfectly polite. Gracious," Signor Speranza had continued. "You will shake his hand. I will bow. And then we will go."

That wasn't what happened.

Signor Maestro fumbled with the paper, unfolding it and squinting in the darkness. Smilzo attempted to cast a light on it with his phone, but Signor Maestro swatted him away, producing instead a cigarette lighter. He hunched over his letter, his lips moving as he read by the flickering flame.

Two minutes, thought Signor Speranza happily. I will be out of here in two minutes, and in another twenty I will be out of this ridiculous costume, and getting into bed.

He was wrong on both counts. For a start, he had, at that moment, only thirty seconds to go until his rapid evacuation from the café.

Signor Maestro came to the end of the letter. Signor Speranza knew this because he could read his lips: *Cordially, The legal representatives of Dante Rinaldi.* That had been Smilzo's idea, *cordially.* Signor Speranza saw the dawning look of stupefaction. Signor Maestro turned the paper over, as if perhaps it might say it was all a joke on the other side.

Signor Speranza gave Smilzo the signal, which was to lean forward in his chair and tap the side of his glasses.

Smilzo stood up.

Signor Speranza stood up also.

"Thank you so much for meeting with us, signore," said Smilzo, pleasant to the end. "On behalf of Dante Rinaldi, I would just like to say—"

But Signor Maestro had scrambled out of his chair. He looked almost to be scrambling over the table.

"Signor Rinaldi!" he said. "Signor Rinaldi, if I could just have a word." He had the lighter in his hand, still alight, and his frantic movements caused the little flame to jerk this way and that, like a drunken firefly. In a second, he was upon Signor Speranza, and tugging at his velour sleeve. "Signor Rinaldi!"

Signor Speranza would remember what happened next until the day he died.

Signor Maestro, small-town Italian butcher and lately unwitting major investor in a fraudulent motion picture project, lunged forward. Signor Speranza, sixty-two-year-old vacuum cleaner repairman, ludicrously disguised in a burgundy velour tracksuit as a twentysomething tank-top-wearing movie star, stumbled. His glasses fell to the ground. His moustache popped over the top of his jacket.

Signor Maestro's eyes widened.

"*SperANza?*"

Signor Speranza did the only thing his frantic brain could think to do.

Pow! Right in the mouth.

❈ ❈ ❈

Sant'Agata's rectory had two doorbells. One was electric and had been installed in 1956. The other, older one, was an actual bell on a string. Rather than take it down, the priest at the time had rechristened it the "confessional bell." Any poor and wretched sinner could ring that bell at any hour of the night in quest of immediate absolution.

"Father!" Signor Speranza bellowed, clanging the bell over and over again. "Are you trying to kill me? Who goes to sleep at eight thirty?"

Two minutes later, he knelt in the confessional.

"Bless me, Father, for I have sinned." It was dark on his side of the confessional box, but he could still make out Don Rocco in his lighted compartment on the other side, his face pixelated through the privacy screen. "If Signor Maestro finds me, this will be my last confession."

There was a long pause.

Signor Speranza squinted through the screen.

"Are you praying now, Father? It has been a while since I have been here. Maybe they have changed the rules?"

Don Rocco sighed. "Would you like to tell me what is going on, signore?" he asked. "You look like Santa Claus in Lake Como in that tracksuit."

Despite his mortal peril, Signor Speranza's moustache bristled. "It's a perfectly serviceable tracksuit, Father," he said coldly.

Don Rocco displayed the appropriate amount of sheepishness. "Please, signore," he said. "What's bothering you?"

The whole story came out, the same as it had to Smilzo. The pipes. The money. The visit to Alberto and his Alfa Romeo. George Clooney. Dante Rinaldi. The lies, lies, and more lies. Finally, he showed him the hand he had used to punch Signor Maestro in the mouth.

Don Rocco, who had been sitting quietly through all of this, his head inclined, could be quiet no longer.

"I *knew* it!" he cried, jumping up from his chair on the other side of the screen. "I knew you were up to something with this movie business!"

Signor Speranza adopted an icy dignity, as he had before, about the *Santa Claus in Lake Como* comment. "Do you really feel, Father, that your conduct befits the holy sacrament of Reconciliation?"

But Don Rocco was not in the least bit penitent.

"Why did you not tell me about the trouble with the pipes?" he asked. "Maybe there was something I could have done to help."

"Did you have seventy thousand euros lying around, Father?"
Don Rocco admitted that he had not.

"Then you couldn't have helped," said Signor Speranza blandly.

"You have to tell everyone," the priest said, in that particular, implacable way only a priest or a nun could muster, as if they spoke the very word of God. "You have to tell everyone what you've done. Lying to them. You must tell them tonight. I will not grant you absolution unless you promise you'll do that."

Signor Speranza considered. He considered all that had happened over the past six weeks. He thought about Smilzo and his screenplay. He thought about Antonella, leading woman. He thought about Ernesto, singing the "Ave Maria" in the middle of that poky little butcher's shop. He thought of Zio Franco and his magnificent amphitheater. He thought of Betta, and her coolheaded scheming, and her T-shirts and earrings and water bottles. He thought about Gemma. Gemma smiling. Gemma laughing. Gemma coming alive again.

Signor Speranza opened his mouth, ready to tell Don Rocco that he wouldn't do it. He wouldn't tell everyone, and Don Rocco could keep his absolution. But then it was as if a wind blew. It was as if, these past three days, all the numbers that had been crowding his head for the past month and a half had lain dormant, like fallen leaves at the bottom of his brain, and now a wind blew, and sent them all swirling again. Sixteen thousand, two hundred and twenty-five euros . . . seventeen days . . . sixteen thousand, two hundred and twenty-five euros . . . seventeen days. It was too much. It was all too much.

He lowered his head and sighed.

"I will do what you ask me to do, Father," he mumbled. "But you must come with me. I don't think Signor Maestro will murder me while a priest is watching."

✻ ✻ ✻

Signor Speranza and Don Rocco approached the hotel for Signor Speranza to get changed. Don Rocco had agreed that it was probably best if Signor Speranza did not confess to his various crimes and misdemeanors while still in the burgundy tracksuit.

But as they approached the hotel grounds, for the second time in a week, Signor Speranza discerned a disturbance looming up ahead.

"Maybe they have come already with pitchforks," said Don Rocco cheerfully. "That will save us the trouble of assembling everyone."

Signor Speranza quickened his pace.

They hurried down the road. They rounded the bend.

Signor Speranza halted, taking in at a glance the throng of excited people. He glimpsed Signor Maestro, an ice pack clutched to his face, and his sons, half in khaki and half in velour. He saw Smilzo and Antonella. He saw a smattering of Trezzas, Bisis, and Zamprognas, as well as Signora Catuzza, in her flamenco skirt. All five members of the Rosary Circle were there, clad in five flannel nightgowns. He saw Betta, Gemma, and Carlotta.

And in the midst of them, wearing a canary-yellow tank top and a lazy, dazzling grin, was Dante Rinaldi.

20

Don Rocco Weighs In

"*I should* be suing you."

That was what Dante Rinaldi's agent, Camilla Gallo, said. She was a middle-aged woman from Northern Italy with aggressively blonde hair and shadowy roots, a professionally tailored suit, and a gravelly voice that matched the many, many voicemail messages Signor Speranza had received over the preceding weeks. She was sitting in Signor Speranza's accustomed seat at the kitchen table, and Signor Speranza and Smilzo, the former still in his velour tracksuit, slumped defeatedly opposite her. Her client had been borne off by a crowd of people to the café, and a scowling Signor Speranza could hear the distant din of celebration.

Signora Gallo lit a cigarette, shaking out the match and tossing it onto Betta's polished walnut tabletop. She had already explained how she had found them: Antonella's posts had kept popping up in her feed, with greater and greater frequency. She hadn't taken them seriously at first, until they had begun to include links to merchandise, and "behind-the-scenes" clips from the set. Now, she leaned back in her chair and crossed her arms.

"Tell me about this movie," she said.

Smilzo began, haltingly at first, and then with increasing animation as he realized she was actually listening. Signor Speranza rolled his eyes to the ceiling.

"A goat? Ha! That's pretty good." Signora Gallo stubbed out her cigarette in the decorative pinch pot Carlotta had made at school. "Do you know where we can find this goat?"

Smilzo's brow furrowed. "*Scusi,* signora?"

Signora Gallo lit another cigarette. "We will have to shoot the scene again, of course. With Dante. We do not have a lot of time." As if confirming this, she glanced impatiently at her small gold wristwatch.

Signor Speranza looked at Smilzo. He looked at Signora Gallo.

"You mean," he said, hesitating, "Dante—Signor Rinaldi— wants to be in the movie?"

It was Signora Gallo's turn to roll her eyes. "Why else would I be here?" She waved to encompass the cramped kitchen and the entire world outside it, her nose wrinkling in disgust.

Signor Speranza's moustache bristled.

"It's true we are a small community, signora—" he began.

Signora Gallo blew a cloud of smoke into his face. "You are a dump," she said flatly. "But my client has gotten himself entangled with a married Swede, so he could use some good PR."

"Is public relations, boss," Smilzo whispered out the corner of his mouth.

"Italian boy returns to his roots." Signora Gallo swept out her hand, as if visualizing a headline. "Makes homespun movie in rinky-dink town." She flicked more ash into the pinch pot and shrugged. "I think it'll work."

"You know," said Smilzo timidly, forgetting for the moment that everything he'd learned over the past month and a half had been an elaborate lie, "Boss knew Dante's father years ago. From the mines."

Signora Gallo frowned. "Fabio Rinaldi never worked in a mine. He is a plumber."

Signor Speranza gazed at the ceiling. *Of course.*

❈ ❈ ❈

It was a sleepless night. At midnight, Signor Speranza awakened to a sharp rap on his bedroom door and a crisp leaflet shoved under the crack. He read it, squinting in the moonlight and barking his shin on Bambolina's pungent playpen. *Call time*, it said, in spindly letters, *nine o'clock sharp*. The *sharp* was written in large print and underlined three times. *Location*, it went on, *that place across from the butcher's shop*.

That place across from the butcher's shop! So agitated was Signor Speranza at having his father's store thus reduced that he could not fall back to sleep until well after four in the morning. Approximately half an hour after that, he was awakened again, this time being summoned to check Signora Gallo's cinematographer and lighting technician, each freshly arrived from Rome, into rooms on the second floor.

"Thank you, signore," said the cinematographer, shifting his bulky equipment bag on his shoulder and appraising the little room. "That is, if this is all you have . . ." And he trailed off, glancing hopefully toward the hallway, as if the really fine accommodations were just an inquiry away.

Since he was awake, and too furious to go back to sleep, Signor

Speranza arrived in the village square at seven, where he found Signora Catuzza manning the café window.

"What do you want?" she asked, her arms crossed over her chest.

Signor Speranza lifted his eyebrows. "Good morning to you, also. I think a sparkling water—"

"No," snapped Signora Catuzza, her arms tightening and white dents appearing on either side of her nostrils. "Those are reserved for Signora Gallo."

Signor Speranza eyed the copious rows of bottles and frowned, but decided it wasn't worth risking a snap from Signora Catuzza's dish towel. "An espresso, then."

Signora Catuzza grunted and set about brewing the coffee, slamming the bag of grounds on the counter and clattering the cup and saucer.

"'Oh, you have sparkling water?'" she muttered to herself in a high-pitched voice that sounded nothing like Signora Gallo, but which captured a certain mood. "'How remarkable! I wouldn't think you could get that here.'"

Nine o'clock came and went. At ten forty-five, Signor Speranza, Smilzo, Don Rocco, and the dentist, Beppe Zello, were all sitting in chairs in front of the dental practice, staring across at the café, where Dante Rinaldi and a group of his friends, who had also checked into the hotel, were sitting.

"Maybe he does not have a watch," suggested Beppe Zello.

"Maybe he does have a watch, but it is set to Roman time," said Smilzo. "What time is it in Rome?"

Nobody said anything.

"Oh," said Smilzo, his cheeks turning pink. "Never mind, boss."

The door to the butcher's shop opened, and Signor Speranza

flinched reflexively. He had not come face-to-face with the butcher since the unfortunate incident of the night before.

"Do not worry, signore," said Don Rocco, offering a staying hand. "He will not attack you. We had a long talk about an eye for an eye."

Don Rocco had not, in his conversation with Signor Maestro, specifically extended his reference to *a tooth for a tooth*, but it had hung there between them. Signor Speranza's blow to Signor Maestro's mouth had, as it turned out, been of sufficient force as to dislodge the latter's left central incisor from its socket.

"Real," Beppe Zello told them, shaking his head with the awe of it. "Those beautiful teeth of his are real after all. Unfortunately, I was unable to reattach it."

Signor Speranza winced. Even at this distance, he could see the purplish swollen spot on Signor Maestro's face.

"What do you think he is doing?" asked Don Rocco curiously. Signor Maestro was nudging his doorstop into place with his toe. Then he went back inside, emerging moments later with a shallow carboard box piled high with a selection of his products.

"Oh no," murmured Smilzo, covering his eyes. "I can't watch."

Signor Maestro made a beeline for the table where Dante Rinaldi and his friends were sitting. Dante was draped lazily in his chair, one arm slung over the back, and obviously aware of the adoring attention he was getting from the surrounding tables full of girls. He did not shift his posture as Signor Maestro approached.

"What do you think he is saying, boss?" asked Smilzo, peeping through his fingers.

Dante and his friends gazed up at Signor Maestro, who was gesticulating in a grand fashion quite out of his usual character. One of the friends leaned over and picked half-heartedly through the box. Then Dante Rinaldi said something, and flashed one of his grins, and Signor Maestro left, leaving his box behind him and doing an odd, ducking bow, twisting his apron in his hands. The occupants of the table watched him go, and, when the door to the butcher's shop closed, they burst out laughing.

Signor Speranza and Don Rocco exchanged glances, and Signor Speranza frowned. This Dante fellow had been considerably less trouble when he had been laser-printed onto corrugated fiberboard.

Beppe Zello was frowning also. "You know," he said, "this guy thinks he's hot stuff. But I can tell you right now, those are veneers."

❊ ❊ ❊

At eleven thirty, Signora Gallo turned up with her requisite bottle of fizzy water and asked them why everyone was just sitting about.

Signor Speranza said nothing, but only pointed across the square at her client, who was still sitting at the café table, but had progressed to unwrapping a packet of diced cured pancetta from Signor Maestro's gift box, and was taking turns with his friends pelting it, piece by piece, at a squirrel.

They got down to business after that.

Antonella was waiting inside Speranza and Son's, as she had been all morning, since eight o'clock. Her hair was painfully curled and sprayed, and as usual one of her plastic hoop earrings was stuck in it. She jumped out of her chair when they came in, sat down, and then stood back up again. This performance provoked laughter from Dante and his friends, and Antonella's cheeks burned.

Signor Speranza briskly intervened.

"Signora Gallo," he said, addressing himself only to her. "I don't know if you have had the chance to meet our leading lady. This is Antonella Capra."

Antonella managed a watery smile.

Signora Gallo, holding her water bottle by the neck, pushed her way over.

"*Ciao,* signora," said Antonella, bobbing an awkward curtsy.

Signora Gallo didn't answer. She was walking in a circle around Antonella, appraising her from all angles. She took a pencil from Signor Speranza's desk and poked it into Antonella's voluminous hair, studying it with a delicately wrinkled nose.

"Perfect," she finally pronounced, tossing the pencil in the vague direction of the wastepaper basket. "She's perfect."

Antonella shimmered, and Signor Speranza let out a breath he hadn't realized he was holding.

Signora Gallo clapped her hands.

"Dante!" she called. "*Andiamo!* Get to work so I can go home."

❊ ❊ ❊

Signora Gallo's skeleton crew made quick work of Speranza and Son's. They pushed all the furniture against the walls, and created a makeshift stage composed of folding green screens and enormous lights on tripods.

"Is so they can make it look as though they are anywhere, boss," whispered Smilzo. "Anywhere but here."

Signor Speranza looked at his assistant and frowned. They were squashed behind his desk on a pair of folding chairs, their view of the soundstage partially obstructed by the spinning rack of replacement vacuum cleaner bags. Smilzo could not keep still. He had a copy of the shooting script with him, and he kept rolling it up and either peering through it, as if it were a telescope, or tapping it against one knee. His eyes, Signor Speranza noticed, kept wandering to the corner near the bathroom, where Dante and Antonella were standing, three feet apart. They were not speaking to each other, so far as Signor Speranza could tell—Dante seemed absorbed in the contents of his phone, and Antonella was standing with an unnaturally straight and rigid posture. Who knew she could be so quiet? Signor Speranza marveled. Every time Smilzo's gaze drifted in that direction, he would give a small, almost imperceptible jump, and look away, blinking rapidly.

"Yes, I'm here now," said Signora Gallo. She was on her phone, pacing up and down the showroom floor, and trailing ash from the end of her cigarette onto the gray-speckled, hundred-percent-wool, low-nap carpeting, which had been installed by Luigi Speranza himself in 1983, and meticulously maintained these four decades by his son and heir, Giovannino Speranza. "Yes, I met the girl," she continued. "She's perfect. She'll be the perfect deflection from all this other nonsense. Salt of the earth, and all of that."

Smilzo and Signor Speranza exchanged tight smiles.

"It's good, Smilzo," Signor Speranza said, even though his heart wasn't in it. "It's good for Antonella. We should be happy for her."

"Yeah, boss," whispered Smilzo. "Is good." His eyes drifted miserably again to where Antonella stood, thirty-six inches from the man of her dreams.

"Trust me. Look, I'll send you a picture." Signora Gallo stopped pacing for a moment and pointed her phone at Antonella, who was unaware she was being photographed.

"Did you get it?" Signora Gallo waited and then started to laugh. "I know." Her laugh expanded to a cackle.

Signor Speranza and Smilzo froze. Signor Speranza could see, out of the corner of his eye, that Smilzo's ear was bright pink, and that his chin was trembling, but he could not turn and look at him. It was too horrible. Suddenly, time and space fell away, and he was standing outside the hotel on the day Carlotta came home from the hospital.

"Luca, come on now," he was saying, trying to sound sure and assertive. "You are a nice boy. I know your mother. You have to give this new life a chance. Gemma needs you. The baby needs you." On his left, he saw the living room curtain twitch, and knew that his daughter was watching. "Don't you love Gemma?" he had asked then, his voice high and tight.

And that was the moment that was burned in his memory forever, the moment that still woke him up sometimes in the middle of the night. Luca Ricci, that stupid, conceited boy, had tipped his head back, just like Signora Gallo, and laughed.

Now, at the shop, Signor Speranza felt a sudden urge to leap up from his chair and turn his desk over and shout at everyone to get out, to just get the hell out. But the same thing happened now as had happened all those years ago. In the face of something awful, something he couldn't even understand, he opened his mouth, and words failed him.

"Boss," said Smilzo hoarsely. He had stood up and was trying to slide through the crack between the chairs and the desk. He fumbled, and tripped, and caught himself. "I have to go home now, boss."

* * *

Don Rocco's fork hovered over his tomato salad. "Is something bothering you, signore?"

"Mm?" said Signor Speranza. They were at their usual table at the café. Signor Speranza hadn't touched his food. Signora Catuzza had just watered the olive tree, and the ground next to them was still steaming. The air tasted like chicken soup.

"It just seems as if something is wrong," said the priest, frowning.

Signor Speranza sighed. It had been a long, demoralizing week. Their movie—the movie they had been making all summer—was effectively gone. Every scene that had formerly featured Smilzo had been reshot with Dante Rinaldi in his place, except one.

"They are cutting the set piece, boss," a morose Smilzo reported. "They say they cannot get the goat to cooperate."

This was indeed true. Signor Speranza had himself witnessed Angelo, Signora Gallo's fancy cinematographer, being pursued down the main street, and without Smilzo to rescue him, either.

"Can't they use our footage? If your face is not showing—"

Smilzo's cheeks turned pink. "They said the goat would make a more believable stunt double for Dante than I would."

Antonella was miserable also.

"*Ciao*, signorina," Signor Speranza had called, the last time she'd arrived on set.

Antonella had jumped, as skittish as a colt. "Fine, signore," she had said, crossing her arms, and blinking, her eyes overbright. "I'm fine."

Then there was the business. Signora Gallo and her crew had taken it over completely, almost to the point of wiping it out of existence. On one occasion, Signor Speranza had been whispering into the office telephone, attempting to remotely diagnose Signor Bisi's wet-dry Shop-Vac, when Signora Gallo had actually ended the call with one long-nailed finger.

"Where do you think you are, signore?" she had scolded, with a simpering smile.

Of course, quite a lot was also going right. The movie was undeniably shaping up, and starting to look like a real, actual movie, which their version never had. Thanks to the crew and Dante's collection of hangers-on, the hotel was fully booked for the first time in years, without even having to count flatulent Pomeranians. And then there was the matter of the pipes. The safe at Speranza and Son's was still short of the seventy thousand euros they needed to pay off the Water Commission, but even that situation was looking up. Signora Catuzza, whose business was thriving, had made a large payment on her back taxes, and yesterday Signora Gallo had taken a photo of Dante and Antonella standing cheek to cheek, Dante grinning lazily with his allegedly capped teeth, and Antonella wearing a wobbly smile. She had posted it to Dante's official social media account, and ticket sales for the premiere had gone through the roof. In fact, they were now overbooked by at least two hundred people, but Signor Speranza wasn't worried about that. Such was the beauty of an outdoor movie theater; the spillover could just sit on the grass. By the time all was said and done, there would be more than enough money to cover Prometto's debt. He should have been elated, but he felt strangely flat.

"I hear there are going to be a lot of people," Don Rocco coaxed, as if reading his friend's mind. He speared a chunk of tomato. "Is it the parking you're worried about?"

Signor Speranza waved an airy hand. "No, Father. You know St. Frances Cabrini handles all my parking issues."

Don Rocco made a coughing sound and took a sip of water, and it was a testament to their friendship and the gravity of the current situation that he did not object to the notion that the patron saint of parking spaces might be free to act as Prometto's own personal parking attendant for the weekend.

"Are there going to be reporters, do you think?" he asked instead.

Signor Speranza sighed again, and shrugged. "I don't know, Father. Maybe you should ask that Signora Gallo. She'll know, probably."

Don Rocco was silent for a long time. He wiped his mouth with his napkin and then folded it on his lap.

"You never asked me, signore," he said quietly, "why I gave you that money. Thirteen hundred euros, even though I knew you were lying to me."

The feeling of listlessness cleared from Signor Speranza's head, and he sat up straight. No, he hadn't asked. It hadn't even occurred to him to wonder. He had just been glad to get it at the time, and then there had been so many other things swirling around in his head that any curiosity he might otherwise have had had been pushed out of the way.

"I gave you that money, signore," continued Don Rocco evenly, "because I know how much you love this town. And I knew that, if you needed money for something, it was for a good reason."

Signor Speranza found that he was nodding.

"And then I saw my friends and my neighbors," said Don Rocco, gesturing to either side. "It was as if they had awakened suddenly, after being asleep for a long time. The old ladies who come to the church. Zio Franco. Antonella. Your Smilzo over there. Ernesto Maestro—singing! Singing with the voice God gave him. And I thought, *This is a good thing here.*"

Signor Speranza felt a lump coming into his throat. A good thing. Yes.

Don Rocco glanced across the way at Speranza and Son's, where the front window was blotted out by a folding screen, and his expression darkened.

"Now these new people have come," he said, frowning. "And it's as if everyone has gone to sleep again."

Signor Speranza narrowed his eyes. He felt the wheels turning in his brain.

"What is it that you think I should do, Father?" he asked slowly.

Don Rocco shrugged. "I am just saying, no one can be here forever. And that is why it matters what you choose to do if God gives you the chance." The priest looked right at Signor Speranza. "Don't you think so, signore?"

❀ ❀ ❀

Signor Speranza lingered at the table after Don Rocco left. It was one of those glorious afternoons in late summer, when the sky was blue, blue, blue, and the heaped white clouds were cut in sharp relief against it, and if one closed one's eyes it smelled of fried oil, and suntan lotion, and overripe bergamots heavy on their branches, and the sound of the children playing was like the chatter of birds. All these things together gave Signor Speranza a strange and fleeting feeling in his chest—a sure feeling that he might not only live forever, but also that he had been alive for a long, long time. It was a day like that. How could it be possible, then, he thought with a frown, that it felt as if he was on the brink of losing everything that mattered?

"Papà."

Signor Speranza looked up. Gemma. He had been so busy, he had not seen her since the day the fake Dante had first shown his cardboard face, even though she and Carlotta had returned to the hotel last night.

"What are you doing here, Papà?" she said. "You have no work to do? Or you are letting Mamma do it all for you?"

Signor Speranza heard the teasing note in her voice and smiled.

Gemma pulled out a chair and sat down next to him. "I heard they changed everything you and Smilzo did." She tipped her head toward the battened windows of Speranza and Son's and flashed a look of sympathy. "Ernesto told me."

Signor Speranza put up his hands. "Well? What can I do?"

"What can *you* do, Papà?" Gemma grinned, and, for a second, she looked just like Carlotta. "Probably anything you want to do."

The statement startled Signor Speranza, and he found he had nothing to say. In a fraction of a moment, all his thoughts dried up. But Gemma didn't seem to mind. He snuck sidelong glances at her, and she just sat there, serene and looking at the sky. He looked at the sky, too.

After a little while, a voice drifted from a nearby table.

"Babbo."

Signor Speranza looked over. It was a little boy—a little boy he had never seen before—talking to his father.

"Babbo," the child said again. "This is my ice cream shop. What do you want to order?" He stood solemnly alongside his father, holding an imaginary pencil and pad.

Signor Speranza and Gemma exchanged glances. *Remember?* he wanted to say. *Remember how we used to play restaurant?* The words didn't come, but still, he could tell she was thinking the same thing.

They looked back at the father, who was eager and young, almost a boy himself, and leaning forward on the table. "All right," he said. "I'll have a cone with one scoop of purple unicorn, two scoops of polka dots, and three scoops of singing kangaroo." He looked at his son and then around at the other tables, clearly charmed by his own vast powers of imagination, and bursting with expectancy.

The little boy frowned.

"I have chocolate, vanilla, and strawberry," he said.

It was Gemma who laughed first, a warbled, almost hysterical whoop, and then Signor Speranza joined in. They laughed so much, and so loudly, that some of the other tables laughed, too, and the young father looked up, surprised and sheepish.

Signor Speranza scattered bills on the table to cover his and Don Rocco's bill, and he and Gemma stood to go. "Enjoy him!" he called to the bewildered young father as they left. "Enjoy your son!"

And that was it. Signor Speranza knew what he was going to do now. He was going to buy an enormous bag of roasted chestnuts from the Emporio, and he and Gemma were going to split it on the walk home and hide the wrapper from Betta, as they'd used to so long ago. Then he was going to play with Carlotta and that dratted puppy, and there wasn't anything Signora Gallo, or the Water Commission, or anybody else, could do about it. As for the rest of it—well, he was just going to have to think of something.

21

The Plan, Part One

Signor Speranza didn't know when the movie had become so important. He only knew that it had. Why should a bunch of big shots come to their town and use it for their own purposes? Why should they take everyone's hard work and throw it away, as if it didn't mean anything? As if it were garbage? He kept thinking of Gemma, laughing in the makeup tent. Of poor Smilzo, who really *did* look a bit like Humphrey Bogart, if you really squinted, or maybe if you closed your eyes. He kept thinking of the day they'd shot the set piece, and of the fireworks bursting in the afternoon sky.

He thought of all these things as he sat on the sidelines at Speranza and Son's over the next week, squashed behind his desk on a folding chair. He thought about it as the voices of Signora Gallo and her crew and Dante Rinaldi receded into the background, and he pored over the *Compendium*, running his finger down each page. He stopped when he got to St. Michael the Archangel, patron of those preparing for battle. Yes. He closed the book with a satisfied snap. That was the one.

The night before the premiere, his prayers were answered.

"Nino! What are you doing?" Betta was sitting up, half-asleep, and shielding her eyes. Bambolina was nestled beside her, having successfully over the past week wormed her way out of the play-pen and onto Signor Speranza's side of the bed, relegating him to a camping cot on the floor.

Signor Speranza was fully dressed and standing at the door of the bedroom, peering through the crack into the hallway. He motioned for Betta to be quiet.

"I think the coast is clear," he whispered. "This is my chance."

Betta sat all the way up. "Nino." She crossed her arms. "I hope you're not about to do something stupid."

Signor Speranza threw his hands in the air and forgot to be quiet. "*Madonna mia*, Elisabetta! I know what I'm doing!"

Betta rolled her eyes. "Don't get arrested."

Signor Speranza crept out of the hotel and across town, and at eleven p.m. on the dot he rapped on the front door of Smilzo's house. It had never before occurred to him to wonder what his assistant wore to bed, but when it was revealed to him now, he looked up at the night sky. *Is he doing it on purpose, Lord?* he asked beseechingly.

"Boss?" said Smilzo, squinting. He rubbed his eye with the capacious sleeve of his flannel nightshirt, which cut off a humiliating six inches above his scrawny ankles; the tassel of his matching sleeping cap swung back and forth.

"Smilzo," said Signor Speranza, in strained tones. "Where did you acquire that nightgown?"

Smilzo looked down, startled. "This, boss? This was my father's."

Signor Speranza frowned. "Don't you have anything else of his that you could wear instead?"

Smilzo started. "No, boss. He"—his ears, that were sticking out on either side of his cap, turned pink—"he took everything else with him."

Smilzo stared down at the ground then, and looked so sad and foolish, with his skinny white ankles, that Signor Speranza's moustache twitched. He pictured his assistant rummaging hopefully in a closet for something that had belonged to his father, and finding only this ridiculous nightgown on a lone hanger, and the thought of it made his throat close up.

"Oh," he said. And then, lamely, "It's very nice."

"Boss," said Smilzo again, rubbing his other eye. "Is something wrong?"

Signor Speranza straightened and took a deep breath.

"Yes," he said. "And we are going to fix it."

❄ ❄ ❄

In eighteen hours, four hundred and fifty-three people would travel to Prometto for the premiere of Dante Rinaldi's surprise pop-up movie. They were, with the presumed assistance of St. Frances Cabrini, patron saint of parking spaces, going to park their cars, file into their seats in the newly constructed amphitheater or on the nearby grass, and wait, in delicious anticipation, for their idol's stupid face to fill the silver screen. Well, thought Signor Speranza grimly, they could wait all they wanted.

He and Smilzo crept down the Via Sant'Agata. Every light in every establishment was extinguished, except for a lone lamp somewhere inside the church, and an orange neon sign at Maestro's that spelled FRESH, like a cattle brand stamped into the night.

Signor Speranza tiptoed to the door of Speranza and Son's, Smilzo close at his heels. He could not see inside because the green screens that had covered the windows for the last week had not yet been dismantled, and a piece of brown butcher's paper had been taped over the door to prevent the intrusion of unwanted light.

"This will only take a minute," he whispered.

He unlocked the door, opened it, dimly perceived the form of Angelo, Signora Gallo's cinematographer, asleep in a chair, and whipped the door shut again.

"Boss!" whispered Smilzo, scurrying after his employer, who was barreling down the street. "What happened?"

"Plan B!" Signor Speranza flung over his shoulder.

❊ ❊ ❊

Ivano Maestro crossed his arms and leaned back in his chair.

"You punched my father in the face, signore."

Signor Speranza's moustache twitched from side to side. "I did do that," he said, bowing his head gravely. "And I feel mostly sorry about it."

"He is going to have a gold tooth," said Ivano, frowning. "Probably he will look like a pirate."

Signor Speranza nearly chuckled at this, as Signor Maestro had already looked overwhelmingly piratical, and it was possible the acquisition of a genuine gold tooth had been more a matter of destiny than anything else. But, as he cast his eyes downward to conceal his merriment, he happened to intercept the alert stares of two of the family's intrepid Dobermans, who were slinking about under the vast dining table, and he immediately sobered.

"If we help you," Ivano continued, "will you put Ernesto's song back in the movie?"

Signor Speranza looked around the polished table at the fifteen Maestro boys, who were all looking expectantly back at him, except for Ernesto, who was staring at his own hands in his lap.

"Absolutely," said Signor Speranza. "Absolutely, I will do that."

❊ ❊ ❊

Twenty minutes later, Signor Speranza and Smilzo were crouching inside the butcher's shop alongside Ernesto and Pietro Maestro. Ivano Maestro was across the street, standing atop the roof of Speranza and Son's, and awaiting their signal.

"Okay," said Signor Speranza. "Now."

Pietro Maestro flicked the switch for the neon FRESH sign on and off three times. Then Smilzo opened the door of the butcher's shop just wide enough to admit the passage of a megaphone.

"Angelooooooooooo!" he said, his voice echoing across the street. "Angelooooooooooooo!"

At first, nothing happened.

"Come on, come on," Signor Speranza muttered, staring at the door of his shop. Then he heard a faint jingling sound. The door opened, and the sleepy, puzzled face of Angelo the cinematographer appeared.

"Now! Now!" Signor Speranza whispered.

Right on cue, Ivano dropped down a length of line from his fishing pole. Attached to the end and bobbing weirdly was Smilzo's mother's toilet-paper doll, bereft of her toilet paper, her staring eyes and oddly billowing peach crochet skirt more bizarre than ever in the eerie neon gloom.

Angelo's eyes widened in terror. He took off running down the street, and Ivano, who, as it turned out, was quite adept at running so long as he wasn't expected to move his arms like blades or pump his legs like pistons, ran nimbly after him down the adjacent roofs of Prometto's shops, so that every time poor Angelo looked over his shoulder, in much the same manner as Tom Cruise, it appeared that the toilet paper doll was in relentless pursuit.

"Quick! Let's go!" said Signor Speranza. He and Smilzo flitted across the street, Signor Speranza dimly aware in his hurry of a light switching on in the rectory. They pelted into Speranza and Son's. Smilzo made for the computer at the back, while Signor Speranza stood guard at the open door.

Smilzo muttered aloud to himself as he powered the computer up and raked through the files. Signor Speranza swept his eyes over the square, and up and down the block, for any sign of Angelo returning. *Go! Go! Go!* he thought, in tune to the rhythm of his heart.

"I did it, boss!" called Smilzo, his voice at a fever pitch. "The Dante movie is erased!"

"Good!" said Signor Speranza, turning around. "Now label our movie as the right one."

"Okay, boss." Smilzo bent over the computer again, and then straightened suddenly, startled by his own thoughts. "But, boss— once they see the wrong movie is playing, won't they force us to turn it off?"

Signor Speranza waved his hand. "Tomorrow!" he said. "We will take care of that tomorrow! Come on!"

Smilzo saved his handiwork and shut the computer with a snap.

"Okay," Signor Speranza whispered. "Time to go."

They were just on the point of escaping when Angelo, out of breath and wheezing, jogged into sight.

Signor Speranza whisked the door closed, and he and Smilzo crouched behind it.

"What do we do, boss?" yelped Smilzo.

"Shhhh!" Signor Speranza ripped a corner of the brown paper covering the door and peered outside. Angelo was ten yards away. Five. Three. Signor Speranza's heart was like a crazed bird banging against its cage. What should he do? What should he do? Lock the door? Hide in the bathroom?

Across the street, there was a piercing sound. Signor Speranza and Smilzo covered their ears. Angelo covered his ears, too, and turned to see where the sound had come from.

A light switched on in front of the church of Sant'Agata. Don Rocco stood within it, along with Ernesto Maestro. The priest lifted Signor Speranza's megaphone and called into it.

"Hey, Mr. Movie Man! Have you heard my friend sing?"

Then Ernesto Maestro, who required no amplification and who could probably be heard from space, burst into "Vesti la Giubba" from *Pagliacci*, and Angelo the cinematographer was so spellbound and bewildered, Signor Speranza and Smilzo were able to slip right past him, and he didn't even notice the priest, flashing a subtle thumbs-up.

22

The Plan, Part Two

$\mathcal{J}$ust before dawn, Signor Spe-
ranza dreamt of when he was a boy. As before, in his dream of
Gemma, he wasn't himself; he was watching from a distance, a tres-
passer tiptoeing at the fringes of a forgotten memory.

"Giovannino! *È pronto!*" It was Nonna Delfina, his grandmother,
toiling over a makeshift stove by the fire.

Giovannino, small, and in short pants and suspenders, hurtled
into the kitchen. He tried sticking his hand in the pot.

Nonna Delfina laughed, and scolded, and shooed him away.
"Lavati le mani, topolino!" Wash your hands, little mouse!

Signor Speranza watched as his younger self scurried to the
sink and worked the pump. He looked on as the little boy whisked
his hands through the water so fast they were barely wet, and then
dried them hurriedly on his untucked shirt. Signor Speranza chuck-

led. That was the way he had used to wash his hands. That was the way. He remembered.

"*Ora,*" called Nonna Delfina, "*aiuti à nonna.*" *Help grandma.*

Giovannino scampered to the stove and obediently, and with great concentration, ferried two bowls of soup from there to the little wooden table. His errand accomplished, he next did something he had always done, and which his older self had forgotten until this moment. He pointed to his grandmother's right hand, which had been withered by a stroke, and which she kept pinned to her side, like a baby bird's wing.

"Give to me," he said imperiously, like the little lord he was, only child of his parents, and thus far infallible in the attainment of his life's ambitions. "I fix it."

Nonna Delfina tipped her head back and laughed, showing her one remaining tooth, like a single standing picket in a fence that has been blown down. "Okay, Dottore Topolino. You fix it." With her good hand, she guided the crumpled one.

Signor Speranza shuffled closer and watched, his heart stuck in his throat.

Giovannino examined his grandmother's hand closely, his tongue sticking out of the side of his mouth. There wasn't anything wrong with it, he was thinking. The thought was plain on his frank, open face. Carefully, one by one, he peeled back the fingers, and then took a step back to examine the fruits of his labor. Nonna Delfina's palm lay open.

Giovannino crowed, and jumped up and down. "Is fixed! Is fixed! I fix it!"

Nonna laughed and laughed. The beautiful, forgotten sound of it rent at Signor Speranza's heart.

"*Topo sciocco!*" she said. Silly mouse. Slowly, her fingers curled back up, like the petals of a flower closing. She kissed Giovannino on the top of his little head. *"Topolino sciocco."*

Suddenly, the dream lurched sideways, like an old projector that had run out of film. The misty kitchen dropped away, and Signor Speranza was in the shop. Signora Gallo was there, and laughing.

"Topolino sciocco!" she mocked. "What makes you think you can fix anything?"

Then the shop was gone, and they were on the edge of a cliff, and Signora Gallo was pushing him over. As he fell, she tipped her head back and cackled, and Signor Speranza snatched at the air and screamed.

❊ ❊ ❊

He woke to Carlotta standing over him.

"Mama said I may use *real* hairspray for the movie tonight, Nonno," she announced. It was six o'clock in the morning. Carlotta had, almost from infancy, an unbreakable habit of talking to people who were sleeping as if they were actually awake. She stood at his bedside now in her mother's robe and slippers, a constellation of hot rollers and their accompanying metal pronged clips sticking out in all directions on her tiny head.

"Do you think you will want to wear hairspray also?" Carlotta asked, nibbling at her piece of toast with Nutella and jelly as Nonno Guido, that incorrigible opportunist, kept watch below. "I can ask my mother for you if you want."

Smilzo's rain, which still hadn't materialized since the set piece was filmed, had come in the night, and the last of it was drizzling when Signor Speranza attempted to take Nonno Guido outside. The dog stopped at the threshold, hopping backward and issuing a warning bark.

"*Che cosa, testa dura,*" Signor Speranza muttered, and dragged him outside, but once they were exposed to the elements Nonno Guido yelped in genuine terror, and tried to scramble up his master's leg.

Realizing what was happening, Signor Speranza scooped him up. "It's okay," he murmured, chuckling softly and nuzzling the tiny head. *Imagine*, he thought. Here was a creature new enough that it had never before seen water fall from the sky.

Shortly thereafter, Smilzo's mother showed up, looking like Smilzo in an A-line dress, and presented Signor Speranza with a crocheted dinner jacket for him to wear to the evening's events. It was not necessary for Signor Speranza to will the tears to his eyes; he just had to recall the welts on the backs of his knees from the director's chair, and they came of their own accord.

"You really shouldn't have done this, signora," he managed to choke. "It's really, *really* too much."

Things got crazy after that. At ten o'clock, a flock of Signora Gallo's people descended upon the hotel—makeup artists, stylists, tent technicians, caterers, decorators, and a phalanx of entertainment reporters—and Signor Speranza sneaked out, bound for a secret meeting at Sant'Agata, with a queasy feeling in the pit of his stomach that perhaps he had made a big mistake.

※ ※ ※

They met inside the dim church at noon, Signor Speranza, Smilzo, Don Rocco, and the Maestro brothers.

"It seems as if this is turning into a very big deal, signore," said Don Rocco uneasily. He was standing at the door, peeping out into the square, which Signora Gallo's people had also infiltrated, and where a crew was setting up an elaborate lane of cones. A pair of men rolled out a length of red carpeting that was to stretch all the way to the amphitheater behind the church, and another two unraveled enormous balls of twinkle lights.

Ivano Maestro was all business. He ignored what was going on outside, staring directly at Signor Speranza. "Tell me what to do," he said.

It was very simple. All they had to do was to convince Dante Rinaldi and Signora Gallo to leave the premiere, before the movie started, and of their own free will.

"That way," said Signor Speranza, "we'll be able to play *our* movie—the movie *we* made—and there'll be no one to stop us."

A little cheer went up from the Maestro brothers, and Smilzo beamed, but Ivano leaned back in his pew, eyes narrowed, and crossed his arms. "And exactly how will we accomplish that, signore?"

Signor Speranza signaled to Smilzo. Smilzo rummaged in his backpack, and produced two objects—a remote control with a single red button, and a small, blinking black box.

There was a clatter just outside, and everyone jumped. Then the door opened and threw a slant of light across the pews.

"Marianna!" rasped Signora Barbaro, peering inside and calling over her shoulder to Signora Pedulla. "Look! Jesus is here! And the apostles, too!"

Signora Pedulla toddled into sight and peered inside as well. Then she flung her hands in the air.

"Ah!" she cried. *"Che bello!"*

❊ ❊ ❊

The plans were laid. Ivano Maestro was going to casually bump into Dante Rinaldi at approximately seven p.m., just before the latter was due to walk the red carpet, thereby providing perhaps three to five seconds of misdirection during which his brother Ignacio was to slip the blinking black box into the target's jacket pocket. They would then wait until the optimal moment, when Dante was in full view of both the assemblage and the press, to deploy the mechanism.

"What if there are microphones, boss?" asked Smilzo, who had lost control of his senses, and could not stop giggling. "Imagine what it will sound like if there are microphones."

"I hope we are doing the right thing, signore," said Don Rocco nervously, as the group disbanded. "Do you think we are?"

Signor Speranza glanced at the altar, before which he had married Betta and his mother had married his father, and at the holy water font wherein Carlotta and Gemma, and every other Prometto baby, including himself, had been baptized for a hundred and fifty years. He looked at Signora Barbaro and Signora Pedulla, kneeling in the first pew, silent for once, and bent over their rosaries, praying the prayers of old ladies, but looking remarkably small from where he stood, like children.

"I hope so, Father," he said truthfully. "But I really don't know."

❊ ❊ ❊

After parting ways with his coconspirators at the church, Signor Speranza checked his watch. It was one fifteen. Thanks to the recent publicity, as of that morning's receipts, the safe at Speranza and Son's contained seventy-two thousand, one hundred and seventy-five euros—more than they even needed. If he hurried, he would have just enough time before the evening's festivities were underway to retrieve the money, drive the hour and a half to the Water Commission's office in Reggio, pay off the pipes, and get back to Prometto without anyone missing him.

"Just under the wire," he muttered grimly, thinking of Monday's looming deadline, just three days away. He hurried across the square, and found the door to the shop unlocked. He pushed it open cautiously, and the bell jingled overhead.

"Smilzo?" he called, frowning. Had Smilzo somehow overtaken him when they were leaving the church?

But Smilzo wasn't there.

"Oh, good, it's you. I was just about to call you." It was Signora Gallo. She was sitting at the back of the shop, at Signor Speranza's desk, flipping idly through the *Compendium*. Her red-lacquered nails clicked together. "Where did you get this thing?" she asked. "It's very funny."

Funny? Signor Speranza's cheeks burned. He hastened over to the desk.

"My apologies, signora," he said, whisking the book out of Signora Gallo's reach. "I should not have left personal things lying around to get in your way." *In my own shop*, he finished furiously in his head. He held the *Compendium* behind his back. "What can I do for you?" he asked, glancing at the clock on the wall, and thinking of the Water Commission and traffic. "I thought you would be getting ready for tonight?"

Signora Gallo laughed. Then she leaned back in Signor Speranza's swivel chair and wagged one sharp-nailed finger.

"You are forgetting something, signore," she said, her voice a teasing, menacing trill.

Signor Speranza looked at her sharply. What was she talking about? His eyes slid over the desk and caught on Smilzo's laptop. *The computer*, he thought, with a well of panic. Maybe she had come here to take a last look at the movie before tonight. Maybe she had figured out what they had—

"Dante's fee." Signora Gallo's words cut across Signor Speranza's thoughts.

Signor Speranza froze. He lost his grip on the *Compendium*, and it slipped from his fingers, smacking onto the floor behind him. His mouth went dry.

"F-fee?" he whispered, and swallowed.

Signora Gallo laughed again. "What do you think we are running here, a charity?" She spun around in the swivel chair so that she faced the safe. "Now, how do you open this thing?" she murmured.

Signor Speranza felt the earth lurch under his feet. No. This was not possible. This could not be happening.

"Signora, please," he gasped, rushing forward. "We are a very small community. We do not have a lot of money. We cannot possibly be expected—"

Signora Gallo's back went rigid. She sat up straight and turned back around in the chair. Her already-flinty face had turned to stone. She folded her hands on the desk.

"Understand me, signore," she said, deathly quiet. "You should be in jail for what you've done. If you don't give me this money today—right now—then I will sue you. I will sue your wife. I will sue your daughter. I will sue that cute little granddaughter of yours. I will sue every person in this godforsaken town." She stared at him, and her eyes burned cold fire. "Is that what you want me to do?"

The next few moments passed in a blur, and, when they were over, Signor Speranza was all alone in his father's shop, staring into an empty safe, and weeping. That was it. After all their hard work, they were done for. Prometto was finished.

❊ ❊ ❊

At five o'clock that evening, Signor Speranza stood in front of the mirror in his bedroom, getting ready for the premiere. He had come now, at last, to the end of things. Prometto was dying, and he felt as though he was dying, too. He wondered what he should say. He had thought a good deal over the years about last words—he even had a book of famous ones at the shop, mixed in somewhere among the vacuum manuals, phone books, and industry magazines. The ones that had always impressed him were the long, assiduously grammatical ones, like Sir Isaac Newton's: "I do not know what I may appear to the world; but to myself I seem to have been only like a boy playing on the sea-shore, and diverting myself in now and then finding a smoother pebble or a prettier shell than the ordinary, whilst the great ocean of truth lay all undiscovered before me." How on earth had he managed *that*? And had there been someone standing by, perhaps professionally trained in shorthand, to get it all down? Signor Speranza had always suspected that Sir Isaac, on perceiving that the end was nigh, had likely read his final utterance from a prepared sheet, and then just clamped his mouth shut and waited it out. Imagine if someone had come in at the end and startled him, and if his last words had subsequently wound up being something ridiculous, like *Shut that door*?

Signor Speranza had always assumed that, when his own time came, he would be able to muster something profound. But as he stood there, wearing the dinner suit he had rented earlier in the week, minus the jacket, contemplating not his own death but the death of everything that mattered to him, nothing particularly brilliant came out.

"I don't want any of this, Betta," he said, his voice hollow. "After tonight, nothing will be the same."

"You look very handsome, Nino." Betta was soft and glittering in the pale gray silk dress she had once thought she would wear to Gemma's wedding, along with her mother's hinge-back earrings with the diamond flowers.

"I'll have to tell everyone now," he said, and his eyes filled with hot tears.

Betta rested her chin on her husband's shoulder. She looked in the mirror, too, and sighed. "Try not to think about it tonight, Nino. Let it be tomorrow's problem, okay?"

Tomorrow. Signor Speranza sighed. Tomorrow, he would have to tell everyone about the pipes. Tomorrow, everyone would hate him.

He reached for the crocheted jacket that was folded in a scratchy bundle on the dresser.

"And here is today's problem," he said wryly, pulling it on.

Just then, one of Signora Gallo's associates, a young costume designer from Milan, happened to waltz past, and stopped abruptly in the doorway.

"That is a sharp jacket, signore!" she cried, without a trace of sarcasm. "Is it Versace?"

❋ ❋ ❋

Via Sant'Agata teemed with people. Signor Speranza could not remember ever seeing it so crowded, although his father had told him of the time before he was born, when the Pope had visited.

"That's why you're here, Giovannino," Luigi Speranza had told his son. "Your mother and I prayed and prayed for a baby. Then the Pope came and blessed the village, and that's why you are here."

Signor Speranza thought of that now, as he shuffled along the red carpet in his crocheted jacket. Betta, Gemma, and Carlotta were lost somewhere in the crowd ahead. He could see Speranza and Son's to his left, but it didn't look as though it belonged to him anymore. Nothing looked the same in this sea of strangers.

"What do you think of all this, Papà?" he murmured aloud, but if his father answered, somewhere away at the back of his mind, then Signor Speranza couldn't hear him.

"I am getting a little nervous, boss," said Smilzo, who was walking beside him. He kept hunching his shoulders, as if hiding, and then suddenly popping up and craning his head to scan the crowd, like a whack-a-mole. "I have not seen Ivano, have you?"

"He'll be here, don't worry," said Signor Speranza, but the truth was, he was getting awfully worried himself. How might a crowd like this react, he wondered, if they came all this way to watch a Dante Rinaldi movie, and were given a Smilzo one instead?

The line halted, and there was a cheer up ahead. Signor Speranza and Smilzo both strained to see. It was Dante. He had stopped in front of a bank of photographers. Now, he grabbed a startled Antonella around the waist and swung her into a dip.

"It's pretend, Smilzo," said Signor Speranza as his assistant flinched. "It's all pretend."

Soon they arrived at a sort of holding area, approximately thirty yards from the amphitheater, where a white tent had been erected, and cocktails and hors d'oeuvres were being served to the cast and crew before the official show began. *How many pipes would this pay for?* Signor Speranza wondered as he entered the tent and was both surprised and relieved to be hit with a blast of air-conditioning. Ivano

Maestro motioned to him from the other side of the tent, and the worst of his anxiety dissipated.

Betta spotted him and waved. "I'm taking Carlotta to get some food, Nino," she called, as Carlotta dragged her away, and then it was just him and Smilzo. A server whisked by with a tray of Campari and sodas, and they each took one. The tent was filled with the soft, pleasant din of people talking, and the clink of plates and glasses.

Smilzo downed his drink. "I think she still likes him, boss," he said, wiping his mouth on the back of his hand and staring balefully at Antonella. She was perhaps fifteen feet away, next to Dante, in a little cluster of people. She wasn't talking. She held a glass, frosted with condensation, in her right hand, and her left hand was clamped tightly around her right forearm. Her neck strained forward as she followed the conversation. She looked, Signor Speranza thought, supremely uncomfortable.

"I don't know if she does, Smilzo," he said, frowning.

A second tray of Campari and sodas passed by, and Smilzo grabbed another glass. He drained it in a gulp.

"I am going over there, boss," he announced, handing Signor Speranza his empty drink.

"Smilzo, I don't think . . ." Signor Speranza tried to snatch at the back of his assistant's jacket, but he was not quick enough. "*Oddio*," he muttered, glancing up at the ceiling of the tent. "Can you hear me in all this racket, Lord?"

Signora Catuzza sidled up beside him.

"Have you tasted these, signore?" she asked, wrinkling her nose with distaste. She was wearing a sequined evening dress, but her dish towel from the café was still slung over one shoulder. She held up a puff pastry with the tips of her fingers. "Are we supposed to *eat* these?"

"Nino!" Betta came hurtling over, wild-eyed. "I think you have a problem."

Signor Speranza snapped to attention. He looked where Betta was pointing.

"*Oddio*," he muttered again.

Smilzo was getting into it with Dante Rinaldi. He was swaying slightly on his feet, and gesturing at Antonella, and poking his finger into Dante Rinaldi's chest. Unfortunately, Signor Rinaldi's underlings had fanned out behind their overlord, the better to witness the current spectacle, and were, in effect, blocking the concerted efforts of Maestro brothers One and Two to deposit an artificial flatulence device in his pocket.

Signor Speranza groaned. *Smilzo!*

"I couldn't do it, signore," said Ivano Maestro miserably, finding Signor Speranza in the shuffling throng when everyone had been instructed to proceed from the tent to the amphitheater for the opening ceremonies. "I could not get close enough."

"Give it to me," said Signor Speranza grimly, and the blinking box switched hands.

❀ ❀ ❀

Signor Speranza and Don Rocco sheltered in the cool vestibule of the church, away from the heat and the tumult of the crowd.

"Do you think this will work, signore?" Don Rocco asked, anxious and hovering.

Signor Speranza did not answer.

"Tape," he said curtly, holding up one hand, like a surgeon calling for his instruments. And then, "Scissors."

When he was finished, he beheld his handiwork.

"Do you see that, Father?" he said, puffing out his chest. "Do you see that, with God, even so evil an object as this can be made into an instrument of His peace?"

Don Rocco frowned.

❊ ❊ ❊

Signor Speranza and Don Rocco stole out of the back door of the church, and scuffled over rock and brush, and through a stunted grove of fig trees, thereby circumnavigating the line of people waiting to get into the amphitheater from the road, and circling around on the other side.

"Boss! Father! Where did you go?" hissed Smilzo, when they joined him in the wings at the side of the amphitheater's retractable screen. The red carpet ended here abruptly. Signora Gallo had brought in enormous speakers that were parked on either side of the stage, and had rigged a microphone that stood waiting at its center. Dante Rinaldi and Antonella were walking, arm in arm, toward it.

"You were right, boss!" Smilzo whispered, his eyes bright. "She does not like him! She says that after tonight she never wants to hear the name *Dante Rinaldi* again!" He grinned crookedly. "I told him he was not so much an actor as an internationally renowned wearer of tank tops."

Signor Speranza looked appreciatively at his assistant and clapped him on the back. "Good for you, Smilzo. I'm proud of you," he said. "Now please stop talking." They had to get the moment exactly right.

Dante began to introduce Antonella.

"Some of you may already know my leading lady," he said, in that studied, drowsy voice, letting his hair fall momentarily over one eye.

There was a shimmer of cheers. The sound of the crowd was light and fizzy, like a carbonated drink. Signor Speranza scanned the rows and rows of people. Wasn't that something? he thought, a little dizzy at the sight of it. Wasn't that something that all these people were here, in Prometto, in a movie theater his own uncle had built? Wasn't that something?

Dante finished talking about Antonella. Then he dipped her again, as he had in front of the cameras on the red carpet, and spun her out, till she spun offstage.

"An ass," Antonella said, straightening her hair, when she was safely in the wings. "He is a colossal ass."

Smilzo beamed.

"I would also like to thank my agent, Camilla Gallo." Dante angled his head slightly toward the opposing wings, where Signora Gallo was standing, in a blinding gold sheath dress. He summoned her to join him, and she did, waving and bowing her head in a self-deprecating manner totally at odds with her actual personality.

"When, signore?" squeaked Don Rocco, who couldn't stand the suspense. *"When?"*

"In a second, Father," Signor Speranza blustered. "Don't rush me."

He waited until Signora Gallo had turned and was heading back to the wings. He waited until Dante adopted a nauseating, in-sincere expression. He waited until he gripped the microphone with both hands and began bleating out the speech Signor Speranza had heard Signora Gallo forcing him to rehearse on the showroom floor of Speranza and Son's.

"This movie was a passion project for me," he began, and the crowd fell silent. "I wished to return to my humble roots, and to work with simple, ordinary people. People like Antonella there," he said, and turned to grin vacantly in their direction.

Antonella crossed her arms. *"Ass,"* she fumed.

"And this village . . ." Dante continued, waving a vague hand. "What can I say?"

Signor Speranza crouched, placing Don Rocco's Roomba, with Smilzo's blinking black box taped to the top of it, on the ground. He gave it a gentle nudge in the right direction, and wished it Godspeed. Then he took the remote control from his pocket.

"Care to do the honors, Father?" he said.

Don Rocco shook his head. "No, signore. I think you've earned it."

※ ※ ※

Two hundred and fourteen. Signor Speranza counted. That was how many people remained in the audience after Dante Rinaldi and his people left, in a trail of fury and expletives. Two hundred and fourteen—just two more than the number of Prometto's own citizens, although Signor Speranza could not determine at a glance, and in the dark, who the extra two were. By some glorious quirk of technology, or semi-miraculous divine intervention—Don Rocco and Signor Speranza were divided as to which—the button of Smilzo's remote had jammed, and the Roomba, which should, by all conventional standards, have embarked on a randomized cleaning pattern, had instead followed Dante Rinaldi at his heels, doggedly and determinedly, until he was out of both sight and hearing.

They had screened Smilzo's movie, and it was great, because everyone knew everyone. The crowd had cheered when the title card lit up the screen—*From Prometto with Love.* "Is a play on James Bond, boss," Smilzo had whispered, and Signor Speranza had nodded and smiled. "Perfect, Smilzo. That is perfect." Signora Catuzza had brought everybody food, and handed out pots and pans and spoons to the children so they could make noise, and when Smilzo and Antonella had kissed on-screen, so did the real Smilzo and Antonella in the audience, and everyone went crazy. When it was over, somebody had handed out sparklers.

"You did a good job, Zio," Signor Speranza said, patting his uncle on the back. "You have driven us all to a state of destitution, but—you did a very good job."

Zio Franco nodded, looking out over the work he had done, his old, wrinkled face unabashedly happy in the light of the dancing sparks. "You did a good job, too, Giovannino. Your parents would be proud of you."

Signor Speranza checked in with his father then, now that he could hear himself think, visiting him at the back corner of his mind and finding him bent over his peppers. "Tell Mamma I miss her," he whispered. "Tell her I said that, Papà."

There was a bang, and a whistling sound, and a stream of fireworks went up from the churchyard. Everyone stood and looked up together, at the sky that was theirs, which hung over their own tiny piece of creation.

"Tomorrow," said Signor Speranza to Betta with a sigh when it was all over. He shifted Carlotta, who was asleep in his arms. "Tomorrow—"

"Shhhh," said Betta, smoothing the little girl's hair. "It is time to go home, Nino."

Ernesto approached, Gemma trailing happily behind him. "She is not too heavy for you, signore?" he asked Signor Speranza. "I can carry her home for you, if you want."

Signor Speranza looked sharply up at him, this impudent Maestro mountain, ready with a retort, but, in that moment, he couldn't say it. He found himself reminded again, for the second time in two weeks, of that dreadful day Luca Ricci had stood outside his hotel and laughed at his daughter, and refused even to meet his granddaughter. This moment, now, felt strangely similar to Signor Speranza, only this time, as Gemma stood watching, it was Ernesto instead of Luca — Ernesto Maestro, strong and dependable, quietly asking permission to give Gemma a second chance at happiness.

"Thank you, Ernesto," Signor Speranza heard himself grumble. "That would be very helpful. Thank you." And he handed his granddaughter over.

Gemma beamed in the dark.

The crowd dispersed. At the bottom of the hill, by the church, Signor Speranza saw Don Rocco.

"Tomorrow, Father," he said, tracing a cross over his heart.

Don Rocco nodded. "I will help you, signore," he promised.

There came a loud screeching sound, and then a bang, and everyone jumped.

"More fireworks, Father?" asked Signor Speranza, frowning.

"No, signore," said Don Rocco, puzzled. "I don't—"

He didn't finish his sentence. He didn't finish his sentence because at that precise moment, and in the ultimate validation of the dire predictions and judgments of junior plumbing inspectors the world over, the pipes along the Via Sant'Agata, which had been installed over seventy-five years earlier, and some of which might or might not have been patched with bubblegum, simultaneously, and *spectacularly*, burst.

23

Six Months Later

"Stop making that face, Nino," said Betta out of the corner of her mouth. It was February, and they were standing on the portico of Signor Maestro's house, Betta holding a glass oven dish of lasagna, and Signor Speranza a bottle of prosecco. The hotel, which had been fully booked for six months running, had been left in the dubious care of Smilzo's mother, who had arrived for her temporary employment cheerfully armed with a brocade bag, protruding from which, Signor Speranza trembled to see, were a pair of crochet hooks. "Don't worry," she had said, glancing over his shoulder, perhaps in quest of unadorned toilet paper rolls. "I will take care of everything."

"I'm not making a face," Signor Speranza said, indignant, lowering his eyebrows even more than before, and expelling two puffs of cold air from his nostrils, like a cartoon bull.

"They're coming," Betta hissed. "Be quiet."

The door opened, and everyone shouted, "Hey!" and bundled them into the house.

"*Nonno!*" shrilled Carlotta, running over. Gemma had gotten her a new red velvet dress for Christmas, with a sash in the back, and she was wearing it now and dashing around in her stockinged feet, trailing a yellow ribbon on a stick, Nonno Guido scampering beside her. Then a pack of Maestro cousins, all boys, and also holding ribbons on sticks, went thundering past, and Carlotta took off after them, whooping.

Signor Speranza's moustache twitched. "Do you see, Betta? Do you see what is happening? They are making her into a hooligan."

"Hush!" said Betta. Then she nudged him in the ribs. "Here's Signor Maestro. Be *nice.*"

Signor Speranza rolled his eyes to the ceiling.

"*Ciao,* signore!" Betta called gaily, kissing their host on each cheek. "I am just going to put this in the kitchen." She and her tray of lasagna whisked away.

Signor Speranza and Signor Maestro stood in the midst of the party and eyed each other. Signor Speranza strained to recall what Betta had told him about making conversation. "Keep it light, Nino," she had said. "Just make observations. Nothing controversial."

His moustache bristled.

"It's cold," he said flatly.

Signor Maestro grunted.

Signor Speranza scanned the immediate area for further inspiration, his eye catching on the folding table next to the door where guests had piled their baby shower gifts for Gemma and Ernesto. Five months ago, the same table had been heaped with wedding presents.

"Could be a girl," he said, shrugging.

Signor Maestro tipped his head back and made a barking sound, and Signor Speranza could see the dull flash of his single gold tooth. "It will be a boy, Speranza," he said. "Believe me."

"Signori!" Don Rocco approached with a tumbler in his hand. *"Come state?"*

"Boss!" Smilzo hollered, with a huge wave. He was on the other side of the room, and had spotted Signor Speranza through the lens of the Betamovie. "Can you go back outside and come in again, boss? I missed it."

Nearly all of Prometto was at Gemma and Ernesto's baby shower. Zio Franco had died just before Christmas, but not before learning that there was going to be a new baby. He had been happy about that.

Signor Speranza had learned who the two extra people were at the screening of their movie. Rilla Bari and Mateo Fiore, a reporter and a photographer from an entertainment magazine. That very weekend they had published a story about Prometto's little home-spun project, and about Zio Franco's magnificent amphitheater, and everything had changed after that.

"Is called a revenue stream, boss," Smilzo had explained archly from the comfort of his own swivel chair and desk, which were now arranged at the back of the shop alongside Signor Speranza's. "Since there are no other movie theaters around here, we have what is called a corner on the market."

Smilzo, Signor Speranza noticed with some consternation, had, in recent days, taken to playing it fast and loose with the word *we.* This was likely owing to a certain rash decision he himself had made, in the emotional aftermath of witnessing his assistant in a hand-me-down nightgown, to take him on as a partner in the business, a decision that was reflected in the freshly printed awning outside the shop, which now read, in cramped script, SPERANZA AND SMILZO'S VACUUM CLEANER MAINTENANCE AND REPAIR AND MAJOR MOTION PICTURE PRODUCTION SERVICES, LLC.

Remarkably, however, the Water Commission had seen the situation the same way as Smilzo, and given Prometto a second chance. *Eligible for payment plan.* That was what the junior plumbing inspector had stamped on their form this time, after Don Rocco had called, urging him to come back.

"Did you also hear his confession when he was here, Father?" Signor Speranza had asked, interested. "I would imagine someone in that line of work is carrying around more than the average number of sins."

"Signore!" Signor Rossi waved from across the room, just as Smilzo had. "Terrible news," he said when he finally reached him.

Signor Speranza frowned. He had known, of course, that this day was coming. If there was one thing that was sure in this uncertain world, it was the reproduction rate of schnauzers.

"A new batch?" he asked grimly.

Signor Rossi nodded. "That's a good way of putting it, signore," he said, wringing his hands. "A new batch."

Signor Speranza considered. He had been thinking about the problem of Bambolina and the schnauzers for some time now—more than half a year—and he thought he might have a solution. The seed of the idea had first been planted during a particularly exasperating conversation with Carlotta several weeks before, when she had claimed that one of the more odious Maestro cousins, Roberto, had the answer.

"Okay," Signor Speranza had said testily. "What did the famous Roberto say?"

Carlotta fluttered her eyelashes. "He said it is simple to solve the

Bambolina problem. He said you only have to find something that scares schnauzers, but does not scare Bambolinas."

"Ha!" said Signor Speranza. "And does Professore Roberto have any ideas what that might be? Does he know that a *Bambolina* is not a distinct breed? Does he know that, *cara mia*?"

Carlotta had shrugged, indifferent to these entreaties, and content in her belief that Roberto was, if not infallible, at least more knowledgeable than a garden-variety grandfather.

"We'll have to go quickly," Signor Speranza said to Signor Rossi and Smilzo and Don Rocco. "If my wife catches me, forget about it."

"I am going, too," declared Signor Maestro, striking his fist to his chest, and Signor Speranza, after conferring briefly with God, didn't try to stop him.

❋ ❋ ❋

It was clear and cold at the top of the mountain. The Bosco di Rudina was cloaked in mist, and a curl of wood smoke went up from the Rossis' stovepipe chimney. It had been a day just like this, fifty years ago, when Signor Speranza had seen his cousin Paolo off at the train station—the day when he had passed up his own chance to leave.

"Don't you want to get out of here, Giovannino?" Paolo had said, his eyes fixed on the distant horizon, as if he were already there, and gone. "Don't you want to get out of here before this place strangles you, too?"

No, Signor Speranza thought now, filling his lungs with the fresh mountain air and looking out, over the crumbling land that had been his father's and his grandfather's before him, and on and on, backward, into the gulf of time. He was exactly where he was supposed to be.

The screen door of the Rossis' house creaked.

"It will not *hurt* Bambolina, will it, signore?" Signor Rossi asked anxiously.

"I assure you, signore," said Signor Speranza, "she will be completely unaffected."

They arranged Bambolina on the chilly ground, and then, on second thoughts, Signor Rossi ran inside to fetch her a blanket. Everything was set.

"This is the dumbest thing I have ever seen, Speranza," Signor Maestro grunted.

"And you are the dumbest thing *I* have ever seen, signore," Signor Speranza muttered.

Signor Maestro's cavernous nostrils flared. "What did you say?"

Signor Speranza waved his hand, impatient. "Nothing. Smilzo, are you ready?"

Smilzo lifted the Betamovie onto his shoulder. "Ready, boss."

"Action!"

Don Rocco knocked on the neighbors' dog flap and whistled softly. At first there was nothing. Then there was the softly accumulating swishing sound of thirty-two infant schnauzer paws scuffling over linoleum. In the next second, the door was breached.

Signor Rossi yelped and bit his knuckle.

"Signore—" he said.

Signor Speranza wasn't listening. His eyes were glued to the schnauzers. They moved as one. He saw the very second their intrepid leader glimpsed Bambolina on her blanket. They streaked toward their soft and furry goal. They were nearly upon her!

Signor Speranza had a remote in his hand. At just the right moment, he pressed the single red button.

PBBBBBBBBBBBBBT!

The schnauzers, startled out of their wits, scattered like bowling pins, and Bambolina, who was, after all, accustomed to such noises, fell asleep in the sun.

✻ ✻ ✻

Having taken care of Bambolina, Signor Speranza and the others went back to the party. When the celebration was over, Betta stayed to drink coffee and talk it all over with Gemma and Signora Maestro, while Carlotta got permission to go back to the hotel with her grandfather, and spend the night in her old room.

"My room from when I was a little kid, Nonno," she told Signor Speranza solemnly, even though she had only moved out five months ago.

The two of them picked their way over the wet, chilly beach, Carlotta stopping to write her name in the sand with the end of a stick.

"Do you want me to write your name also, Nonno?" she asked.

Signor Speranza opened his mouth to spell *Giovannino*, but Carlotta was too quick. *NONNO*, she wrote, in tall, wobbly letters.

Signor Speranza looked at his name, crooked in the sand, and laughed. He had forgotten that, to a child, Mamma is only Mamma; Grandpa is only Grandpa. He had forgotten what it was like to think like that.

They made their way up the mountain, just as they had on another wet February day, and, just as before, they came to the battered village sign.

PROMETTO
POPULATION: 212

"Zio Franco is still up there," Signor Speranza said, pointing. "Maybe tomorrow I'll send Smilzo to change it."

Carlotta shook her head. "You don't have to do that, Nonno. Pretty soon my brother or sister will get here, and then the number will be right again."

Signor Speranza's chest tightened, and he felt suddenly as if he might be dreaming. *Lord?* he asked, and looked up at the misty sky. There was no answer but a lone drop of rain splashing into his eye. He yelped and scrubbed it away. How long had he wanted a second chance at this conversation?

"Do you think that's all right, though?" he said carefully. "If Zio Franco holds the baby's spot for now? Maybe the baby won't like it."

Carlotta yawned and shrugged. "Babies don't care about things like that, Nonno. They have more important things to do with their time." Then she lifted her arms, the way she had when she was a tiny thing. "I'm too tired," she whined.

Signor Speranza laughed, and he scooped Carlotta up, boosting her onto his shoulders. He continued walking, past the sign that kept tally of the revolving door of life, and toward the hotel. His heart was light, and his conscience clear. He did not know what the future held, but Prometto was safe, for now, and that was all he could ask for.

Grazie, Signore, he said, glancing up at the sky. *Mille grazie.*

ACKNOWLEDGMENTS

I hope you enjoyed reading this book as much as I enjoyed writing it. As ludicrous as the story is, so many bits and pieces of it are real. For starters, I can attest by personal experience that it is difficult to remove slug from the beard of a miniature schnauzer. More seriously, if I close my eyes and picture my main character, the person I see is the late Italian author Giovannino Guareschi, from whom I borrowed Signor Speranza's voluptuous moustache as well as Smilzo's name. The *Compendium* is real also; the glorious *Comprehensive Dictionary of Patron Saints* by Pablo Ricardo Quintana is the only place I have been able to find St. Barbara specifically identified as the patron saint of death by cannonball, a designation which is as silly and joyful as the invention of wrapping paper.

Prometto is real, its location and topography based on my grandparents' village of Ferruzzano in Calabria, a place I've only seen in photographs, but which, luckily, my grandparents somehow packed up and brought with them when they moved to Cliffside Park, New Jersey. I've let my *nonna* have run of the café as Signora Catuzza, and it's her *pane pazzo*, or "crazy bread," that Don Rocco is eating in chapter fourteen. I tried and failed to find a place for her emergency ricotta, which is exactly as it sounds—a recipe for turning milk and vinegar into ricotta if you do not have any on hand AND IT IS AN EMERGENCY. If you would like to try making *pane pazzo*, let all your bread go stale. Then heat a bit more than a coating of olive oil in a shallow, high-sided pan the internet is telling me is called a *sauteuse*. Add around a cup of black olives and some diced scallions and let them sauté for maybe five to seven minutes. In the meantime, open a fifteen-ounce can of tomato sauce. Add that to the pan and then thin with approximately a canful of water. Season with basil and a few red pepper flakes. Once it's simmered for around fifteen minutes, add the hunks of bread to the sauce, letting them soak a few minutes before removing to a plate. Don't worry if it doesn't turn out right; this is the way of Italian grandmothers' recipes—they do not contain measurements. My other grandmother inspired Signor Speranza's ongoing conversations with his father, because even though Grandma Babe has been gone for some time now, we somehow hear her voice all the time—fitting, since in life she found it distinctly difficult to stop talking.

Thank you to my mother, Pauline Ragosta, who spent many years in the 1980s and '90s tracking down every Beverly Cleary, L. M. Montgomery, and Nancy Drew book she could find, and who delighted, as only a mother could, in the not-at-all annoying game I devised of saying a word and then loudly reciting all the synonyms I could think of. She also shared stories about her own grandparents that helped give Prometto's zany cast its flavor. Thank you to my father, Joe Ragosta, who makes everything funny and is a consummate storyteller as well as an inveterate Finder of Movies We Would Like. Thank you to my sister Gina for making me short ribs[°]

[°] I am expecting a fresh batch when you read this.

every time I accomplished a writing goal and for pointing out that my faux fur robe made me look less like Mariah Carey and more like a madam running the numbers in the Bronx. Thank you to my brothers: Joe, for coming up with his own version of what he thought I was writing; Michael, for his insights into basically every film ever made; and Robert, who will answer the phone when I call with a random question in one of his areas of expertise, even if he is standing on a ladder or on top of a roof. Shout-outs to Jason, Dana, Chelsea, Quinn, Rachel, Everly, Bianca, Joey, and Charlie, as well as Karen, Ed, Evelyn, and Audrey.

Thank you to my husband, Shaun, for many hours of talking shop and solving story problems—it's amazing work can be that fun. Thank you to Jack for inspiring me with your unrivaled skill in character creation—you deserve a bucket of fish crackers and a pail of juice. Thank you, Juliet, for taking my author photo and for throwing me a party when I had to go to the dentist. Thank you, Zoey, for your profoundly inspirational and only somewhat aggressive pep talks—I couldn't possibly fail to get my work done after one of your speeches. Finally, thank you to Emily Claire Simon, who has instructed me to stop just short of listing her social security number so as to avoid any confusion as to her precise identity. Thank you for bringing me sneaky snacks, refreshing my email, and acting as quality control so I do not spend all day writing trash.

QueryTracker helped me connect with my lovely and unstoppable agents, Allison Hunter and Hellie Ogden, who in turn brought Signor Speranza to my wonderful editors, Kaitlin Olson in the US, and Darcy Nicholson in the UK, both of whom I liked from first Zoom. Thank you to the entire team at Atria, especially Maudee Genao, Karlyn Hixson, Jade Hui, and Megan Rudloff, and many thanks to production editor Tamara Arellano, copy editor Janet

Rosenberg, and proofreader Kristen Strange for polishing the words to a shine. Thank you to Janklow & Nesbit on both sides of the Atlantic, and especially to Natalie Edwards, Kirsty Gordon, and Lianna Blakeman. You all helped a first-time author feel so confident and comfortable.

I owe several debts of gratitude to the world of films and filmmaking. I was fifteen thousand words into a much different version of this book when I happened to watch *Waking Ned Devine*, and the plot was so simple and straightforward, with Jackie O'Shea and Michael O'Sullivan's single-minded pursuit of their goal, that the next morning I trashed all my words and started over. The other two films that guided me were *The Full Monty* and, my favorite of all time, *Big Night*. If I ever write a scene as good as Secondo asking Primo to make a side of spaghetti for the lady who ordered the risotto, then all of my professional goals will have been realized. I also want to thank Blake Snyder for *Save the Cat! Goes to the Movies*. For the initiated, *The Patron Saint of Second Chances* is a Golden Fleece.

Now that I've gone on at least as long as one of Dante Rinaldi's speeches, I'd like to wrap up by thanking writing and imagination itself. I wrote this novel over forty-three days during lockdown and early quarantine, when it wasn't possible to go anywhere but the grocery store, and I will be forever grateful for the escape it provided. I like Prometto best during happy times, but I can imagine what it would be like during the pandemic, too. I can see Signor Speranza's consternation when his mask wilts his magnificent moustache. I see him delivering baskets of food to the ladies of Don Rocco's Rosary Circle on the end of a stick. Finally, I see him at his desk at Speranza and Son's, composing a Very Important Bulletin to illustrate social distancing for his constituents. *I want for you to imagine my assistant, Smilzo,* he writes with a flourish. *Only imagine he has been turned sideways, and suspended in midair.* We must always remain *one Smilzo apart.* And then I see the natural progression this bulletin takes in Prometto society, and how, for this strange little village of two hundred and twelve souls, a "smilzo" becomes a standard unit of measure, and then, just like that, I am back there, and I am laughing. *Grazie,* signorè.

ABOUT THE AUTHOR

Christine Simon grew up in a very large and very *loud* Italian family, where it was considered a major milestone among her countless siblings and cousins to surpass their *nonna*'s towering height of four feet, ten inches. She lives with her husband and four children, who are also extremely loud, and the crowning achievements of her life are learning to read knitting patterns and teaching her otherwise unscrupulous miniature schnauzer to ring a bell when he wants to go out.